Praise for
The Spying Moon

"The subject matter of this lucid police procedural may be grim, but the Canadian sensibility is refreshing."
—*Publishers Weekly*

"With a keen eye for Canadian detail, Ruttan crafts a grim thriller with a unique social conscience. We need more stories like this one. Kendall Moreau is a Mountie you won't soon forget."
—Sarah L Johnson, bestselling author of *Infractus*

"*The Spying Moon* is a welcome, gritty addition to Canadian crime fiction. Ruttan is a thoughtful and original writer, and Kendall Moreau is a compelling detective in the vein of Jane Tennison and John Rebus."
—Sam Wiebe, award-winning author of *Cut You Down*

THE
SPYING
MOON

ALSO BY SANDRA RUTTAN

Harvest of Ruins
Lullaby for the Nameless
The Frailty of Flesh
What Burns Within
Suspicious Circumstances

SANDRA RUTTAN

THE SPYING MOON

Copyright © 2018 by Sandra Ruttan

All rights reserved. No part of the book may be reproduced in any form or by any electronic or mechanical means, including information storage and retrieval systems, without permission in writing from the publisher, except by a reviewer who may quote brief passages in a review.

Down & Out Books
3959 Van Dyke Rd, Ste. 265
Lutz, FL 33558
www.DownAndOutBooks.com

The characters and events in this book are fictitious. Any similarity to real persons, living or dead, is coincidental and not intended by the author.

Cover design by JT Lindroos

ISBN: 1-948235-27-7
ISBN-13: 978-1-948235-27-3

*For Brian, the #metoo movement
and the people who have to fight to overcome
prejudice and discrimination every day.*

Chapter 1

Political correctness had taken a detour on the backroads of Western Canada and bypassed Maple River. Constable Kendall Moreau found her path to the breakroom of the police station blocked by a man in jeans and a green T-shirt who'd either been skipping the donuts since he earned his badge or had a metabolism worth killing for. His wavy brown hair brushed the top of the doorframe and his hazel eyes glinted.

"Whoa there, woman. I've been known to make time for reporters outside office hours." He summoned a smile. "But you aren't supposed to be here."

Pit Bull. She had an affection for the misunderstood breed, so instinctively likening this man to these normally intelligent and loyal dogs struck her as odd. She suspected that he had the potential to exhibit many positive characteristics but with the wrong influences could turn deadly.

He was right about one thing. She wasn't supposed to be there. The plan had been a post more than a hundred miles north, in the heart of the province, where women had been disappearing for decades.

Where her mother had been before she vanished.

For years she'd worked to earn her degree and be accepted to the Depot, where Royal Canadian Mounted Police officers trained. She'd graduated near the top of her class. Everything she'd done or hadn't done since the day she'd become a file in the foster care system had been motivated by her desire to find

THE SPYING MOON

out the truth about what had happened to Willow Moreau.

Now, instead of being in Burns Lake, she stood in the Maple River RCMP station and stared at a man obstructing the doorway so she couldn't get inside the meeting room. Part of her wished she could turn on her heel and walk away. Clearly, they didn't want her here any more than she did. Moreau reached into her pocket, her fingers brushing her keys. She could leave. Even if that voice inside her that always told her to do the right thing prompted her back to this station on Monday she could take the weekend and talk to her new contact about her mother's case.

She'd begged to go on that trip with her mother but Willow Moreau had left her with the Thompsons instead so that Kendall wouldn't miss the first day of school.

Mama had hugged her goodbye. She remembered the feeling of her mother's arms wrapped tightly around her, how Mama's silky, black hair felt as she pressed her cheek against Mama's head. She remembered Mama telling her school was important and that when you have a choice between doing what you want and doing what's right there was really no choice at all.

Willow Moreau's words echoed in her mind as she made her choice, pulled out her ID, slid to Pit Bull's right, wormed her way through the tiny gap between the man and the frame and entered the room without a word.

Sergeant Freeman had tried to entice her to Maple River before she'd received her posting. He'd shared his vision for a task squad. Big city crime wasn't restricted to the streets of the metropolitan centers like the greater Vancouver area anymore, and with her own reasons for wanting to work the BC interior it hadn't been hard to get Moreau's interest initially, but it was her fallback position, and it had fallen all the way to the back of her mind when she'd been offered Burns Lake.

After years trying to make headway in her mother's case, Moreau had earned her badge and had a chance to see her mother's file for herself. When the clerk approached her with the thin folder she'd felt as though all the juices in her stomach were on spin cycle; her skin had tingled and for a second she almost thought she could hear her mother's laughter, feel the warmth of her touch as she held Kendall in her arms on a warm summer day by Lake Muskoka, where they'd shared a picnic lunch just days before Mama had told her she was going on a trip.

The mix of emotions in her when she finally held that file swirled like the blur of events that had followed the social worker's visit. House after house, school after school, it all spun together until it was hard to separate where she'd stayed when she turned eleven or thirteen or which house she'd gone to after her first day of work.

She'd tried to temper hope with reason but her knees had buckled when she'd opened the file and found a single page staring back at her. A cursory form partially filled out, dated after Willow Moreau had been missing for more than a month.

Whatever trail there may have been had already turned cold, a trail nobody had ever really tried to find. Her mother was just another forgotten woman added to a long list of possible abductions from Highway 16. There'd been one arrest and a few people were considered suspects, but that was overshadowed by the lack of concern for the victims. They were mostly Aboriginal, with a few pretty white girls sprinkled in the mix. There were those that thought that the white girls may have been innocent victims of a perpetrator who was simply taking out the Native trash. Indigenous lives held little value to some people.

She hadn't given up and had finally located a source. One of the other missing women had a family member that was willing to talk. The woman thought she might have a lead about where her relative had been before she went missing but so far Moreau's contact remained anonymous and only called Moreau from pay phones or disposable cells that couldn't be traced. She'd promised if Moreau was posted near Highway 16 that she'd meet with her.

Moreau had been on her way. She was parked at one end of a lookout, near the Icefields Parkway south of Jasper, Alberta, when her phone rang.

THE SPYING MOON

She answered a call confirming her start date in Maple River. "I was going to Burns Lake," she'd replied.

"Change of orders. You'll be getting an email about the new assignment."

It was a cloudless, clear day, but she stepped outside into cutting air gusts coming off the mountain, the sunlight amplified by the sea of snow that had arrived early this fall and covered the earth. Snowblind, pelted by razor-sharp wind, she could almost fool herself into thinking the tears she was fighting were weather-related instead of echoes of the loss she'd felt when her mother had slipped from her life the first time.

Just when she'd thought she might not be able to hold herself back anymore and opened her mouth to scream with the wind a car had pulled over.

A happy couple. Glowing, holding hands, laughing as they snapped their selfies together.

Moreau did what she always did. She pushed her feelings down inside and told herself it was a temporary setback. Once she was back in her vehicle she checked her messages. The email covered every member of the team assigned, as well as the loose thread of cases that Freeman had strung together to push for this task force. They would be focused on tackling trafficking in the area. The more border security at major crossing points, the more cross-border crime shifted to the small towns without the resources to stop it.

A recent incident had created a vacancy and two last-minute additions had been abruptly transferred to the team. She couldn't tell if she was replacing Willmott or if Nate Duncan was, but she gleaned enough to know that neither of them had put in for this post.

The email also indicated that Freeman was out of town at a conference, and wouldn't be able to brief the team on her assignment until he returned.

With every mile of highway she drove she had to fight the urge to turn north and head to Burns Lake anyway. Now that

4

she was in Maple River she wished she'd taken the weekend to meet her contact.

When she'd arrived that night there were only a few officers in the building, at the far end of the station, near the main doors.

One of them had pointed her in the direction of the lunch room and explained that the renovations meant that the old conference area was being used for storage while things were shifted to make space for the contractors. The members of the task force were meeting in the only place that had a table big enough to seat all of them.

As she'd sidestepped boxes on her way through the building all she'd absorbed was shades of brown and shadows from the looming stacks that wobbled as she walked by. There was something about the station that reminded her of the makeshift room she'd stayed in at the Thompson's, a borrowed space she slept in that was nothing more than a nook on the far side of the laundry room, separated with a pale yellow sheet tacked to the top of the door frame.

She'd noted a few rooms with desks that were covered with boxes and she had to weave her way around everything that had been jammed into the hallways until she reached the door, where she had to snake her way around a plainclothes officer with an attitude that needed adjusting.

The station had a restless quiet hanging over it and her forced entrance had caused an uneasy stillness in the room. To her right a wide path led to an old, white refrigerator, which was at the end of a kitchenette with basic oak veneer cabinets, a brown laminate counter with flecks of yellow in it and a pantry closet on the far side that was comparable in size to the fridge and ran floor to ceiling with a single door for access. A microwave was housed on a ledge above a stainless steel sink in the center of the counter, and the appliance was flanked by open shelves on either side. At the far left end of the counter there were stacks of trays with files and paperwork. The right end of the counter held a coffee maker, which dripped a fresh brew

THE SPYING MOON

into the pot; sporadic *sploshes* were the only sound that dared to break the awkward silence. Every wall was station-issue white, judging from what she'd seen as she'd worked her way from the entrance, and the carpet was a dirt-stained gray.

There was a long table that was off center, pushed more to her left to make the access to the fridge easier, surrounded by conference room chairs with blue padded seats.

The left wall hosted a bulletin board, which had some information about drug-related arrests posted on it and the words Task Force taped at the top. They were printed in a bold Arial font on faded yellow paper the same color as the sheet off the laundry room that had separated a small space for her in the Thompson house all those years ago.

Like that sheet it felt as though this assignment represented another obstacle keeping her from the woman who'd been the only family she'd ever known.

She turned her attention to the men at the table, who she'd heard snicker at Pit Bull's remarks before she'd entered.

If the man who'd tried to block her at the door was a Pit Bull, the fellow by the left side of the table with his forearms resting against the back of a chair was more of a Jack Russell Terrier. He was shorter than average, slight and bristled with energy. His fingers fidgeted with the folder he clutched.

Moreau couldn't access that side of the table and Pit Bull now blocked the wider path that led to the fridge, ready for round two. Jack Russell scanned every inch of the room as he avoided looking her in the eye.

She cleared her throat and he turned instinctively before his shoulders slumped as he glanced at Pit Bull. Moreau stepped forward as Jack Russell moved back and she sat in the chair in the middle of that side of the table before anyone could stop her.

A stocky blond pulled mugs from the cupboard along the wall by the sink. He had meaty hands and the body of a bear with the bearing of a gerbil. After he sniffed a cup he rinsed it quickly, reinspected it and tried to stick his fingers inside to scratch at something. That was followed by a shrug. He set the mug down and filled it with coffee.

From the other side of the breakroom door she'd noticed his hollow eyes as he'd laughed at the remarks Pit Bull directed at her.

Another man entered. The gerbil spoke.

"Coffee?"

"No, thanks." This newcomer had dark brown hair that looked like it was a breath of wind away from falling into his blue eyes. He had the kind of face that appeared chiseled, like it was etched in stone.

Pit Bull blew out a breath. "There's a woman on the team now, Alec. No need for you to be in the kitchen."

He clearly wasn't interested in offering an apology or changing her impression of him. Moreau didn't avert her gaze. She stared straight back, but otherwise ignored the taunt. The latest arrival sat beside her. His eye twitched as Jack Russell and the gerbil laughed. Something about the newcomer struck her as a man trying to follow the rules. Like a Labrador Retriever: well-trained and capable of effective socialization, but there was something else there, too. A sense that he could run with the wolves, a wildness within him.

She knew who he was. Moreau had read everything emailed to her that day her life detoured away from Burns Lake and the answers she sought. After she'd finished digesting the files she'd googled each member of the team.

Nate Duncan. If his history and her initial impression were accurate, Duncan's transfer to this team had likely been as welcome to the other constables as her own. They were the new additions, neither of them there by choice.

Freeman entered. She'd seen a picture of him with an article he'd written about overcoming racial bias as a black officer in command. He reminded her of Wayne Brady, but without the dance moves or quick grin. The elegance and authority of a Doberman were present in his movements, and when he sat

THE SPYING MOON

down at the end of the table the others filled the rest of the seats without a word.

"The number of drug-related arrests are up all throughout BC's lower interior. What's connecting the cases is the batch of product retrieved, but we have no information about the new drug source. The first thing we're going to focus on is identifying the source. Let's start with you." He turned to the man who'd blocked her entry. "Give us the run-down on your progress."

"You know all of this."

"Pretend I don't," Freeman snapped. "I want to make sure that we aren't overlooking anything, and that every member of this team is up to speed, otherwise you'd still be at home, jerking off in the comfort of your own bed."

Moreau saw a few sets of eyes turn her way. So much for team spirit.

Had they known she'd compared them to animals they might have thought her sexist, but from what she understood her people believed everyone had a spirit animal that revealed their character. Most canines were held in high esteem, which was why she couldn't think of comparing Alec to an Irish Setter; she hated to infer the breed lacked intelligence.

Freeman opened his mouth to say something when he looked at her and paused.

"Constable Moreau," she said.

"You weren't due until Monday."

"I arrived early and wanted to check in."

"At eleven at night?"

Moreau could see Freeman had a knack for subtle shifts on his face that hinted at his thoughts. There was a mix of amusement along with approval, although she felt certain he didn't believe she'd shared the whole truth. She offered a thin smile. "I heard the meeting was going to be late this evening because of the renovation work."

Nate Duncan turned to her. "They've been cutting down drywall and it's the only time we can talk without shouting."

"Yes, well, it's good you checked in." Freeman tapped the stack of papers in front of him. "There've been some developments. First, this is the team."

Scott Saunders was the short one that overflowed with energy and suffered from restless leg syndrome.

He'd moved to the other side of the table and sat beside Alec Chmar, the gerbil, who still seemed more interested in studying his coffee mug than acknowledging her presence.

The man beside her, Nate Duncan, was the curiosity. Nate Duncan came with rumors of a past that was in the public domain. The information she'd found when she'd googled the other men was standard issue; a history of education and arrests with no personal details. Duncan was originally from Maple River and she'd pieced together some of his past. His family was alleged to have numerous criminal enterprises that stretched back to Prohibition, and he'd left town after being arrested years ago.

The wildness she sensed lurking beneath the surface.

The reason the rest of the team might not be eager to have him back home.

She found it curious that Freeman had chosen a constable with a questionable history and a family connection to trafficking and inserted him on a task force focused on taking down the local drug trade.

After Corporal Phil Willmott had been injured in a suspicious accident the transfers for Duncan and Moreau had been approved. Moreau's start date was delayed, because she was transferring from out of province. Duncan had been transferred abruptly, with no time to prepare. He'd finished his shift one day, been given his transfer papers and told to report in thirty-six hours, leaving one day for him to pack up his life and move hundreds of kilometers back to the hometown he'd been forced to leave years before.

That left the man with the attitude who had dug himself into a hole with a backhoe instead of a shovel, with both her and Freeman. Levi McIver winked at her when their boss said his name.

THE SPYING MOON

A knock at the open door gave her an excuse to look away from McIver.

"I'm sorry, sir." Zadecki, the uniformed officer who'd directed her to the breakroom when she'd first arrived, stood at the entrance. "There's been a report of a body found on Holt Hill."

Chapter 2

They had to walk on foot from where Duncan parked his Rodeo and the blanket of night nearly swallowed Duncan as Moreau followed him along a path, through the trees. Her flashlight did little to hold the long shadows at bay.

An officer darted out in front of Moreau and blocked her path.

He fussed with a light he was setting up along the trail. The extension cable was pulled so tight it was level with her waist. Moreau bent underneath it.

"Oh, sorry," the officer said as she straightened up on the other side of the cord, as though he'd only just noticed she was there. She had to admit that that was possible, given how thick the darkness was.

Moreau quickened her pace to catch up to Duncan.

The ground was littered with the remnants of beer boxes. Kokanee bottles, Molson Canadian cans and a half-full bottle of Jack Daniel's rested on the camp table. Crime scene techs scoured the area and set up more lights to make sure nothing was missed in the darkness.

Of all the nights for a call like this it would be one without a bloody star in the sky.

"Jesus fucking Christ."

Saunder's voice was thin and strained. He had his face turned away from the lights and it blurred into the black night sky.

Moreau surveyed the alcove at the crest of Holt Hill. It was nothing more than a patch cut out of the thick brush off the

THE SPYING MOON

road accessed by a narrow trail that anyone could easily miss if they didn't know what they were looking for.

Fortunately Nate Duncan was familiar with the area. He'd driven in silence while she studied street signs and tried to memorize the route from station to scene. She suspected she couldn't have found the site on her own, not in the dark on her first day in town.

Moreau turned to look at the body. Youth and promise still resonated in the half of the boy's face that remained, though it was hard to see past the mangled mess of brain and blood that spilled out of the orifice the bullet had torn into the left side of his head.

The coroner nodded at them and knelt beside the body. He barked orders to officers and demanded more light for his cursory examination with a voice like sandpaper.

"Creaser," he gruffly offered as an introduction when he finally turned his attention back to Duncan and Moreau. White hair stuck out in various directions, overgrown eyebrows concealed the large forehead and his eyes were wells of darkness surrounded by pasty white skin. There was a weariness in his tone, like he'd seen too many bodies, too much death. "Not much light to work with here, I'm afraid."

"Powder burns?" Duncan asked.

Creaser adjusted a hand-held light that had an intense bulb. "Tattoo pattern."

"So he was shot from between six inches to two feet away."

The coroner nodded. "Entry was the bottom of the chin, at a bit of an angle. Assuming gunshot is the cause of death it would have been instantaneous."

"Sure, that makes it better." Saunders walked away from them with an arm bent up across his mouth, as though he was trying to hold something back. He stumbled on something and caught himself on a tree.

"I don't think he's ever taken a call like this before," Creaser said. He turned and looked at Moreau, then focused on Dun-

12

can. "You must be the one back from the city."

Duncan didn't deny it. "What else can you tell me?"

"The gun was in his left hand. We'll do a GSR test to see if he shot himself. Judging from what I can tell here—" Creaser looked around the alcove at the sea of techs photographing and tagging evidence, "—he could have been drunk. Maybe even high."

"Do we have an ID?" Moreau asked.

"Sammy Petersen," Duncan said.

She glanced from cop to coroner. "Confirmed?" How had she missed Creaser telling Duncan that?

"He's right," Creaser said. "There's no doubt about that. Anyone from around these parts could tell you it's Sammy."

Moreau swallowed. Duncan knew this kid?

Duncan shook his head slowly. "It's him, but none of this sounds like Sammy."

"I thought you'd been gone from here for a while, Constable Duncan." Her words betrayed her knowledge of his history with the town and she wondered if that was a miscalculation on her part.

Duncan didn't blink. "I have. But this family—" He looked at the coroner.

"It doesn't sound like Sammy," Creaser confirmed.

"Any witnesses?" she asked.

Duncan nodded at the picnic table. "By the look of things he wasn't here alone." He sighed and turned his face down as his hair fell over his eyes. When he lifted his head a second later there was a look that reflected reluctance, resignation. "And if he wasn't alone I probably know who he was with."

She turned and her eyes scrutinized the area around them. Signs of a party. Shoe prints in the sand that were being photographed.

Something awkward about the way the gun rested in the victim's hand.

"Do you really think he fired it?" She crouched down beside the body, across from Creaser, and nodded at the weapon.

13

THE SPYING MOON

The coroner swallowed. After a quick glance at Nate Duncan, Creaser stood and packed his hand-held light away and fussed with his bag.

"Do you?" she repeated.

The answer was a shrug so short if she'd blinked she would have missed it.

"Bullet entry was the right side of the chin, on an angle, and the exit wound was on the left side of his head, where most of the damage is. But the gun is in his left hand." She titled her face, formed a gun shape with her fingers and demonstrated. "Holding a gun in my left hand, I'd shoot left to right. Not right to left."

Duncan and Creaser exchanged a glance, but neither said anything.

Moreau stood up. "Who's lead?"

"That's the sergeant's call," Duncan said.

She could hear Freeman's voice from down the trail as he rebuked the officer who apparently still had that cable pulled tight across the path several feet off the ground. Freeman approached them and looked around the scene with nothing more than a glance at Saunders, who leaned against a tree and, after another look at the body, retched.

Duncan confirmed the victim's ID for Freeman. The sergeant's eyes closed for a second.

When he reopened them he asked, "Suicide?"

"It's not impossible," Duncan said.

Freeman turned to Moreau. "It doesn't seem like Saunders is up to talking to the family. Can you handle this with Duncan?"

"Yes, sir."

"What about Chmar and McIver?" Duncan asked.

"I don't want to pull everyone off the drug investigation just when it's getting started. Not unless I have to. I'll have Saunders handle the scene, if he can pull himself together."

Freeman left them and went to talk to Saunders.

"I assume you know where the Petersens live," Moreau said.

14

Duncan nodded. Moreau turned toward the path and then looked back when she realized Duncan wasn't following her. He was studying Freeman and Saunders, his eyes narrow, his mouth set into a hard line.

"Coming?" she asked.

He turned and walked past her. She followed him back to the road at the top of the hill where at least half a dozen vehicles were now parked. He unlocked her door before he walked around to his own.

"How do you want to handle this?" he asked.

Freeman hadn't put either of them in charge, officially. If Moreau had been with Scott Saunders or Alec Chmar she would have assumed command because she already lacked confidence in their abilities. Within ten minutes on the job she had a pretty good idea why the task force was spinning in circles. Willmott had the most experience and had been sidelined by injury. Saunders couldn't even handle a body yet and Duncan hadn't been there long enough to make much of a difference.

She would have fought McIver just because he acted like a jerk.

However, she was with Nate Duncan, who hadn't offended her and had shown nothing but attention to detail at the scene. "I believe you have the seniority and you know the town. I'm prepared to follow your lead."

Duncan offered no response. He kept his focus on the road. The world around them was as black as molasses with a feeling in the air almost as thick. Moreau felt like she was fighting for each breath; the darkness of night was like a physical force that had closed in on her and was choking out all the oxygen from the sky. Her sense of dread escalated as they drove through town and she anticipated the anguish about to be unleashed in the Petersen home.

Moreau thought she'd come prepared, but she hadn't expected this on her first day in Maple River.

Duncan slammed on the brakes and Moreau reached out to

THE SPYING MOON

brace herself as her body was thrust forward, toward the dashboard. The seatbelt tightened, snapped her back against the seat and pushed out the air that was in her lungs.

"Sorry. You okay?"

She breathed in and out, glad to at least have a physical excuse for feeling short of breath. "Yes." As her heart rate slowed it occurred to her to ask, "You?"

"Yeah."

Moreau stared out at the reason for the abrupt stop. A coyote stood in the center of their lane, the headlights creating a blurred edge of light around him. His gaze was fixed on Moreau.

Duncan honked the horn.

The coyote didn't move anything but his eyes. It seemed he looked at Duncan with irritation. Moreau told herself that was ridiculous as the coyote shifted his gaze back to her. His head bobbed a nod before he turned, looked out into the darkness for a moment and then walked across the road, unbothered by the hum of the engine, the lights from the vehicle or the sound of the horn.

"Cheeky," Moreau said.

"There's a lot of wildlife in the area," Duncan said. "More now because of the fire."

Even with the sudden stop it didn't take long to reach the pristine neighborhood where the Petersens lived. House after house boasted new siding, high efficiency windows, manicured lawns and decorative touches that made for great curb appeal. Unlike Holt Hill, the streets were well lit and the pavement smooth. They parked at the end of a driveway and got out of the vehicle in front of a two-story home with white siding and dark trim.

"We'll just cover the basics," Duncan said as they walked toward the front steps. "Notification, arrange for someone to formally identify the body and find out who he was with, if we can."

She nodded and took her ID out of her pocket as she followed him. Just as he started to climb the steps to the door an orange cat dashed out in front of her. It was as out of place in the Petersen's neighborhood as it would have been to see Queen Elizabeth buying hot dogs from a street vendor. The cat was about two feet long and mangy. She moved to the right to try to go around it, but the feline hissed and swiped at her leg with his claws. Moreau stepped back just in time.

Duncan glanced at her as he reached for the bell and paused. The cat hissed again, and then ran around the side of the house and disappeared into the darkness. Moreau sprinted up the remaining steps.

Three rings later, Duncan knocked firmly with his fist. A light went on in the hallway. Shuffled footsteps were followed by the turn of the lock on the heavy wooden door in front of them.

The tired eyes widened as recognition sank in. "Nate. I heard you were back in town, son."

Duncan drew in a breath and held up his ID. "I'm very sorry, Mr. Petersen, but we're here in an official capacity." He introduced Constable Moreau.

"What's this about?"

"Can we come in?" Duncan moved forward to cross the threshold. Mr. Petersen stepped back as his look of confusion gave way to one of concern. Although not all of Sammy Petersen's facial features were intact, it wasn't hard to imagine Cal Petersen as the older version of the youth. They shared the same jawline, cheekbones and a similar eye shape.

A voice called from down the hall. "Cal, what's going on?"

Cal Petersen looked at Duncan, his question unasked.

"You should have Mrs. Petersen join us," Duncan said quietly.

Cal's shoulder's sagged as he turned and went down the hall. Duncan walked into the living area and sat down.

Moreau followed. The basic entryway opened up to a simple room with a comfortable flower-printed sofa and matching chair, a beige, inoffensive shade of paint on the walls and a collection of family photos that lined the mantle of the fireplace.

THE SPYING MOON

Strings of fall leaves had been hung around the window frames and pumpkin candles dotted the coffee table and window ledges.

Signs they were ready for the holiday. There would be no celebration for the Petersens now. This may have been the start of the Canadian Thanksgiving weekend but their arrival at the Petersen home was certain to push that fact from their minds and mark it as a time of mourning rather than a time for appreciation.

She paused and looked at one of the photos. Sammy Petersen held a video camera away from his face and smiled with promise and vigor.

Moreau turned as the Petersens entered. They were as normal a couple as you could imagine. Aging gracefully, perhaps a little thicker around the waist, more gray in the hair than one might hope for, but deep creases around the eyes hinted at the years of laughter and happiness that she'd noted from the family photos.

It was a happiness not reflected in their older son's demeanor in the few pictures he was in. She wasn't sure if it had been fully realized in Sammy's smile yet, either.

Duncan got them to sit down on the couch as he perched on the edge of the chair across from them.

Moreau stood in the corner of the room near the fireplace.

"What...what's this about?" Mrs. Petersen glanced from her husband to Duncan and clutched her housecoat closed. It was already tied tight with the belt. "Is it Jimmy?"

Moreau noted how when some people faced fear they tried to take charge of something physical that they could put their hands on.

The same way she'd pushed herself through the pale yellow curtain that day, pulled out her small duffel bag and started to pack.

As though doing something put her in charge. Pretending that what would follow wouldn't be a series of orders she had no say in, a stream of events beyond her control.

18

Mrs. Petersen clutched that robe closer. To Moreau, it was a subconscious way of holding out hope that by keeping that fabric in place Mrs. Petersen could prevent her world from being pulled apart.

"Constable Moreau—" Duncan pointed at her and then turned back to the couple, "—this is Cal and Laura Petersen."

The couple nodded at her.

"We've come about Sammy," Duncan said.

"Sammy? Not Jimmy?" Cal said.

Duncan shook his head.

Laura Petersen's mouth hung open for a split second. "He's upstairs, asleep." She sprung to her feet and ran up the steps. "Sammy? Sammy? Sammy?"

Moreau imagined what Laura Petersen was feeling. Her need to believe that two police officers would wake them up late at night for some reason other than a tragedy.

Cal covered his face with his hands. The sound of his wife's footsteps were all that broke the silence as she ran down a hall above them, still calling her son's name. A door creaked open, and she cried out.

After a few moments Laura Petersen came back down the stairs at a snail's pace. When she reached the landing she shuffled into the living room.

Robe unclutched. Face a ghastly white. Her hands trembled as she reached out for Nate Duncan.

"Where's Sammy?"

Duncan stood up as Laura Petersen grabbed his arms. Moreau took a step toward them, but he shot her a look and she stopped.

As he held Mrs. Petersen's arms, Duncan led her to the couch.

"I'm very sorry," he said. "I'm afraid we have some bad news."

Chapter 3

Moreau drew a deep breath and inhaled the fresh air the way she'd seen smokers suck the last dregs of a cigarette into their lungs. She sensed Duncan's glance as she exhaled slowly, though she kept her own gaze focused on the road straight ahead.

"It never really gets any easier," he said.

How could it? It felt like they'd just torn the flesh back from Mrs. Petersen's chest and hauled out her heart. Moreau had choked back a lump rising in her own throat. Laura Petersen had dropped to her knees and cried. Eventually, Duncan helped Cal move his wife to the bedroom, which meant he'd observed more of their reactions and their home than she had while she stood idly in the living room and re-examined the same photos she'd seen when she entered. After the men returned, Cal Petersen had tried to wipe his tears away, his lower lip quivering as he stared out at them vacuously and forced himself to answer their questions.

He hadn't known anything helpful. They'd only prolonged his suffering.

"What now?" she asked. It was probably too soon to follow up with Creaser, and the crime scene techs would still be at the scene.

"We talk to Kenny Jensen."

The person Cal Petersen was certain his son would have been with if he'd snuck out on his own.

"He's a minor and it's the middle of the night. I'm sure his parents—"

"Can be handled," Duncan said.

She arched an eyebrow. "You're in charge, Constable Duncan."

"Call me Nate," he said. "What do you want me to call you?"

"Moreau."

If he was bothered by her unwillingness to move to a first-name basis with him he didn't show it.

As they drove the bumps in the pavement increased as the number of streetlights declined. The headlights exposed structures of varying shapes and sizes and a few mobile homes. Duncan pulled over when the SUV's headlights revealed a house that was tired, worn around the edges, with gray paint that peeled off the window frames. Duncan killed the engine and led the way along a few pavers sparsely spread between grass that swallowed their calves, peppered with brittle leaves that crunched as they walked over them. He rang the bell. When they were waiting at the Petersen's house Moreau had felt the heat of an adrenaline surge. Now she felt cold, like the touch of death lingered on her skin. As though anyone who looked at her would know she had been on the hill examining the mangled half of Sammy Petersen's brain.

Feet stomped toward them from inside the house. "What is so goddamned impo...?" The words died on the woman's lips as the door screeched open. Her dirty-blonde hair was partly restrained in a ponytail, while the uncollected locks fell across her hard-angled, lean face. The silence didn't last long.

"What the hell do you want?" she said.

Moreau wondered if the only tone this woman spoke in was pissy, iced with irritation.

"Mary, Constable Moreau and I need to speak with Kenny." Duncan held up his ID.

She looked at him like he was a dead rat a cat had left on her doorstep and about as welcome. "Like I don't know who you are."

The woman didn't move and Duncan didn't respond.

THE SPYING MOON

Moreau said, "I'm sorry, but it's important."

Mary barely glanced at her and sneered as she pushed the screen door open, turned on her heel and let go, without waiting for one of them to grab it. She pulled her frayed, yellow sweater around her thin frame as Duncan reopened the door and stepped inside.

Mary Jensen disappeared. Duncan led the way and Moreau followed him silently. Unlike the Petersen house, this one didn't seem to have a real entryway and dark halls led past a dining room and kitchen to the back of the house to a room with paneled walls. A long, faded couch that may have once been a rich chocolate brown sagged in the middle, a matching set of rust-colored chairs flanked a small sofa that was closer to mocha and a threadbare rug all embraced an oversized, flatscreen TV. No photos of family or proud, smiling youth adorned the mantle. The only thing that covered the ledge above the fireplace in this house was dust.

It couldn't be more different from the Petersen's living room. That space had been bright, and even in the dead of night it was clear it would be filled with light during the day. This room seemed to breed shadows; even the single bulb did little to illuminate it.

The Petersens had highlighted their family with pictures of their life and their children. The Jensens had showcased their TV.

Duncan clearly knew the Jensen family, which was why he'd been certain a middle-of-the-night intrusion could be handled, although Mary's reaction made Moreau wonder how it was that he knew them.

Had he miscalculated when he decided to knock on their door at that hour?

Mary Jensen reappeared. She led a heavy-eyed teen, who was dressed in pajama pants and a faded blue T-shirt that looked like it was two sizes too big. Kenny Jensen had Mary's height, thin frame, and dirty-blond hair that flopped down over his eyes. The edges of his face were softer, though. He started to shake off the drowsiness when he saw them.

Kenny sank into the small sofa and Mary disappeared back down the hall and around the corner. Moreau guessed she was in the kitchen.

"Constable Moreau." She held up her ID. Like Duncan, she remained standing, facing the couch and chairs.

He acknowledged her presence with a glimpse and nod before he turned to Duncan.

"What's going on?"

"Mr. Petersen told us you were likely out with Sammy earlier."

"Yeah." Kenny shrugged. "We were at the outer camp on Holt Hill."

Duncan glanced at Moreau. "Sammy was grounded."

"So?" Kenny shrugged. "That ever stop you?"

Duncan ignored the question and lowered his voice. "Were you drinking?"

Moreau was surprised by the blunt query. From the other room she could hear water run into a sink, then fill something smaller before the sound of running liquid stopped. The slide of a filter tray and sprinkle of something light but solid being poured suggested that Mary was making coffee. There was a lull in the activity when Duncan spoke, despite his quiet tone.

"No. Not me, anyway." Kenny blinked. "What's this about? Don't you wear a uniform?"

Duncan shook his head. "We work plainclothes."

"Oh."

At that moment another teen, this one older than Kenny, emerged from the hall. He was wearing a basic black shirt and jeans, and his arrival coincided with an acrid campfire aroma that filled the room. This teen wasn't as lean as Kenny; he was athletic and filled out with muscle. His hair was darker, his face fuller.

"Heard you were back," he said to Duncan.

THE SPYING MOON

"Hello, Randy."

"Has something happened?" Randy moved toward the sofa where his brother sat. Kenny had shaken the sleep off fairly well but was still a little sluggish. Randy wasn't struggling to get out from under a drowsy fog. He perched himself on the arm of the nearest chair and tried to look relaxed, but his fingers were wrapped into fists, his shoulders stiff and his eye twitched.

"What makes you think that?" Moreau asked.

Randy's eyebrows arched as he stared at her. "Nate's not exactly on the most-welcome list around here and I don't know you."

"Constable Moreau," she said.

"Police. Something has happened."

"There's been an incident on Holt Hill," Duncan said. "Was anyone else up there with you tonight?"

Kenny half-shrugged and snuck a look at his brother. Moreau saw their gaze meet and when they turned back it was Randy's narrow eyes that focused on the constables as Kenny studied the floor.

"I was there, for a while," Randy said. "But we left hours ago."

"Was Sammy still there when you left?"

"Yes."

"Anyone else?"

"I think pretty well everyone left when we, I, did."

"Who is everyone?"

"Well, Kenny left first. Early. Seven-thirty, seven-forty, something like that. Ma expected him to come home and help clean the garage. I haven't a clue why it had to be done just then, but it did. Or so she said."

"That's hardly late enough to be considered going out."

"Tell me about it."

"When did you leave?"

"Maybe fifteen, twenty minutes later." He offered a feeble half shrug.

24

"Maybe twenty-five or thirty?"

Randy lifted his hands up with palms to the sky or, in this case, the sagging nicotine-stained ceiling. "It wasn't like I was paying that much attention."

"Who was with you?"

"Some guys from school. George, Arnold, Doug."

Kenny's head spun around and Randy shrugged. "Came after you left."

Moreau watched Kenny as he looked back down at the carpet. His hair flopped over his forehead, but not before she saw the lines of confusion that formed in his skin.

"George Jacobs, Arnold Hardee, Doug Terry."

"I know who they are," Duncan said.

"They're good guys."

Moreau saw Duncan's eyes narrow just a touch and wondered about Randy's unsolicited defense of his friends.

"You all left before, say, nine?" Duncan asked.

"Earlier. Like eight, I think. We split for a bit and met up later at George's place. His parents are out of town."

"All of you? Except Sammy?"

"Except Sammy and Kenny."

"Any reason why?"

"Why what?"

"Why Sammy didn't go with you," Duncan said.

Kenny's knee shook.

Mary entered with a mug in her hand. She didn't offer anything to anyone. "Do I need to call their father?"

"I don't feel that's necessary at this point," Duncan said.

"Then what the hell is this about?" Mary slammed her drink down on the coffee table as she sat on the chair nearest Kenny, the one Randy was perched on the edge of. She glared at Duncan as though it was his fault the hot liquid had sloshed over the rim of the cup, onto her hand.

"I'm afraid we have some bad news," Moreau said. She told them about Sammy and hoped the revelation would distract the

THE SPYING MOON

Jensens from their history with Nate Duncan, and keep them just off balance enough for her to assess their reactions.

Kendall Moreau fell back against the closed door and sighed. She shut her eyes and started to sink down to the floor, ready to collapse right there, but forced herself to launch her body upright with her shoulders. After she bolted the lock she dragged herself through the sterile space. To her right was a basic kitchenette and to her left there was a serviceable living space with a beige couch, matching chairs and a wall-mounted flatscreen.

The only décor in the entire space was an oversized framed photo of a coyote that was centered on the wall over the sofa. She'd added nothing to the cabin since her arrival Friday except a suitcase, still packed and tucked under the bed, two bags of groceries that didn't even fill the fridge and one cupboard, and a robe, towel and toiletries set on the bathroom vanity, meant to be put away in the morning.

Straight ahead was a tiny hallway, the door to the bathroom to the right and the entrance to her bedroom on the left.

Moreau tugged her long, black jacket from her body and left it where it dropped as she made her way to the bathroom. The coat was stylish and functional, with two oversized pockets on the front that held her phone, notepad, ID and wallet, and a long pocket inside that came in handy when she had paperwork she wanted to protect.

The taps creaked as she turned them on. She let the water adjust to the right temperature as she peeled her jeans and teal sweater off and tossed each article of clothing onto a pile on the floor.

Moreau stepped into the hot shower; the steaming water massaged her muscles, and worked on the knot in her left shoulder as it pulsed against her. She closed her eyes, tilted her head back and soaked her hair. Her upturned face smarted from the sting of the spray against her cheeks.

26

Bruises were forming along the lines where the seatbelt had snapped into her. Those points on her body were tender and each drop of water felt like a pin pricking her skin.

Maple River was a study in contrasts. It was scenic; that was her first observation when she'd arrived and it surprised her. It wasn't the town so much as the location. The mix of rolling hills and craggy, towering mountains gave it a unique postcard-potential setting in every direction.

The town was beautiful, but it was also broken. Any photos would be perfect as long as the dilapidated houses in the poor neighborhoods on the outskirts were cropped out of the picture.

Until she'd arrived Moreau hadn't thought of Maple River as idyllic because of the darkness that lurked beneath the face of each report she'd read. Comics and movies could make one think that unspeakable acts and atrocities happened in places that emanated with evil in the air. Crime was supposed to be a toxin that blackened trees and cast dark clouds over the earth. It created an oppressive force that sucked the joy from people's lives and filled them with fear and warned good people to stay far away. She'd looked at the spirit of the place, saw the sinful ills that plagued the core of the community, and forgot that on the surface Maple River could appear to be as normal as any other town anywhere in the country, with its mix of new and old, rich and poor, polished and tarnished.

Local papers focused on progress and sidestepped the reality of the ramshackle homes that sagged with age and indifference, the abandoned businesses that littered the older streets and the crime rate, which had climbed steadily in the last sixteen months. The gloss in the travel guide she'd seen in the grocery store was the projected image that masked the grimy underbelly of a town peppered with tired people just putting in time before they got their headstone.

Shot right, Maple River could appear clean and pristine, but it was soiled beneath the surface, and there was no way to bring tourists to town and keep them from seeing that life here was

THE SPYING MOON

far from perfect. Freeman was already under pressure about the crime rate, a pressure he'd used as leverage to get his task force approved. He'd have his hands full now as he took the brunt of blame for a crime that would hamper the town's foray into international tourism, a development that the town councilors had invested months working for. The death of a local teen never made for a good headline, whether it was murder or suicide. Both hinted at problems in the community that people didn't want to have touch them, particularly during their vacation days.

She'd arrived earlier than Freeman expected, but later than she'd hoped. Roadwork clogged the highways and a detour had sent her several miles off course. After she finally made it to Maple River she'd silently cursed her way through the maze of one-way streets that steered her away from her destination before she located her rental cabin. After she got the keys she found the grocery store, stocked up on supplies and located the Royal Canadian Mounted Police detachment. What she hadn't told Freeman was the source of the conversation she'd overheard outside the RCMP station earlier. Her hand had been on the door when she heard two men talk candidly about the task force meeting that evening.

Two men she could now identify as Scott Saunders and Alec Chmar.

A glance at her wristwatch as she stood with her hand on the door to the RCMP station had confirmed that she would have hours to wait if she timed her arrival for the meeting. There was a chance if she'd walked into the office earlier she'd be ordered to report Monday like she was supposed to.

Her fingers had lingered on the steel handle as she debated her options. The weekend was time she could use to look into the missing person's case that was never far from her thoughts, a small consolation for being ordered to a border town in the mountains instead of the heart of the province where she could look into the string of cold cases that she was determined to solve, on the books or off.

She'd dropped her hand down to her side, left the station that afternoon and returned at the time of the meeting. It was a way of regaining control. Maybe if she got to work she could overcome this obstacle and move on, to where she really wanted to be.

One way to see the real team was to arrive unexpectedly, which had paid off. There was no air of pretense or illusion of fake welcome that met her when she'd approached the breakroom a few hours earlier.

The team had one member that was a follower and another that seemed to be a sexist jerk. Scott Saunders couldn't hold down his dinner at the crime scene while Nate Duncan had pushed his feelings out of the way and focused on the job at hand. She winced as she turned off the water and stepped out onto the bathmat. It had been her first dead body on the job. Sammy appeared to have committed suicide. There would be an investigation and alcohol might be a factor, maybe even drugs. There would be questions about where the teen had gotten the liquor and likely a public outcry against the willingness of people to supply booze to minors.

There were doubts she had, things that didn't sit right, but so far nobody had been willing to call it murder.

Still, the sight of Sammy Petersen's half-face lingered, his one discernible eye still looking vacantly on the world around him…

No, not vacant. Surprised, like he hadn't expected it.

She dried herself off, hung the towel on the single bar on the wall across from the shower and reached for her robe.

That look had flashed through her mind when Freeman mentioned suicide. Her gut instinct had almost pushed a protest right out of her mouth.

Goddamn kids. What were they thinking?

How old did you have to be to understand that life was precious, that death was the end? Okay, maybe it wasn't. Maybe Sammy was already back in Maple River as a gnat. Maybe his spirit embodied that mangy cat outside his home and he'd been

THE SPYING MOON

trying to stop her from tearing his parent's world apart.

Maybe, but she wasn't about to debate religion with herself after a night like this.

She couldn't grasp the notion of a loving force in the universe when she saw the senseless waste of a young life, some fool kid who'd blown himself into oblivion for no apparent reason at all, no supreme force interceding to guide him to his senses.

If there was a God, she must be on his shitlist to be stuck with the team she'd been put on in Maple River. Levi McIver, Scott Saunders and Alec Chmar seemed to form a boys' club, and she had no doubt they were more interested in her body than her brains.

They probably thought she'd gotten this assignment because she was a woman and not because she'd earned it.

Freeman didn't even seem aware of the tensions within his team. And then there was Nate Duncan. He walked a fine line; unlocked her door but didn't open it, avoided the use of any of the gentlemanly phrases she so often encountered and stuck to the business that had called them out into the night.

He was an enigma. Even with the response from Mary he'd remained calm, despite the rumors of a temper, but she could see the tension in his face as Mary taunted him. His demeanor didn't seem like a mask, but more like a second skin that was still emerging, not quite formed.

She walked to the bedroom, pulled her suitcase out from under the queen size bed that swallowed the space, grabbed a cotton nightshirt and pulled it over her head. The soft fabric fell against her skin and she was thankful she'd cut her hair short enough to not need to pull it out from the collar. It was one less thing for her to focus time and energy on. For five years her goal had been to become an RCMP officer and get assigned in the BC interior near Burns Lake.

She'd been so close.

As she pulled the sheets back on the bed she thought about the coat she'd left in the living room and the clothes on the bathroom floor. It only took a minute for her to retrieve them, and she fished her cell phone out of her jacket pocket, dug back under the bed and into the suitcase for the charge cord and plugged it in by the nightstand on the left side of the bed.

Her phone lit up with an alert she'd clearly overlooked earlier. One missed call, one voicemail.

She didn't recognize the number but as she sank down into the bed she realized she couldn't ignore it. After a few taps on the screen she heard the sound of a familiar voice.

"I-I trusted you."

One single statement, followed by static before the message ended.

Maple River was a setback. If she could work through this case maybe she could work her way back to the goal.

That voice on the phone had rebuked her absence and reminded her of her goal. She wasn't the only daughter to have a mother disappear. Moreau wasn't the only one looking for answers.

That day the social worker came was the day that Moreau's life had been put on hold. Her dreams had been redefined. No longer did she think about traveling to Asia or South America. Gone were the thoughts of a career teaching.

Since that day everything in her life had been filtered through her need for the truth and Kendall Moreau didn't intend to let anything stand in the way of her real mission.

Chapter 4

The Saturday morning edition of the *Gazette* reeked of headlines that were already stale, bitter in the aftertaste of the sudden death of a local boy. It had been too late to include that development in the morning paper's hard copy; instead, word traveled via social media. What Moreau gleaned from the various posts was that the Petersens were prominent in their church, block parents, the type of well-liked, respected community members with a clean image that others either applauded or cynically likened to the Cleavers.

A family that seemed so healthy they were an anomaly.

Now they had entered the ranks of modern normality, a home shattered by grief, ripped apart by God, karma, fate or whatever other force you wanted to blame.

Ministers never recommended the bereaved read Job, did they? God's screw you letter to mankind; he was willing to let even the loyal be abused if it suited his purpose, which meant there was little hope the godless would avoid suffering.

Less significant local news filled the pages of the paper instead. The clash between Councilor Stothers and Mayor Veitch was heating up as the election approached, and the *Gazette* wasn't above printing gossip about the relationship between the two of them. Apparently they'd had a prolonged affair, but Stothers was now being touted by the news as the local gay candidate, with pictures of her and her alleged lover inserted as proof. After Stothers and Veitch had split up, Stothers had gotten involved with a doctor who was on leave for treatment for an addiction to painkillers after being attacked by a patient. Moreau guessed Stothers liked drama.

There were stories about crime, city development and more proposals for tourist attractions.

The town and Abe Holt were arguing over property lines.

A forest fire just outside of Maple River was under investigation. The cause was unknown, and it had destroyed a few acres of vegetation on the slope of the mountain near the old mines. Crews had secured the damaged trees but people in the area were cautioned to be on the lookout for unusual animal behavior as wildlife adjusted to the loss of land and food from the area that had burned. Bears had been seen closer to town than usual on that side of the city.

Corporal Willmott had been injured in the same area just hours before the fire. The cause of that accident was also unknown, although his condition had been upgraded to stable.

Moreau found that interesting, since she'd been assigned to take over the cabin he'd recently occupied.

Other insignificant news. Adam Gilchrist had been elected as an honorary member of Similkameen town council, which was just across the border from Maple River. Gilchrist had moved there after his marriage to an American woman. He owned and operated the town drug store, worked as the local pharmacist and oversaw shipments between his U.S. stores and affiliates in British Columbia and Alberta.

Moreau rubbed her forehead. It was hard to be interested in the trivialities of life when you were faced day in and day out with undeniable depravity and death. It was clear the job was affecting Freeman. He'd entered the breakroom where she was using her own laptop to follow the local social media trail. The man looked so tight that a flat soccer ball could bounce off of him and he didn't say a word to her as he yanked a cupboard open, struck the counter with a cup, whacked a spoonful of sugar into the mug and sloshed coffee so quickly it spilled over

THE SPYING MOON

onto the counter. After he tossed the coffee pot back on its burner he left without acknowledging her presence, or cleaning up his mess.

She'd come in early. Freeman had ordered her and Duncan to go home and sleep, since the coroner's preliminary report wasn't expected until the afternoon at earliest, but she was unable to stay in bed for more than a few hours. After she combed through the print news, online editions and all the Facebook postings and tweets she could find, Moreau wondered if she should start inquiries on her own. Duncan wasn't due for another few hours, and while the information she'd gleaned was probably helping her begin to understand the town's issues and interests, she was anxious to interact with the real Maple River and its residents, to get a feel for the place through contact, and make evaluations about this case based on something more than words on paper or a screen.

She may not have wanted to be there, but if she was going to do the job she was going to do it right. If you weren't willing to strive for that standard there was no point in doing it at all.

A drive through town wouldn't do any harm. She closed her laptop as Freeman reappeared in the doorway without his coffee.

"You're up."

She paused. Did he mean—

"I need you to take a call with McIver." He seemed to be studying what he'd spilled on the counter and hadn't looked at her since he'd spoken.

Worry lines were etched into his face and assured her that he wasn't joking.

Levi McIver. There was a God and he was an asshole.

"Is it about Sammy Petersen?"

Freeman crossed the room to the fridge and opened it. "No. It's a break and enter."

Moreau chewed her lip for half a second while he rummaged through the contents of the shelves.

"Related to the drug inquiry?"

34

Freeman's head snapped around and he looked at her for the first time since she'd arrived at the station that day. "Is there a problem?"

"Not at all, sir." She grabbed her notepad and stuffed it and the laptop into the blue canvas case with K. C. Moreau embroidered on the flap as the sergeant closed the fridge. She swung the bag over her right arm; her shoulder protested and she removed it and grabbed the handle instead.

The bruises had fully emerged by the time she'd risen from her nap.

Levi McIver entered the breakroom and was so focused on Freeman that he didn't seem to realize she was there until the sergeant tipped his head in her direction.

A split-second scowl slid across McIver's face and smoldered beneath the surface of his skin. Moreau could see it in his eyes.

"Scott—" McIver said.

"Do you have a problem with my orders?" Freeman appeared to grow an inch as he spoke.

McIver's millisecond pause suggested hesitation, despite the words that followed. "No, sir."

"Really." Freeman glanced at Moreau. "I'm sure you can handle this."

Whether he meant the two of them could deal with the case or that Moreau could manage McIver was unclear, but she'd seen the way Freeman's eyes shriveled into slits as he'd asserted his authority over them and she had no intention of getting on her superior's bad side.

There was no polite formality offered, no pause in McIver's step to ensure she kept pace with him and no indication of which vehicle he was heading to until the remote opener caused the alarm to beep and the lights to flash on an unmarked four-door SUV.

Her view of the town was limited by the speed at which McIver could take corners, even inside city limits. Instead of structures she noted a blur of colors. He turned down a road and

THE SPYING MOON

there was a quick cuss under his breath, so soft she almost missed it. She looked up and saw the construction worker holding a stop sign and a bucket truck that blocked their path.

Since her arrival there had always been something in the way of progress. McIver wove along a side street and went the wrong way down a lane. A vehicle pulled out into his path and honked at him. McIver accelerated and swerved around the car. The driver backed up into the adjacent alley and flipped them off as they drove by.

Another distraction. Every second lost was another one standing between Moreau and her goal. It was starting to feel like her chance to find the truth was slipping away.

The speed McIver drove at helped to make up for the detour. They came out onto a quiet street that Moreau guessed was near the edge of town, with potholes so old they were crusted with dirt and debris that had settled into them and the street lacked lights to ward off the darkness of a mountain night.

A sharp turn to the right sent them up a steep incline. Moreau looked out the window and saw an overview of the town from above. From that vantage, the spires of the local churches and straight lines of the older buildings artfully meshed with the trees and roofs of houses, while all the grit and grime the city had acquired was concealed through the angle of her focus.

It was possible at just that second to look down and think Maple River was idyllic, which was hardly how she would have described it after her first night on the job.

They turned the corner and she saw a blue Dodge pick-up truck sitting in front of a rustic cabin perched partway up the mountainside. McIver parked and the crooked screen door opened. A stout and wrinkled woman with short, white curls emerged, spouted a stream of verbal diarrhea, and gestured with her hands to convey her annoyance over the inconsiderate crime she'd endured.

"In my day we would'a hunted them down and tanned their hides ourselves and we wouldn't be making excuses for this type of nonsense, breaking into a woman's house and taking her food and looking through all her drawers."

McIver glanced at Moreau and opened his mouth as the woman's monologue continued. He looked as though he was about to say something, but he didn't.

The woman's face froze mid-whine as she glared at McIver. Mabel Cook stretched herself up to her full height. All five feet of it, Moreau estimated. Mabel stomped down the front steps, marched up to them and wagged her finger at McIver. "What are you going to do about this?"

"What we can," he said.

Mabel hmmph'd and glanced at Moreau before she poked McIver in the chest. "You damn well better do everything you can."

She shoved her keys into his hands, turned and stomped off up a path, yelled at a mongrel tethered just down the slope from the front porch, and disappeared into a small shed while the dog whined at the shed door.

Moreau followed McIver up onto the porch. She watched as he studied the door. There were no marks on the frame or scuffs on the metal. McIver pulled out a glove and snapped it on before he twisted the handle and then tried the lock with the keys he'd been given. Everything worked.

She followed him into the cabin.

Every drawer had been pulled out, rifled through and dumped. Moreau could see through the doorway to a bedroom off the kitchen. Clothing spilled from the dresser. Between those points, where the hands of the thief had not been busy, there was a bed made so properly it rivaled the tension of a trampoline, a small cloak area to the side of the entrance with shoes set neatly in a row, hooks where coats hung smartly, and gloves lay across a shelf above the jackets. Even from the entrance she could see that the tap on the kitchen sink sparkled. A pristine counter shone around the area where things had been knocked down from the upper cupboards.

THE SPYING MOON

The inside of the cabin stood out in contrast to the outside, which bore the effects of exposure to the elements and eluded the immaculate presentation it was easy to assume Mabel Cook offered inside when her home had not been ransacked.

"This will be our point of entry." McIver nodded at the far window, the one at the end of the kitchen nook area, which didn't overlook the porch. "Perp used tape to keep the glass from shattering."

He pointed to the sheet of glass on the floor; the broken pieces were held together by adhesive and maintained a neat square.

Moreau hadn't known exactly what she expected from McIver once they got to the scene, but open communication wasn't it. She scrambled to respond appropriately. "That suggests they came prepared."

"Why here and not one of the living room windows?" McIver looked outside at the area below the window and nodded.

Moreau walked over. There was about a five-foot drop from the bottom of the window to the top of a hilly slope of loose dirt and brambles that had sprung up around the outside of the cabin. "Blackberry bushes?"

McIver shrugged. "We should be grateful this guy was dumb enough not to come in off the porch. Not the sharpest knife in the drawer."

The area on the other side of the bushes was muddy and the bushes were thick. There was a chance their perp had drawn blood from the prickles or left impressions of his footwear. "It does beg the question though, doesn't it? Avoiding the dog?"

"What's the point of that? There wasn't anyone around to hear the dog bark." McIver paused. "Unless he thought Mabel was home."

"Which would make this a robbery to cover up what, exactly? With this point of entry, it was planned. Unless he's over six feet tall he would have had a hard time prepping the glass from the ground. It was taped up pretty high," he said as he pointed to the upper edge of the glass, almost two feet from the bottom part of the square that had been broken into the window pane. "And even at that height it would be hard to pull yourself up through the frame."

McIver shook his head. "It makes no sense. He taped the glass, which keeps it from shattering, so he won't be wounded entering or make as much noise. That suggests experience. But then he walks through mud where he might leave footprints and climbs over prickly bushes that may cut him. He picked the window farthest from the dog but all he took was canned food."

"After he made a hell of a mess."

McIver turned as the crime scene techs that had just arrived came in the door. "Which makes your job much more interesting."

"Were you born heartless?" the first tech said.

McIver forced a smile. "I got a double dose of sarcasm instead."

Creaser turned as Moreau followed Nate Duncan into the coroner's office. He grabbed a file and a sugar-coated donut. "Cherry filling." Creaser took a bite and held the pastry out for inspection while red ooze spilled down the sides. "Help yourselves."

It was the only color that stood out in the part of the otherwise sterile room that Moreau could see from the entrance. A narrow hall led to a desk; the chairs, table and cupboards were stainless steel, offset by the bright white walls and coat that Creaser wore over his clothes, which consisted of a pair of beige pants and a pale white polo shirt.

Moreau swallowed against the bitter taste of bile rising in her throat. She couldn't move. It seemed like the smallest disruption in the aura of the room would be enough to send her stomach contents spilling forward, like that day when she'd finally held her mother's file in her hands.

It's all in the mind. Find a way to regain control. She drew a

THE SPYING MOON

deep breath through her mouth to minimize her exposure to the scent her nose was responding to.

Duncan glared at the coroner.

"You two aren't any fun," Creaser said. "Right down to business. Guess what killed him?" He led the way around the corner, where the room opened up. At the far end of the space there were doors to each of the compartments where bodies could be stored. To the right, the remains of Sammy Petersen lay on an examination table.

When neither responded right away, he said, "Nobody's going to take a shot at it?"

Duncan groaned. Moreau swallowed again.

"Last night, it seemed cause of death was a single gunshot wound to the head." Creaser popped the last bit of the donut in his mouth. "But not so."

"What do you mean?" Duncan frowned. "We thought..."

The coroner walked to the sink, washed his hands, dried them and wiped his mouth. "As did everyone, but that's what they pay me the little bucks for."

He went to the body, picked up Sammy's right arm and turned it over. A bruise at the joint circled a small hole.

Moreau hadn't realized how thankful she should have been for the darkness at the scene the night before. It had minimized the graphic shock value of the gaping wound.

In the clear light of the examination room nothing softened the edges of the chasm in Sammy Petersen's skull.

However, the darkness had also concealed some of the details, and the injection site was one of them.

Duncan bent closer and looked at the spot on Sammy's arm. "Blood had to be circulating in his system in order for his skin to bruise, which means he was still breathing when the metal pierced his vein," he said.

"Very good." Creaser's smile hadn't waned as he put hand to stiffened flesh. "There is a certain amount of satisfaction in establishing that a boy his age didn't simply blow his brains out

40

for no apparent reason one night after a few beers."

"Are you saying he was murdered?" Moreau asked.

"This isn't the psychic hotline. I merely assert the medical factors. Whether or not he was murdered is a question for you to answer." Creaser put Sammy's arm down and retrieved the file, which he flipped open.

"You're the one that determines cause of death."

"Quite right. This is what I can tell you. It was after midnight when we all met on the hillside. Rigor was beginning to show in the facial muscles that were left to examine, as well as the neck and the shoulders."

"He'd been dead for at least two or three hours, possibly a bit longer," Duncan said.

"He could have had an elevated body temperature if he was running or doing something causing exertion before his death, which would taint the timeline," Moreau said.

"Thank God for *CSI*." Creaser mocked a praying man, with hands pressed together and held toward the heavens, file sandwiched between them. A quick smile flickered across his face as he winked at Moreau. "You're right, technically, but there are no other indicators of physical exertion or elevated body temperature. In my opinion, Sammy died between eight and nine on Friday night."

Moreau glanced at Duncan. Kenny claimed he headed home around seven-thirty. Randy said he'd left not long after Kenny...

Add in the fact that Sammy was killed by drugs before half his head was removed by a bullet and there were some concerns about Kenny and Randy's account of the night's events.

"There's something else I can tell you. Postmortem hypostasis indicates he was sitting upright when he died. The discoloration around the buttocks is more pronounced than the lividity around the shoulder blades and back."

"What about his chest?" Duncan pointed at the unusual crisscrossing of lines on the photo of the body Creaser had passed him.

THE SPYING MOON

Moreau looked at Sammy. The lines from the photo weren't on the cadaver now.

"It seems to indicate he was slumped forward for some time after his death. Blood was beginning to settle around the contact points where his torso pressed against his arms, which were likely supported by his knees. Similar marks were found—" he extracted another photo and passed it to Moreau, "—on the legs, hence my assertion that he appears to have been bent over. He would have needed to be in this position for some time in order for us to find this level of postmortem hypostasis. I decided to re-check the body after you left the scene. Sometimes, a delay in moving the body can come in handy.

"And, of course, since lividity hadn't settled and shifted when we moved him at one-thirty a.m., we know that he died within six hours of that time, which narrows your window on the time of death to between seven-thirty p.m. and nine p.m. at the latest. Any later and we wouldn't have seen the rigor progress to the point it had."

A uniform had taken the call at 11:08 p.m., about what sounded like a gunshot. That had prompted an officer to do a drive by. Moreau had read Constable Michaels' report that morning. He'd stated that he expected nothing serious. It could have been a hunter, or even a car backfiring. Instead, he'd found a body.

With the time of death now established and the fact that it occurred hours before the gunshot, as well as the conclusion that Sammy had died of an overdose, someone had to have been up on Holt Hill not long before the first officer had arrived.

"How do you know he died from the needle and not the gun?" Duncan asked.

"In toxicological terms, he was LD50. That means—"

"It means he took enough to consistently cause death," Moreau said.

"And then some. You know a thing or two about drugs, which I suppose is why you're here. Sammy was way over the limit. Death was a certainty." Creaser passed them the file, complete with pictures and his preliminary report. "And there wasn't enough blood at the scene. If the heart had been pumping when the bullet pierced his brain he would have bled like a stuck pig. As it was, most of what we had to retrieve was brain tissue.

"By the way, the poison of choice..." The arch of Creaser's brow hinted at more.

"Don't hold back on us now," Duncan said.

"Not only was there more than enough drugs in Sammy's system to kill him, but the combination of alcohol and cocaine would have been enough to ensure death already. This was overkill."

"He was already dead when somebody faked his suicide. We picked up on the excessive measures already," Moreau said.

"Yes, yes, there is that. But it's what they don't teach you about illegal substances that I get paid to explain. When alcohol and cocaine are combined, they create cocaethylene in the system."

"Okay, I'll bite." Duncan said.

"Cocaethylene is more toxic than drugs used independently. It affects the brain longer than cocaine or alcohol alone. It's a lethal mix. This is the most common combination that results in drug-related death."

"Are you saying—?" Moreau began. Creaser put up his hand to stop her.

"All I'm saying is that, with the alcohol in his system, Sammy didn't need the overdose to die. He could have stopped halfway through shooting up and it wouldn't have made a difference."

"This isn't a case of a long-term user who kept pushing the stuff because he wasn't getting the buzz he wanted?" Moreau asked.

Creaser shook his head. "There's no physical evidence that he'd ever used drugs before. No traces in his system, no long-term damage to the heart, liver, kidneys, no other needle marks.

THE SPYING MOON

I think Sammy's first time was his last."

Moreau drew in a breath. "Is there any way to know if he injected himself?"

"Short of finding the needle and matching fingerprints?" Creaser paused. "I did find bruising around his right wrist and left shoulder."

"Consistent with the age of the bruise around the injection site?" Duncan asked.

Creaser nodded. He pointed to the marks on Sammy's body. "I'd say a lot more pressure was used, though. You can see the bruises are more extensive."

"If you had to make a call, what would you put this death as?" Moreau asked.

"Suspicious. I'm not willing to conclusively rule it a homicide at this time, because all of these factors could be explained away. It's possible Sammy Petersen overdosed deliberately or by accident; it's possible someone helped him take the trip from this life to the next."

Duncan and Moreau left in silence. They were halfway down the hall when Moreau spoke.

"What do you think?"

Duncan sighed and shrugged. "Like he said, there's plenty of room for doubt."

"Sounds like the Jensen boys weren't being straight with us. How do you know them?"

"We'd better go talk to Freeman," Duncan said. "He isn't going to be too happy about this."

Moreau's phone beeped and she pulled it out of her pocket. "First, we're wanted in ballistics."

Chapter 5

A thin, Asian male in his mid-twenties with black-rimmed glasses and a soft smile identified himself as Greg when they walked into the ballistics lab. It was a sterile room of gray shadows accentuated by the light reflecting on the stainless steel desks and workspaces, and it hadn't been overtaken by boxes or stacks of furniture. A steel wall topped with a plexiglass partition separated Greg's workspace from the area where test shots were performed, obstructing their full view of that space.

Moreau guessed it was a sound buffer.

"You have something for us?" she asked.

"Not what you expect. The gun recovered at the scene wasn't the gun he was shot with."

"You're kidding," Duncan said.

Greg shook his head and extracted a photo from a tray on a desk by an oversized computer monitor. "It's all in the report, but if you look here you can see the bullet recovered from the scene, and on this side is a bullet fired from the weapon he was holding. The lines and grooves don't match."

"What kind of gun we are looking for?"

"It was a 9mm. Stop at the lab to talk to Benji about the prints."

The lab was just down the hall from ballistics. Benji was an Asian male with dark spiked hair, glasses with black frames and chubby fingers. He looked like a slightly rounded version of Greg.

THE SPYING MOON

"Constables Duncan and Moreau," Benji said.

They nodded.

He apologized for the towers of boxes spiraling toward the ceiling that surrounded them. "The renovations. Our storage facility is being rewired. Until then it's like walking between Jenga games played with cardboard boxes and hoping you don't bump one of them the wrong way."

Moreau may have been petite but she slid sideways anyway. One wrong move could have a chain reaction that would send dozens of boxes crashing down around them.

"We checked the gun for prints."

"And found nothing?" Duncan said.

"Precisely. However, we did confirm that there was insufficient GSR on Sammy's hands to suggest he fired the weapon. We tested both right and left hands, to be certain."

"Which confirms what we already know, since he was dead when someone pulled the trigger," Duncan said.

Benji nudged his glasses up his nose. "The serial number was filed down. We can't raise it. I started a search to see if the bullet that was fired from the weapon matches any cases in our system. I haven't gotten a hit."

"But?" Moreau prompted, sensing there was more he hadn't said.

"There was a gun store theft in Okotoks last month. A number of models were stolen, including the type of gun recovered from the scene."

"Okotoks, Alberta?" Duncan said.

Benji nodded.

"I doubt Freeman will send us on a road trip to check it out." Moreau took the report Benji offered. "But we appreciate your hard work."

"Yes, thanks," Duncan added as they carefully twisted through the maze of boxes back to the door.

"We don't know it was murder," Freeman said. Duncan and Moreau hovered over him because he hadn't invited them to sit down. His office could have seemed spacious but it was crammed full of boxes and chairs stacked with more boxes that towered precariously around the sergeant, like cardboard versions of the Leaning Tower of Pisa, except Moreau suspected that the leaning tower could outlast any of the spires in this room.

"We don't know it wasn't," Duncan said.

"Kenny and Randy Jensen stated everyone left around eight o'clock. If that was true then Sammy was by himself on that hill," Moreau said. "But the medical evidence is clear. There's no way he was alone. Someone pulled the trigger of a gun and it wasn't Sammy Petersen."

"And he wasn't even shot with the weapon recovered at the scene," Duncan said. "The gun we found doesn't match the slug from Sammy. It was planted."

Freeman leaned back and rubbed his palm against his forehead. "An unknown person could have wandered through the cut-out, found Sammy's body slumped over on the picnic table and decided to stage a suicide."

Moreau swallowed as Duncan responded. "Why would anybody do that?"

"Kicks. Maybe they thought, since he was dead anyway, they'd see how good our investigative techniques really are." Freeman scratched his head. "Hell, maybe they were just bored."

"Let's go way out on a limb here and say it was some random person who thought they'd mess around with a dead body. They're complicit in tampering with evidence from the scene of a crime." Duncan looked at Moreau. "The techs didn't come up with a syringe, did they?"

Freeman's face creased as Moreau shook her head. "There's no trace of the drugs found at the scene. The other issue is that there was bruising consistent with Sammy being restrained while injected."

"But there could be another explanation for the injuries."

THE SPYING MOON

"It's possible, but it's certainly suspicious."

Freeman rubbed his chin for a moment. "Still not conclusive."

"Drugs in his system, bruises on his body, a staged suicide and switched guns." Duncan tapped the stack of reports that lay on Freeman's desk. "Look, I know we can't be certain it was a murder. Sammy could have injected the drugs himself. It could have been an accident. Maybe he even knew it was a lethal dose and had it planned."

Freeman arched an eyebrow. "I get enough sarcasm from McIver."

Duncan sighed. "We owe it to the family to ensure we consider all the possibilities."

"Out of everyone here I would have thought you'd be the one who'd want this to blow over so you wouldn't have to deal with these families."

Moreau held her breath as the two men stared at each other.

Duncan's face tightened. "Respectively, sir, I may not be happy to be here, but I'm not going to let that get in the way of the work."

Freeman seemed to process that for a few seconds before he nodded. "You still haven't convinced me this is a homicide."

"I know a murder with a drug connection wouldn't be good for your—"

The sergeant stood up and slammed his hand down on the desk.

"This isn't about me. This is about making sure we handle the situation properly. Not getting ahead of ourselves and jumping to conclusions we can't support with evidence."

"Respectfully, I don't feel this is something we can dismiss out of hand."

Freeman looked at Moreau. "I have to agree, sir. And this is a drug connection." Moreau watched his face as she spoke. He'd gone from the flush of anger to pale resignation.

"Not once did I say I wanted you to wrap this up quietly. But we have to consider how we approach this. You already have a statement from two boys saying that they left Sammy alone on that hill around eight o'clock. If it was murder you need to prove they lied or that someone else was there. You need to track the drug source. At least from that perspective this ties in with the bigger investigation at play. If we can establish that someone gave Sammy a needle that they knew contained a lethal dose or prove someone else was on that hill with him when he died, then we have somewhere to go with this."

"If this is ruled a suicide and it turns out to be a murder it will be a lot harder to get a conviction," Moreau said. "And at the very least, we have someone firing the gun hours later, which seems to be an attempt to conceal the true cause of his death. That could have been someone tied to the drug trade, someone who didn't want us to connect the dots between the cocaine in Sammy's system and their crimes."

Freeman rested his hands on his desk, but remained standing. "We aren't making a ruling yet. Track down the other boys who were there and get statements."

"The crime scene techs said they had DNA and fingerprint sources to work with. Should we ask for voluntary samples, just to piece together the scene?" Moreau asked.

"Not yet. Go with the statements first. Get everything the techs can give you. If we start bringing teenagers in for voluntary DNA samples and fingerprinting we'll cause a panic. And at this point the only reason we can offer is a question of curiosity. Thanks to Facebook everyone thinks we're closing a file on a suicide. Don't tell them otherwise." He glanced at Duncan. "It isn't just about politics. Parents get defensive when a kid dies, especially if it's a kid they knew. We need to be careful about alienating potential suspects who might be critical to our investigations."

"You make it sound like they're a bunch of hardened criminals instead of teenage boys out for some kicks," Moreau said.

Freeman sank back down into his chair. "If one of those boys put the drugs into Sammy's hands they know where you can get

THE SPYING MOON

your hands on enough cocaine to take a one-way trip into the afterlife. You said yourself it could have been someone involved with the drug trade. If the dealers get wind of us pushing down hard on them we might have a clear homicide on our hands instead of a suspicious death, which, at this moment, is all we do have."

"I don't suppose you'd like to send us to Alberta for some field work," Duncan said.

Freeman's eyes bugged out, and he looked like he was ready to jump back up, leap across the desk and throttle Duncan. "What the hell for?"

"There was a theft from a gun shop in Okotoks," Moreau said. "A number of weapons were stolen, including ones that match the make and model we recovered."

"That's hardly enough to justify a trip out of province."

"We can ask someone local to handle it," Moreau said. "But the gun's serial number has been filed off, and without a physical inspection, we may be left with a guess at best."

"The gun's serial..." Freeman didn't need to finish. He leaned back in his chair and rubbed his forehead.

"I know none of it on its own is conclusive," Duncan said. "But it is suspicious."

Freeman nodded slowly. "Do what you can for now. I hope to hell we aren't dealing with gun smugglers here on top of everything else."

Duncan swallowed and turned to leave but before his hand reached the door handle the sergeant spoke again.

"Not a word about the possibility of murder to anyone." He cleared his throat. "As far as everyone else is concerned, you two are pushing hard to clear this routine investigation so that you can get back to the drug investigation."

"What about Saunders?" Duncan asked.

"I'll take care of him."

"And Creaser?" Moreau asked.

Freeman reached for his phone. "He won't be a problem either."

50

***

Outside Freeman's office Moreau noticed a woman sitting at a nearby desk. She looked up, her gaze drawn straight to Duncan like a magnet to metal.

The woman's auburn hair fell over her shoulders. She had dark eyes and fair skin, and Moreau saw the color creep up the back of her partner's neck as the woman stared at him.

A nameplate on the desk identified her as Alyssa Everett. "I guess I lost the bet," she said.

Alyssa's voice was crisp and direct; she wasn't flirting with Nate Duncan, but Moreau still didn't want to be there, hearing this conversation. She was just about to sneak past Duncan when a delivery man stopped in front of him, which left Moreau wedged between him and the sergeant's office door.

"Oh?" Duncan said.

"I put one hundred dollars on the certainty that there must be more than one Nate Duncan who would live in Maple River in my lifetime because there was no way you'd be coming back."

He almost smiled. "Ouch. Stiff bet."

"Next time I feel sure about something I'll think twice. At least where you're concerned."

There was something in her tone that hinted at layers of meaning. Moreau wondered about their history and wished she could escape. It was none of her business, just another place she didn't want to be that she was trapped in.

"I would have made the same bet. There were better odds on Jesus returning before I did."

Alyssa got up, signed for the boxes and added them to the stack of cardboard squares behind her desk.

The delivery man moved and Duncan walked away. Moreau followed. A glance back confirmed that Alyssa's intense eyes watched them go.

Chapter 6

"Here we go." Duncan nodded at the three males he'd already identified for Moreau. The older one sat on a car while the two thin nerve-bundles shifted weight from one foot to the other and averted their eyes after they saw Nate Duncan.

Their friend on the car had dark hair and eyes that were as cold as steel on a December day and he stared at Duncan as they approached.

He sat with one foot resting on the car's bumper, the other dangling against the grill. Once he pulled his gaze away from Duncan he seemed more interested in the color of air than the approaching RCMP officers. He had a cigarette snug between his fingers, which were stiff as stone.

The lanky lads had scraggly hair, the lazy-boy look of indifference in their deliberate scruffiness. From a distance it was hard to tell them apart, but when you got closer you could see that Arnold Hardee had a thin mustache that looked more like a smudge of dirt and his hair was closer to a sandy brown. Doug Terry's hair was darker brown and it didn't reach his shoulders. The black-haired one on the car was clean-shaven, hair neat and trim, his clothes tidy. He wasn't living clean, but he knew enough to maintain an image that could fool the optimistic elders who still believed in goodness of youth today.

He was probably responsible for every bad thing his bookends did, but the average person who didn't look far beneath the surface would think he was more respectable.

His focus turned to Moreau, almost as though he knew what she'd been thinking. The skin around his eyes pinched as they hardened and she felt a chill trickle down her spine. There was something unsettling in his gaze, perhaps because of the way he stared with a smile on his lips and ice in his eyes.

"Well, well. Should we feel honored that you've been seeking us out? You the park bench police, ensuring the youth of today sit on properly designated public structures?"

His friends sputtered a quick laugh as they studied their toes.

"Big words, George. I'm impressed, but I'm sure you know what this is about."

George's eyes gleamed. "What do you think I know about drugs?"

"What makes you think this has something to do with drugs?"

"It's been all over the news." George arched an eyebrow. "You can read, can't you? No uniform, so you're plainclothes, which means you're part of Freeman's precious little task force."

Moreau saw Duncan's shoulders stiffen, but his face remained a blank slate. "You're keeping up on public affairs, George. That's impressive."

George lifted the cigarette to his mouth and sucked in hard.

"Actually, Constable Moreau and I are here about the death of Sammy Petersen."

"Care to tell us what you were doing last night, Mr. Jacobs?" Moreau asked. If Duncan could keep his cool with the little smartass, she could too, and she was tired of the banter. More filler that stood in the way of clearing this case.

George lifted what was left of the cigarette to his lips. He exhaled as he studied her through the smoke he discharged. His eyes hardened, as though he'd sized her up and reached some conclusion about her that he didn't like. "Hanging out with my friends." He nodded at the bookends.

"Just the three of you?"

His mouth twisted cynically. "Obviously you know that's not the case or you wouldn't be here."

THE SPYING MOON

"Why don't you tell us your version, for the record?" Duncan flipped his notebook open.

"Why don't I call my folks and have them meet me at the station with a lawyer?" George sucked hard on the end of the cigarette before flicking it on the sidewalk. The butt rolled within an inch of Duncan's shoe.

"This doesn't have to be formal. You can give us a statement and be on your way. Or we can take you all down to the station. We can call Arnold's parents and Doug's mom, but for you—" Moreau smiled, "—we don't need to call your folks. You're legally an adult."

Arnold's head snapped up and he stared at her with his mouth hanging open in the shape of an O. Moreau counted to three and then took a gamble. "Or like I said, we can take door number one and keep things simple."

George scowled but his shoulders dropped down just a touch. "A bunch of us boys were up on Holt Hill, having a few drinks on a Friday night. But we left early."

"Any special reason why?" she asked.

"Why what? That we were drinking on the hill?"

"That you left early."

George shrugged. "My parents were away."

"Where were they?"

He paused with his mouth open for a moment as he turned to look at Moreau. "Some hotel in Vancouver, for their anniversary. You know, walking in Stanley Park and movies at the IMAX, shit like that."

"Your parents were out of town so instead of having a party at your place you went to Holt Hill with Arnold, Doug and Sammy, had some drinks, and some of you left early." She looked at George and waited.

He smirked and drummed his fingers against his knees. "Arnold, Doug, Sammy, Kenny and Randy were there. Kenny had to leave early 'cause of his mommy." The bookends snickered. "Everyone else left not long after that."

54

"Everyone but Sammy?"

"Sammy wanted to stay to hang out."

"So he stayed on the hill?"

"That's right."

"He was alone?"

George pointed his index finger at her. "You're catching on."

"And you went straight to your house? No stops?"

"Nope."

Duncan spoke. "Did he have the gun out when you left?"

George's mask slipped at the unexpected interjection, but only for a split second. Doug spun around so fast he was probably dizzy. Arnold froze. They both looked at George, who focused on Duncan.

"What gun?" George finally said.

"You watch enough news to know about the task force and drug investigation but you didn't know that Sammy was found with a gun in his hand and had been shot in the head?" Moreau arched an eyebrow.

"Look, I don't know what was going on with the kid. He wanted to top himself it's nothing to do with me."

"Everyone else left by eight and Sammy was fine."

George looked at her with a cynically puzzled glare that inferred the answer should be obvious. "You slow or something? That's what I said."

"And how did you come to believe that Sammy had committed suicide?"

"That's what the news said, isn't it?"

"I don't know. Is it?" Moreau replied, her voice equally cool.

"Look, yeah, I heard he shot himself, okay? It's all over Facebook. But I wasn't there."

"You guys were just drinking?" Duncan asked.

"What else do you think? Jacking off?"

"We'll know if you were," she said. "Crime scene techs took samples of everything at the scene."

The corners of George's mouth had that doubtful pull, his

THE SPYING MOON

eyes widened and his face paled. Then he put his mask back on, control regained.

"Won't help much without samples to compare it to."

"A technicality, George. After all, we have statements saying that there were only six of you up there Friday night and that Kenny left first. Right now, that makes you three of the last four people to see Sammy Petersen alive."

"Nobody's going to bother the golden boy."

Duncan smiled. "Which is why you have our attention at the moment."

George's mouth twisted. "What are you getting at?"

"Me?" Duncan's face feigned innocence. "I was just telling you that it won't be hard to figure out who was doing what, especially since we have you on the record saying nobody else was there."

"It's not like we're the only ones who know about the place," Doug said. He glanced at George and red heat filled his cheeks. His mouth clamped shut and turned away.

"Doug has a point." George folded his arms across his chest. "Anyone could have come along. There were like, three hours between when we left and the gunshot."

Curious. George hadn't said when Sammy shot himself, which is what she would have expected someone who wasn't there to say. George said the gunshot. He was referencing the sound, which was something she'd expect from someone who'd heard it themselves.

Duncan shook his head. "That may be true, but Sammy didn't die three hours later. He died between seven-thirty and nine."

The bookends' heads snapped up.

"Really?" George's voice pitched with a nervous tinge.

"Really."

George's shoulders drooped as he stared at Duncan but the look of fear on his face evaporated with the ring of a phone. George reached into his pocket and pulled out his cell. He muttered something under his breath, reached for his back pocket and took out a second phone.

"Hello? Oh, good. Yeah. We'll be right over, Max." He snapped the flip phone shut and hopped off the hood of the car. "My truck's fixed."

"How long has it been in the shop?" Duncan asked.

"What's it to you?"

"Why's it a secret?"

George stared at Duncan and then scowled. "I don't know. Like a week and a half."

"That's pretty long for your vehicle to be out of commission."

"It's been gone longer than you've been back. Satisfied?"

Duncan nodded. "Do you need a lift?"

George's mouth hung open for a few seconds before he forced his head to shake. "No. We'll be fine."

"I am curious about something," Moreau said.

George had regained enough composure to look her up and down. "I like white meat."

"Pretty finely tuned racial radar, George. I've got my mom's black eyes and hair, but otherwise, most people don't see it."

"Well, there's lots of squaws 'round here and a pasty squaw is still a squaw. I like cream." He paused. "No half and half for me, if you know what I mean."

From the corner of her eye, Moreau could see Duncan's face harden and darken. She took a step toward George Jacobs that put her between him and Duncan.

"You knew the time of the reported gunshot."

"I told you, they said it on the news."

"For someone who was hanging out with him on a Friday night you don't seem that upset, or that surprised."

She stared into George's eyes and watched him try to hold his face in check and not react to her words, but a look of fear had crept in. From the corner of her eye she could see that the bookends were perfectly still.

George faked a cough and turned his head away from her as

THE SPYING MOON

he put his fist over his mouth. He used the maneuver to twist his body away from her. "Let's go," he said, and cut sharply around the end of the vehicle, walking away so fast that the bookends had to scamper to catch up.

Duncan tapped his pen against his notepad. Once George, Doug and Arnold were out of earshot, he asked, "What do you think?"

"He doesn't like you." Moreau extracted a plastic bag from her pocket and bent down by Duncan's foot.

"Besides that?"

"Well, he didn't nail down a timeline, exactly, but then he definitely thought he'd given them a three-hour window between leaving and Sammy dying." She scooped the cigarette butt into the bag and stood up.

"He didn't seem to like the fact that we had already disproved the alleged time of death."

As they turned to leave, Duncan stopped. He walked over to the vehicle George had been sitting on, pulled out a bag from his pocket, and picked up something beside the wheel of the car.

"The news did report the initial speculation that Sammy had shot himself shortly after eleven, by the way."

"I know," Duncan said. "They relied on the report of a gunshot in the nine-one-one call."

"Sammy's death didn't seem matter to him." Moreau turned that over in her mind and chewed her lip. "You seemed surprised about his truck being away for repairs."

Duncan nodded.

"Any special reason?"

"Just that it means they were walking or riding in Randy's car. Doug and Arnold are younger than Kenny, so they can't drive. George lives just on the other side of Bearspaw Bridge."

"I take it that isn't close enough to have heard the gunshot themselves."

"Not a chance. The good news for us is that Holt Road is pretty busy, with the bar on the corner of Main and a convenience store on the corner of Front Street. And there's usually something going on at the church Friday night, too. If he went home with his friends there should be a lot of witnesses who can corroborate that."

Moreau arched an eyebrow subconsciously. "George likes to spend his time with boys that are considerably younger than he is. I guess it helps that you know this town."

"That's why they sent me here."

She thought about the exchange between Freeman and Duncan earlier, where Duncan had made it clear he'd rather not be there and Freeman had acknowledged his awareness of Duncan's feelings. "Just because you know the town?"

"No."

It was a one-word answer that made it apparent Maple River wasn't something he wanted to talk about.

Neither of them wanted to be there, neither of them wanted to talk about it and neither of them would solve the case if they let that get in their way.

She pushed that thought aside. Considering the details they had so far on Sammy's death it seemed like a good idea to spend some time following up on George Jacobs and checking his story.

"Wait a second," Duncan said as he walked past the vehicle, down the block.

She followed his path until she saw two other teenagers who couldn't have been more different than George Jacobs. They were scruffy and wore grungy clothing that hung loosely on them. Moreau moved closer so that she could hear the conversation.

"Charlie. Remember me?" Duncan said.

The boy's eyes narrowed and then widened. "What the hell you doin' here?" He tucked his hands into the pockets of his pea green coat.

"Transferred."

"Kicked you out of the city, huh?"

Duncan ignored the comment and nodded at the other man.

THE SPYING MOON

"Not going to introduce me?"

"He don't need no trouble."

Duncan pointed at the backpacks that hung from their hands. "What have you got in there?"

"Food."

"Looks like you guys could use a good meal. There's a diner around the corner."

"After last time? Forget it, man."

"You know that wasn't me that screwed up."

"I don't know shit except I'm still breathin' and I plan on stayin' that way."

"You change your mind, you let me know." Duncan pulled a card from his pocket and held it out.

Charlie looked at it for a second, snatched it and then swung his bag over his shoulder. He walked away with his friend and didn't look back.

Duncan stood still and watched Charlie walk away.

Moreau got her phone and pulled up a number. Charlie disappeared into an alley several blocks down the street as she hung up from her call.

Duncan didn't comment on Moreau's proximity as he strode past her and led the way to the SUV.

"What was that about?" she asked after she'd buckled her seatbelt, wincing as it pulled against her bruises.

"Nothing."

She bit her lip. Duncan had been pretty decent to work with so far, but he had his moments where he was as closed as the southern U.S. border would be if Trump got elected. "Well, while you were doing nothing, I called Max's auto shop and checked. George's truck was towed in a week ago Wednesday from Mining Road #2. The guy said that's out of town."

"Up near the old mines," Duncan said. "I know where it is."

"Any reason they'd be hanging out there?"

Duncan shook his head curtly.

"It isn't a popular teen party place or something?"

60

He glanced at her and some of the tension seemed to seep out of the lines in his face. "It wasn't when I lived here."

"What's on the agenda for tomorrow?" Moreau asked.

"I'm sure there'll be a somber service at the Anglican Church."

"What's special about that?" she asked before she realized what he meant. "Oh, I guess you mean more somber than usual."

The twinge of a smile flickered across his face. "I take it you won't be attending regularly?"

"Gee, I don't think I even own a dress." She saw his bemused look. "I'm not really a church-going gal."

"I'm sure even the atheists will play the part so they can indulge in the emotional display tomorrow."

"Sick, isn't it?"

"Maybe just evidence that we're all so numb we need a tragedy to remind us that we're still breathing."

"I had you pegged as a realist, not a pessimist."

"You see half a teenager's face splattered over the ground and you don't feel like it isn't real, that it can't possibly a kid you know lying dead before you like that?"

She didn't mention the fact that he knew Sammy, but she had not. "Bet you're a cheerful drunk."

There was an almost imperceptible hardening of his eyes at her words, though his face was placid as ever when he responded. "I abstain. I've been told I don't need to indulge in order to cast a shadow over a party, anyway."

"The cop's lot in life, I suppose," Moreau responded wryly. She felt her left eyebrow arch instinctively. "We're either shockingly inappropriate or morbidly depressing."

Duncan nodded. "What would you do tomorrow? If you were off."

She wasn't going to tell him the truth, so she stuck with the case instead. "Get up on the mountain."

"You climb?"

He misunderstood what she meant. She wanted to check out the place where George's truck had been towed from but she

THE SPYING MOON

didn't have the heart to tell him that. "I trained a bit, but most of my experience before that is from climbing rock cuts in Ontario. I've always wanted to try climbing out here."

"The challenge is all psychological."

"And muscle tone has nothing to do with it?"

A cynical grin flickered across his face. "I didn't think it was an issue for you, given your apparent level of fitness."

"Ah." She knew she was failing to keep the corners of her mouth from turning upwards. "Does that mean I've demonstrated some mental deficiency?"

He started to speak and then paused, smiled again, this time with a small degree of genuine warmth. "Perhaps I should climb out of this hole before I dig it any deeper."

She chuckled. Duncan showed more discernment than McIver had. "Why do you do it?"

"It clears the mind." His eyes were hooded as he kept his focus on the road. "It's a distraction from the mental replay."

He turned and looked at her. "The only thing that you really have to contend with is your own fear, whether you control it or it controls you. Everything else just fades into the background when you're climbing."

He'd offered such a simple statement, but between the lines it told her more about Nate Duncan than anything else she'd heard or observed to that point.

For him, the ghosts still lingered.

Chapter 7

As Moreau walked into the breakroom, McIver tossed a file back on the table and swore under his breath.

"Can I get you anything?" she asked as she opened the fridge.

McIver glanced at the door before he turned to look her in the eye. "You got a break on this case for me?"

She stared back. "No."

"Then there's not a damn thing you have that I want." McIver grabbed the file, jumped up and turned to leave with such force he knocked over his chair.

Duncan stood in the doorway and McIver's steps faltered for a split second. When Duncan moved aside, McIver disappeared down the hall.

Moreau opened the fridge, grabbed two bottles of water and handed one to Duncan after he picked up the fallen chair.

"Thought you were partnered on that thing at Mabel Cook's."

"We are." Moreau avoided Duncan's gaze as she stared down the hall. What had McIver so bent out of shape? He'd been a sexist jerk when she met him, a professional at the crime scene, and now he was back to ass mode.

She recalled his glance at the door and wondered if Duncan had been standing there when McIver had looked over. Was it genuine frustration or was it a show?

What would be the point of such a performance?

"Do we have anything new?" Duncan asked as she rifled

63

THE SPYING MOON

through the tray with her name on it that was stacked with the other team-member's trays on the far end of the counter, near the wall with the bulletin board.

She extracted a piece of paper. "An assessment of Sammy's handwriting."

"Let me guess. He was right-handed," Duncan said.

"There was no doubt in the analyst's mind."

"Seems a stupid mistake to make, since most people are right-handed." Duncan snapped his fingers. "His camera. He always carried it in his left hand."

"So whoever planted the gun thought that meant he was left-handed?"

Duncan frowned. "Could be. He always had a video camera on him. Filmed everything. I'd like to know where that camera is."

An amateur filmmaker? Moreau wondered about that. Wouldn't someone who had a camera stuck in their hand that much have it with them if they were committing suicide? "This report doesn't really help us much. We already knew he didn't die from the gunshot wound. The gun was wiped clean. No other prints."

"What about the shell casings?" Moreau asked.

"None at the scene, further reinforcing the fact that somebody else was up there. We should have caught that earlier. It suggests they had a guilty conscious."

Guilty of trying to cover an accidental OD by making Sammy's death look like a suicide? Or something else?

"And we already know that it wasn't the same gun."

"When can we get into the Petersen house to search Sammy's room?"

Duncan looked at his wristwatch. "I suppose we should do that next."

The impression Moreau had of the Petersen's neighborhood was strengthened by driving through the streets during daylight. Every home was the picture-perfect image the town councilors would want to represent the idyllic life in Maple River.

Duncan parked on the street near the end of the driveway. There was no sign of the mangy cat as they walked to the front door.

It only took one ring for Cal Petersen to answer, almost as though he was expecting them.

"May we come in?" Duncan asked.

Cal stepped aside wordlessly and they walked into the living room. Nothing had changed in the hours since they'd been there, except that Cal was wearing pants and a shirt that he'd only partially tucked in, which didn't strike Moreau as normal for the man. The house had everything in place, every picture showed a well-dressed couple, whether they were laughing at the park or posing at a school event.

She noticed one of the photos of Sammy, his video camera snug in his left hand and held down at his side. When she'd seen it the night before she hadn't realized he loved to film. As she scanned every photo she noticed the camera was present in each one.

Not even put away for a family photo.

"Laura still isn't feeling well."

"That's all right. We'd like to take a look in Sammy's room."

"What do you need to do that for?"

"It's just procedure."

"Procedure?" Cal Petersen's voice lilted into the high notes as his cheeks flushed red.

Moreau glanced at Duncan before she spoke. "Mr. Petersen, we have to be thorough. We want to make sure that we look at everything, consider all the facts, so that we can provide a clear picture of what happened."

"What happened is that my little boy killed himself." Tears streamed down Cal Petersen's cheeks now and snot bubbled out from his nostrils. "Something was wrong and I-I didn't see it."

Moreau swallowed. They couldn't even tell him that it was

THE SPYING MOON

possible Sammy hadn't killed himself. Would that console him? Would it make a difference?

Was she the one who'd experienced mercy by being left without answers about where her mother was, why she'd never returned for her all those years ago? She'd thought the Petersens deserved the answers she desperately sought herself, but maybe there was no peace in knowing what had happened.

No. She couldn't believe that. For almost fourteen years she'd lived with the fear and the hope, the unanswered questions gnawing at her, never far from her thoughts.

"Please, sir, we just want to be sure haven't overlooked anything," she said.

"Wh-what does that mean? What difference does it make?" The look that was creeping into Cal Petersen's face was one of wild-eyed desperation and when he ran his hand threw his hair he left it tousled, adding to the appearance of a once-strong man descending into madness. "I have to go down to the coroner's office and tell them that's my son lying there, dead."

Duncan put a hand on Cal's shoulders. "Is there someone we can call for you?"

The doorbell rang. When Cal didn't move, Moreau went to answer it.

A woman about Cal's age, with graying hair and laugh lines around her eyes stood there with a casserole dish in hand. A graying, plump man about the same age was walking up behind her as he dragged a suitcase to the door.

"Can I help you?" Moreau asked.

"No." The woman swept through the gap between Moreau and the frame without apology and marched into the living room. She set the casserole dish on the coffee table, pulled Cal down on the couch beside her and wrapped her arms around him.

Moreau stepped back and let the man with the suitcase pass without comment, closed the door and followed him into the living room.

"Mrs. Benson," Duncan said. "I'll leave you with your brother. We're just headed upstairs to search Sammy's room."

She mashed her lips together, looked from Duncan to Moreau, and offered a curt nod.

"Someone else will be coming. We may need to take some things to the station as part of our investigation."

There was no response to this.

Duncan led the way up the stairs. At the top they went to the left, and pulled on gloves before Duncan opened a door on the left that led into a bedroom.

The lower half of the walls were dark blue. The upper half was cream, and the two sections were separated by a yellow chair rail.

A small bookshelf featured graphic novels and books about film and photography.

The bed was casually made. Underneath it, the only thing that Moreau could see was dust.

Duncan opened the closet, which was along the wall near the door. He worked his way through hanger after hanger of basic shirts and sweaters. There was no ledge above the clothes.

Moreau moved beside Duncan. A few boxes on the closet floor held toys: a remote controlled helicopter, a stuffed monkey, a race track set. Remnants of the childhood Sammy had outgrown.

The dresser contained nothing more than clothes and the only other things in the room were his desk, which held a computer, and a table filled with a thirty-two-inch TV. It didn't take long to confirm that neither piece of furniture concealed anything out of the ordinary.

"No diary, no notebook, no idea what this kid did with his time."

"He filmed things. He had his camera glued to his hand most of the time, even back when I lived here."

"You said that before. Then where's the camera?"

Duncan frowned. "Did we find a school bag?"

THE SPYING MOON

Moreau surveyed the room again, and then swung the door closed. On the back a blue backpack hung on a hook. She unzipped it and emptied it onto Sammy's bed.

A calculus text, copy of *Heart of Darkness*, notebook, pencil case and a piece of paper folded into a square fell out.

They flipped through the books. "Nothing interesting so far," Moreau said as she picked up the paper.

A doorbell rang. "Could be our techs. I'll go downstairs and see," Duncan said.

Footsteps faded down the stairs as she felt her phone vibrate in her pocket. She pulled it out.

Unknown number.

Moreau clicked to answer it. The voice from the message the night before responded. "You promised."

"And I meant it. If it was up to me I'd be there right now."

"I told you that there was a party this week. I thought—"

"I know what you thought and if there's any way at all I can make it, I will. But you're going to have to be patient."

"Be patient? It's been ten years."

It had been longer for Moreau, but she didn't say that. "I want answers just as much as you do."

"And I bet you won't be willing to bust your cop ass to find them. Your boss will tell you how much our mothers don't matter and you'll let it slide like everyone else."

"The whole reason I became an RCMP officer was to find out what happened to my mother." Moreau struggled to keep her voice from rising. "I'm doing everything I can."

"From hundreds of miles away. Right."

"Look, I promise you, as soon as I can get to Burns Lake I won't rest until I find out what happened." The statement was met with silence. "I need you to believe me."

"And this week? The party?"

"It would help if I could call you. I—"

"I'll call you."

"Just promise me you won't take any risks if I can't make it. I—"

68

There was a click and Moreau pulled the phone away from her ear. The call had been cut.

From the lower level of the Petersen house she heard a door open. She slid the phone back in her pocket and as she smoothed out the paper that had fallen from Sammy's bag. On the paper an infinity symbol had been drawn in black, with a red letter S in one loop and a pink E in the other.

Feet stomped up the steps and down the hall. Laura Petersen burst into the room, still in the same attire she'd worn hours earlier when they'd been there. Her eyes were red-rimmed, there were black smudges beneath them that suggested she hadn't gotten much rest and her hair stuck out in dozens of different directions.

"What are you doing? Leave his things alone. You can't take my Sammy."

As Moreau stepped forward to try to calm her down, Duncan entered, followed by Mr. and Mrs. Benson.

"Mrs. Petersen, it's all right. Your family is here now. Let's get you downstairs," Duncan said as he gently touched her shoulders. She collapsed as though the weight of his fingers was too much to bear.

He stood back as the Bensons approached. Mrs. Petersen bent down as though she was praying, her body shaking as she wailed. The Bensons froze and looked at each other, questions clear in their eyes. Should they move her or let her be? Laura Petersen rose back up to her knees and the Bensons pulled her to her feet. She didn't resist. After they left the room Moreau passed Duncan the note.

"Maybe he had a girlfriend."

Duncan turned it over and studied both sides. "It isn't signed."

"Which doesn't give us much to go on."

The techs entered, and Duncan directed them to box up the computer and bag the letter.

Moreau followed Duncan down the stairs. Mrs. Benson met

THE SPYING MOON

them at the bottom.

"Do you really need to do this?"

"Yes," Duncan said, "we do. I'm sorry—"

"You're sorry? You? For the grief you bring families here? One might think you enjoy causing people pain."

"Ma'am, respectfully," Moreau said, "right now it's our responsibility to see that this family gets answers about Sammy's death."

"What difference will that make? It won't bring him back."

Mr. Benson stepped out to the entrance. "Come now, Carol. They're only doing their job."

They turned away and Moreau shut her eyes for a second before she spoke.

"Someone needs to bring Mr. Petersen down to the morgue."

The Bensons stopped walking, but didn't speak.

"It's a formality," she said softly. "To identify Sammy."

Moreau heard what she was sure was a small gasp from Mrs. Benson before Mr. Benson nodded. "I'll drive him," he said, but he didn't turn around.

"Thank you."

Moreau followed Duncan out the door. They started to walk to the vehicle in silence, but that was disrupted by the sound of a car zooming around the corner and screeching to a stop just in front of the Petersen's driveway.

A man exited from a faded blue Civic. "Seth Gorden, with the Maple River Gazette," the man said. He was average height, with brown hair and brown eyes. The most distinct feature the man had was a smattering of freckles across his face and he was a little thin, although Moreau realized that may have been embellished by the baggy dark blue pants he wore.

"No comment," Duncan said.

"You're Nate Duncan, right?"

Duncan started walking around the front of his Rodeo and the reporter stepped in front of him. "You have no comment about that or about Sammy Petersen's death?"

70

"Either."

Moreau was almost at the passenger door but she hesitated. With Duncan's path blocked and the redness creeping up the back of his neck she wondered if she might have to intervene.

"Look, isn't it time people around here knew the truth? Everyone thinks Sammy Petersen's a great kid because he comes from a good family and you're a bad egg because you were sent away, but that isn't the whole story, is it?"

"It would be a shame if my story here ended with punching you in the face because you wouldn't get out of my way."

Seth Gorden leaned back. "You don't mean that."

"These people are grieving. They just lost their son. The last thing they need is for a reporter to be snooping around their house trying to take advantage of their pain."

Gorden's eyes widened and he stepped back just enough for Duncan to get by.

"That's not what I was…I wanted to give you a chance to tell your side of things," Gorden said. "It might help heal some old wounds."

"Let's save the therapy for Dr. Phil," Duncan said as he got into the Rodeo.

Moreau opened her door and jumped in. She hadn't even fastened the buckle when Duncan started backing up, away from the reporter.

She'd heard more than enough in less than one day to know that Nate Duncan wasn't happy about being back in Maple River, and now she'd seen enough to know that to some people his return home was newsworthy.

And like Duncan, some people in town weren't happy about his return, either.

Chapter 8

Before they'd left the station to search Sammy's room Duncan had marked out the most likely route George and his friends had followed on Friday night. Wanda Griffin was the first person on their list to talk to and when they arrived she was raking leaves in her yard, which bordered the street that went up to the top of Holt Hill. This was the only road a vehicle could take.

Duncan told her most of the land on the hill belonged to Abe Holt, who had it fenced and guarded by dogs that did not take kindly to unwanted guests. The road was the only access point by foot that wasn't within reach of Abe's canines.

Mrs. Griffin was one of those frail-looking older woman who seemed to have withered with time, like she was sinking into herself. But that was the deception of the face. Wanda Griffin glanced up as they approached and drew herself up to her full height.

"I heard you were back in town." She stared at Duncan, followed her statement with *hmmph* and barely looked at Moreau. "What do you want?"

Moreau held up her ID.

"I'm Constable Moreau, and this is Constable Duncan."

She noted a slight change in Mrs. Griffin's face. The startled look faded and her expression softened, the corners of her mouth sagged and her eyes also appeared weighed down. Then that look passed, replaced with the hard edges of suspicion and annoyance at being interrupted.

"Mrs. Griffin, we're following up on the death of Sammy Petersen," Moreau said.

"Wondered when you'd be back."

"Be back?"

"The other one who was here, asking questions. He said someone else would come by. I didn't care for him much."

"That's quite all right, Mrs. Griffin." Duncan looked at Moreau, who gave the tiniest shake of her head in response. "I didn't think Constable Saunders had made it here yet."

"Saunders? No, that wasn't the name. What is it you want?"

"We're wondering if you saw anything unusual on Friday night. If you happened to see any vehicles go by or people walking down the road."

"I'll tell you what I told the other one. I was sitting in my living room, which does have windows on this side of the house." She gestured to the bay window that faced the road. "The town's too busy printing pamphlets to be bothered installing streetlights, so I finally got one with a motion sensor." She nodded at the post, which extended from the fence that bordered the road. "Whenever anyone goes by after dark it goes on.

"I noticed the light a minute or two before eight last night. It was odd, because usually at that time of night it's a car full of boys skidding their way up to the top for a bush party. I guess that's why I remember seeing one of them young ones walk by, on his way down from the hill."

"Just one? Are you certain?" Moreau asked.

"Of course I am. I pay attention. Those damn kids are always smashing bottles against my fence, tossing crumpled cans into my yard, or causing a racket. In my day people who let their kids run wild like that were too embarrassed to look you in the eye. Now the parents couldn't care less.

"Or," she said, as she studied Duncan, "their parents are useless and abusive and the better part of the reason the kids are on the street in the first place." Again, all the pointed angles of her face seemed to melt and then, as quickly as the softened ex-

THE SPYING MOON

pression had appeared, it was gone.

Moreau noticed Duncan's shoulders stiffen and wondered how close to home Wanda Griffin's words had struck.

When he responded, Duncan didn't acknowledge what she'd said. "Can you tell us anything about the boy?"

"I can tell you it was Randy Jensen."

"You're positive?" Moreau asked.

Mrs. Griffin glared at her. "I know Randy Jensen when I see him. He left his car parked down here on Friday night."

"Do they usually park down here?" Moreau asked, undaunted.

"I'd be lying if I said they never parked down here, but more often than not they take the car up and come speeding down later. Mr. Price told me that after the stunt the Jensen boys pulled they had to fix the suspension. Randy might not have wanted to do any more damage to it by driving it up the hill."

"How did Mr. Price know about the suspension work?" Duncan asked.

"How do you think? They had to order parts from him to fix the car."

"They went to Price Auto Repair instead of Max's?"

"I would expect so if Mr. Price ordered the parts."

"We can't jump to any conclusions, Mrs. Griffin. We have to be certain we're getting the facts."

"And he just happened to mention this to you...?" Moreau let her voice trail off. She didn't know if there was a reason for Mr. Price to be talking to Wanda Griffin about anything in particular, and she didn't want to infer anything that might offend her.

"He's fixing my snow blower for me. And no, that's not a metaphor for anything else. Lord knows I can't manage shoveling the entire walk all winter. We were chatting about the stunt the Jensen boys pulled, with the Petersen boys in tow, no less. Lou told me their joyride set them back a few hundred dollars."

"Sounds like just desserts," Moreau said. She made a mental note to ask Duncan if he knew what Mrs. Griffin was talking

74

about. Something about the look in his eye told her that he did. Another thing he hadn't shared.

Like how he knew the Jensen boys.

"Yes, well, the police don't seem to be able to do anything about it, do they? Those boys weren't even given a hand-slap. They could have killed somebody, racing down the hill like that. When the Halvstrom boys did that they couldn't sit on their backsides for a week and the one driving had his license suspended. To think, that wasn't even ten years ago."

"I remember," Duncan said. "That's where Randy and Kenny got the idea. They used to talk about it when…" His voice trailed off, and whatever he was remembering, he didn't share. "Did you see anyone else walking or driving by your house on Friday night? You're sure you didn't fall asleep?"

"I always wake up if the light goes on. The police went by. After I called nine-one-one there was a lot of traffic."

Moreau frowned. "I didn't realize it was you that made the call."

"I was only one of many. My neighbors may be old but they're nosey. And they're light sleepers."

Duncan smiled. "Fortunately for us." Then he frowned. "You're absolutely certain nobody else came down the hill? Just Randy?"

"That's what I said, isn't it? I was in that room from seven-thirty on, watching *The Newsroom*."

"Is that still on?" Duncan asked.

"It's on one of the streaming services."

"Do you remember who was around asking you questions before? We should have a word with him for making us waste your time," Duncan asked.

"That one seemed to think being older was the same as being senile. And daft. I'm afraid the name that stuck is McIdiot."

"I believe we know who you mean. Thanks for your time," Moreau said.

Duncan echoed the sentiment as they turned to leave.

THE SPYING MOON

Mrs. Griffin started to rake again, but then called after them. "Do you remember what Confucius said about success, Nate?"

He slowed his stride, stopped and turned. "Something about the glory in rising when we fall."

"The point is that glory doesn't come from not making mistakes. It's what you do about them that counts. Do you still read?"

He arched an eyebrow. "Crime scene reports and street signs, on a daily basis."

She shook her head but there was a hint of a smile on her face. Moreau followed Duncan back to where he'd parked.

"What was that about?" she asked.

"I used to spend a lot of time in the library."

Moreau's brow wrinkled. "Okay..."

"She was the librarian. Volunteered for thirty years to see that the local kids had a safe place to go filled with good books to read. Started it from scratch after the old town library burnt down."

"I guess that might explain why she's a little bitter about how some of the local youth have turned out."

As soon as the words were out Moreau bit her tongue and cursed silently.

His mask was back, the expressionless face that kept all the thoughts concealed, the dark shadows of the past beyond reach. She didn't press him further when they got into the vehicle.

"We now have doubt about Kenny's story, as well as George's."

Duncan frowned as he turned the key in the ignition. "We'll have to talk to Mary and Kenny. If Kenny substantiates his claim about leaving around seven-thirty then it throws Mrs. Griffin's statement into question, which doesn't help us disprove George's assertion that he left the hill before Sammy died."

Moreau tapped her pen against her notepad thoughtfully. "Well, there are at least a few things that help us."

"What would those things be?"

76

"One is that Randy said Kenny was still cleaning out the garage when he got home," she said.

"Yes," Duncan said. "Which makes you wonder what time Randy got home at. And why he was still dressed when we arrived in the middle of the night."

"Right. The other thing is that there's something about this case that's caught the interest of Levi McIdiot."

"Don't say that around me," Duncan said blankly as he turned down Holt Road. "I'm liable to slip and say it to his face."

Chapter 9

"What the hell is it now?" The words reached the door before Mary Jensen did. "Oh, it's you." She swung the door open and the hinges groaned in protest as she turned on her heel. "Kenny's not home."

"That's okay. We were hoping to ask you a few questions," Moreau said as they followed her into the house.

"Me? I don't know nothing about the gun or the Petersen boy's problems."

Moreau couldn't miss the glare Mary fired at Duncan as they went into the living room to sit down or the way she talked about Sammy Petersen, who was supposed to have been her youngest son's best friend.

"What time did Kenny get home last night?"

The skin between Mary's eyebrows puckered for a second. "Oh, I guess it was around eight. I'd been on the phone with my..." Her voice trailed off as she looked at Duncan and then turned her focus back to Moreau. "She was gonna watch some show that started at eight. I'd hung up and gone out to the garage when he turned up." She looked from Moreau to Duncan. "Why?"

"It's just routine, Mrs. Jensen. We have to understand the movements of all of the boys who were on the hill that night so that we can make sure our report accurately reflects what happened."

"Don't ya think you oughta spend more time on the streets

chasing after these thugs instead of writing reports about a suicide?"

Duncan frowned. "What do you mean by that?"

"Those Petersen boys ain't the little angels everyone says they is. Jimmy's been into more and more trouble. Sammy wasn't so bad at first, but he was following his brother around with that damn video camera, taping everyone and everything. It doesn't surprise me he'd been drinking. Oh, but don't say that in front of the Saint Petersens."

Your kids were there too. Moreau suppressed that thought. Mary struck her as one of those women who was always on the edge of letting their temper take control, like the snake in a can gag: open the lid and the oversized stuffed toy inside springs forth and scares you half to death if you aren't expecting it.

Only this snake had venom and teeth. Mary Jensen was wound up so tight there was no doubt she'd snap. The only question was when.

"I wasn't aware that Jim Petersen had a record." Moreau glanced at Duncan to see if this was something he knew.

Duncan shook his head. "He doesn't."

"Not for lack of trying. He's a shifty one. Heard he got kicked out of the bar for assaulting one of the girls in the hall outside the bathrooms. Wasn't going to take no for an answer." Mary bit her lip as she looked at them. The lines on her face stiffened and her features hardened even more.

"She didn't press charges?" Moreau asked.

"Against a Petersen boy? Sissy knew better than to bother."

"You're fairly certain Kenny was home just after eight?" Moreau asked again.

"Yeah."

"Do you remember when Randy came home?" Duncan asked. He was calm, composed and his tone had no resentment or doubt in it. For a moment Mary was perfectly still as she looked at him.

"He came home around eight-thirty and then he went out

THE SPYING MOON

again later. Ten-thirty or eleven, I think. The news came on not long after he left."

"Where was he going so late?" Moreau asked.

"He was supposed to go out earlier but his friend called and said something came up. He texted later and said he was on his way home so Randy went over."

Mary reached across the coffee table and picked up her pack of cigarettes. She lit one, sucked in a deep breath and let the nicotine filter into her system. Moreau watched the woman's twitching slow to a crawl until Mary looked sedate, despite the presence of two police officers.

The squeak of the hinges on the screen door echoed through to the living room. Moreau found herself willing the arrival along. She listened to the click of the latch as the door finally swung shut, the footsteps on the landing, the double-thud of shoes being dropped off someone's feet. The shuffle into the kitchen was followed by the fridge door opening. Adding to the hum of the fridge motor was a clank on the counter, the *glug-glug* of a beverage being poured, the sound of the fridge door sealing shut and the snap of a cupboard.

Randy Jensen walked into the living room, cup in hand. His white jersey shining brighter than anything Moreau had seen in the Jensen house.

She studied the team logo. A coyote, much like the one that had blocked their path only hours earlier. The Maple River Tricksters.

Randy's stride broke when he saw his mother sitting silently across from Duncan and Moreau.

After his two-second hesitation he forced a quick smile, sat down in the nearest armchair and took a drink without saying a word.

Not curious about why they were there. Not happy to see them, but not really surprised, either.

"Have you fixed your suspension yet, Randy?" Duncan enquired. The unsuspecting teen snorted milk up his nose.

80

Duncan had shared the story on the drive over; the Jensen and Petersen boys had raced a Mustang through town and right across the border in record time, something she suspected Randy might not be too anxious to talk to two RCMP officers about.

Border patrol had already made them regret it, a fact Duncan had confirmed with a quick call. Nothing formal that barred them from the U.S. this time, but they received a strict warning that if it happened again they'd be classified as illegal immigrants and formally deported.

Which would be a problem for the potential hockey star.

"No. Why?" Randy asked as he wiped his face with the back of his hand.

"I guess that means you still have to walk up and down Holt Hill," Duncan said.

Randy sighed. "Okay, you know. I left Sammy on the hill with Arnold and Doug. George wasn't even there. I left alone."

Mary's head spun to the side so she could look at him. "Why the hell did you lie?"

Randy took a breath and half-shrugged. "George called me. He said something was going on, something was wrong with Sammy. His parents warned him not to get in any trouble while they were away so I said I'd cover for him."

"He called you the first time or the second time?"

Randy glanced at his mom, rolled his eyes and sighed. "Both times. The first time was to tell me something had come up and he was late. Then he called later and told me to meet him at his house."

"Why you?" Moreau asked.

Randy set the empty glass down on the coffee table. Mary swatted him, and he reached back, lifted it up, slid a coaster under it and put it back down. "Nobody would pay much attention to Arnold or Doug would they?"

"You weren't suspicious when he called you?" Duncan asked.

"No. I was supposed to go over there anyway."

THE SPYING MOON

"Randy, do you think George could have been lying to you?" Duncan leaned forward.

Duncan had adopted a different tone, with more authority, the kind you associate with a father giving his son one last chance to confess whatever he'd done. Since she'd never met Mr. Jensen Moreau wondered if that would help elicit an honest answer. The teen sheepishly shook his head before responding.

"If I thought George had something to do with Sammy shooting himself I wouldn't have lied for him. He wasn't even there. I thought he was coming and that's the real reason we all left early. George didn't show."

"Do you know where he was?"

Randy shook his head and held up two empty hands with a shrug.

"So George didn't show up and you don't know why. Then he asked you to cover for him and you weren't even curious? It didn't occur to you to ask why?"

"Look, he probably got into a fight or something. I'm sure it's nothing. He wasn't even on the hill so what's the big deal? That's what you're here about."

"Why ask you to lie for him?"

Randy sighed and collapsed back against the cushion. The indifference that had been in his eyes had given way to resignation, as though he'd finally realized they weren't going to let this go. "He thought it would sound better if we said we left together. George said he was worried about Doug and Arnold."

"Because they were there with Sammy when he died?"

"He said Doug and Arnold left Sammy alive and alone at the hang-out. George swore they had nothing to do with it." He looked from his mother to Duncan, the lingering silence contributing to a fearful gleam as his face lengthened. "I'm telling the truth."

"Sammy Petersen was grounded," Duncan said.

"Yeah, because of our joyride. How dumb is that?"

"If he'd stayed home he'd still be alive."

82

A flicker of something flashed across Randy's face. Regret? Moreau wasn't sure what it was, and the teen didn't respond to Duncan's words.

"What was he doing on the hill?" she asked.

Randy ran his fingers through his hair and scratched his head. "Skipping out. He was sick of his parents treating him like a little baby. I thought he wanted to hang out longer because he was trying to get into George's little gang."

"Gang?" Moreau echoed.

Randy proffered a half-shrug indifferently. "Gang, group, whatever."

"Was Sammy drinking before you left?" Duncan asked.

Randy nodded. "It wasn't like it was the first time, but I'd never seen him drink so much before. Arnold just kept egging him on."

"You mean he wanted Sammy to get drunk?"

Randy shrugged. "I don't know."

Duncan exchanged a glance with Moreau. "Do you have any idea where the gun came from?"

Moreau observed the subtle shift, something about the lines around the eyes and the shape of the mouth. Randy pressed his lips together and shook his head firmly, refusing to verbalize an answer.

"What time did Kenny go out?" she asked.

Randy looked puzzled. "He didn't go anywhere. Kenny helped with the garage and then he went to his room. He was probably reading."

The door banged shut again. Moreau barely processed the thudding of shoes falling from feet before Kenny flew around the corner, his wide eyes bursting from his pale face.

"Where the hell have you been?" Mary lit another cigarette as soon as the words were out. She exhaled. "Well?"

Moreau noted Mary hadn't grilled Randy when he came home. Wherever he'd been, she either knew, approved or didn't care.

THE SPYING MOON

Why the special interest in her younger son? Was it because of Sammy's suicide, or something more?

"I, uh, went to the Petersen's house, to see how they are." Kenny's eyes welled with tears as he spoke and his voice trembled.

"You shouldn't go over there. It's just going to make you feel bad," Mary said as she vaulted off the chair and marched out of the room into the kitchen.

Kenny looked at Moreau then and it was a moment that unnerved her. It was the look of a puppy that had been kicked on the side of its head and goes to its mother for comfort, only to have her turn away from him.

It was a look that reflected how she felt every time she thought about the day the social worker had pushed back the faded yellow curtain and grabbed her hand.

"We'll find you a new family," the woman had said.

"I don't want you to find me a new family. I want you to find my mom."

"If she was worth finding she'd be here."

A twisted circular logic. Moreau could see it now, but as a child she'd felt hopeless and alone and part of her had wondered if the woman was right.

She glanced at Duncan and forced herself to think about the case instead of the confusion she saw in Kenny's eyes as he sank into the chair Mary had abandoned.

Duncan turned back to Randy. "If there's anything else, anything at all, this is the time to tell us. Don't let us find out you're lying again later. It won't look good."

Kenny's head snapped up. "Randy?" He glanced at Duncan before turning back to his brother. "What does he mean?"

"Look, it's nothing, Kenny, all right? I've told them everything there is to know about Friday night."

"But what didn't you tell me? Were you up there when Sammy died?"

"Of course not! You know that. I was here."

84

"But you left before eleven."

"Sammy didn't die at eleven, Kenny," Duncan said. "Sammy died shortly after eight."

Randy's head snapped up at Duncan's words.

Startled? Surprised? Scared? Moreau wondered at the emotion driving the action.

"Wh-what are you talking about?" Kenny finally managed to push the words out. Randy stood and placed an arm on Kenny's shoulder.

"He died shortly after eight. And we have an eyewitness who says that the only time someone came down the hill that night was around eight." Duncan looked at the younger brother. "Which has us wondering about whether you were really up there, Kenny."

The boy swallowed and sank down into the chair behind him. "I walked down through Uncle Abe's property."

"You what?" Randy said. "Ma is gonna tan your hide."

Uncle Abe? Moreau started to connect the dots in her mind; the picture was taking shape. Moreau knew Nate Duncan was related to Abe Holt.

"Randy, Arnold and Doug were the last people to see Sammy alive. Sammy died just after Randy left him on that hill with Arnold and Doug," Duncan said.

"You said..." Kenny fell silent.

"George wasn't even there," Moreau said.

"Arnold and Doug didn't leave with Randy, either," Duncan said. "They stayed behind, with Sammy."

Kenny sprung from the chair as Randy stepped back and put his hand up, but Kenny's fist connected with his chin and sent him reeling before Randy could stop him.

The younger brother's anger propelled him forward. "You lied? You lied about this? What the hell is wrong with you?"

Duncan and Moreau ducked punches and sidestepped the elbows raised defensively as they tried to stop the fight. Moreau winced as Kenny pushed Randy into her, but she still grabbed

THE SPYING MOON

his shoulders and yanked him back as Duncan stepped in front of Kenny. The younger Jensen's arms waved frantically as he tried to squirm his way past the man Moreau now knew was his cousin, who managed to wrap his arms around Kenny's torso as Kenny tried to jump past him. Mary stomped in from the kitchen and cuffed Kenny on the side of the head.

"What the hell? This is a goddamn house, not a bloody boxing ring. Go to your room!"

Duncan let go of Kenny and he snorted air out of his nostrils as he stomped three steps down the hall, turned on his heel and marched back toward them, gaze fixed on his brother. Mary raised her hand and took a step in his direction and the red flare of anger in his face faded to a pale shade as tears started to fall. He spun again and stomped out of the room.

Mary turned her glare on Randy. "You too. You should know better. You screw up your hand and you can kiss that first-round draft pick placement goodbye. No Canucks or Flames or Leafs jersey in your future then, boy. You won't be the hometown hero. You'll be a has-been before you were anything."

Moreau released Randy. He glanced at her, then looked at Duncan, who paused. One look at Mary seemed to help him decide. Duncan nodded at Randy, who wordlessly disappeared down the hall and out of their sight.

The three adults who remained in the living room stood still until the latch to Randy's door clicked shut. Mary lunged at Duncan.

"Goddamn you, Nate, you sonofabitch," she said as she beat her fist into his flesh. Duncan raised his left arm to shield her blows from reaching his head, which was where she seemed to be aiming, and he stepped away from her.

She kept coming. What had started as a one-fisted assault turned into both hands pounding at him and her fists unfurled as she clawed at him. Duncan pulled his head down behind his bent arm to shield it as much as possible, and kept moving back, away from her. He twisted away so he wouldn't be pinned between the woman and the wall, which meant that Mary had to spin around as Duncan raised his right arm as well so that she wouldn't have a clean shot on that side.

"I hate you, I hate you, I hate you." She didn't scream, but the words came out with a tone that burned. "We all hate you, you sorry sack of shit." Mary stopped swinging her arms long enough to spit at his foot.

Moreau lunged forward now that Mary's back was to her and she wasn't in motion. She grabbed the woman around the waist, picked her up and spun her back toward the large sofa before she grabbed her gun.

Mary looked up at Moreau through slanted eyes that showed she still had some fight in her. A red anger had crept into her face, highlighting all the sharp lines. Her blonde hair was half out of her ponytail, with the wisps pointing in all directions.

"Mary Jensen, you've assaulted a police officer."

"Yeah? That what he is to you?" Mary glared at Moreau, her mouth drawn into a tired, hard line. "He's nothing to me."

"Nothing but a ticket straight to jail."

"Moreau."

She kept her gun and her focus directed at Mary Jensen and didn't turn when Duncan spoke.

"Moreau, let it go."

Mary sneered. "If you ask me you're wasting your time and mine. My boys have nothing else to tell you."

"This visit stopped being about that when you chose to put hands on a police officer. I'm charging you—"

Duncan stepped in front of Moreau. "Let it go."

"Give me one good reason why I should?"

"Everyone's just—" he turned to look behind him at the woman on the couch, who was crouched on the edge, knees bent and ready to propel her into round two in a split second, "—a little tense right now. Things got out of hand. It won't happen again. Will it, Mary?"

THE SPYING MOON

She gave him a look that, to Moreau, said she was still thinking about taking another swing at him, but then Mary looked at Moreau, who still had her gun out.

The lines on her face smoothed out a little and Mary sank back. She didn't relax fully, but the tension in her body subsided just enough to tell Moreau that she wasn't going to make any sudden moves.

"Just go."

Duncan nodded at her and she tipped her head toward the hall that led to the exit. He started walking in that direction and Moreau followed as she slipped her gun back into its holster.

Then Duncan turned and walked around her, back to the living room.

"Thank you for your time and cooperation, Aunt Mary. I hope we won't need to bother you again."

The only response from Mary Jensen was a cold stare. Moreau's hand had gone straight to her gun again.

Mary stiffened and looked at Duncan.

His aunt, his cousins. Some family.

Duncan turned again, glanced at Moreau's hand resting on her weapon and then went around her and led the way outside.

"You've been holding out on me," Moreau said once the door had creaked shut behind them.

Duncan looked her, brow puckered.

"You never said your family reunions were so much fun."

The lines in his face smoothed but he offered no other response.

"Are you sure you made the right call in there? Not bringing her in?"

Duncan gave her a firm look that made it clear the subject wasn't up for discussion. "I made the only call I could."

What did that mean? He clearly had no intention of elaborating and walked around to the driver's side of the vehicle wordlessly.

Once they were both in and had their seatbelts buckled she

finally broke the silence. "What's next?"

Duncan turned the key in the ignition but didn't answer.

"I'd really like to know why George felt he needed Randy to fib for him, especially since he wasn't even there," Moreau said.

"You already know what he'll say. He'll flash that beguiling smile and tell you that the word of the beloved future NHLer of Maple River is gold and he didn't want to get into any trouble. Just the sort of crap that a jury would buy."

"Jury? You think George had something to do with Sammy's death?"

"I don't know."

Moreau considered all the facts. No evidence of previous drug use, no hardening of the veins, no needle tracks.

Nothing. The absence of evidence became evidence itself.

What they did have was a lie, prompted by a person who hadn't even been on the hill that night.

Moreau leaned against her hand, her elbow propped up by the armrest on the door. "There's something about George Jacobs. Why ask a friend to protect you before the police are even asking questions? My gut says there's more to this than meets the eye."

That vaguely familiar ghost of a smile flitted across Duncan's face. "I wouldn't recommend repeating that around Levi McIver or he'll start hailing the powers of women's intuition."

"How much do you want to bet that Randy and George are on the phone right now as we speak, getting the new story straight?"

"You don't believe Randy?"

"I'm not convinced he's lying but I'm also not sure he's telling us the truth. He wasn't honest before and that's a mark against him." She felt the bruises protest as the seatbelt pulled against them. Randy and Kenny's scuffle hadn't helped much.

"The statements we have from Mary and Mrs. Griffin both corroborate parts of Randy's statement. We know he left around eight p.m. We have Randy and Mrs. Griffin stating that he left alone."

THE SPYING MOON

"I'm not talking about whether he left when he said he did. I'm talking about why George asked him to lie and…what's going on there?"

They were driving along Holt Road, the route George, Arnold and Doug should have taken home on the night in question. A group of people, some with shopping bags in hand, others dangling smokes between their fingers, were gathered around the sign at the edge of the property of St. James Anglican Church. The crisp black letters spelling out the catchphrase "Jesus Paid For Our Sins" were still clear against the white backdrop at the top of the sign, but the information below about service times was blocked out by the bold red letters proclaiming "So let's get our money's worth" below.

Duncan glanced at her, and she fought to hold back a cynical smile. "At least nobody can say the youth of today can't spell."

"I'm sure Mrs. Griffin would be happy to know that," he responded dryly.

Chapter 10

"Where are you two at on the robbery?" Freeman asked while he sorted through the mounting pile of paperwork before him. The office seemed even smaller than when she'd been there with Duncan; the boxes and files were swallowing the desk Freeman sat at.

Moreau and McIver hadn't been invited to sit down, and Moreau was glad Freeman's attention was elsewhere, because he couldn't see her glance at McIver.

McIver took the hint and responded.

"Virtually at a dead-end. We have fingerprints but we don't have a match. No eyewitnesses so no working description. There wasn't anything conclusive at the scene to work off of, other than the MO. A comparison hasn't turned up any similar crimes within two hundred kilometers yet."

Freeman glanced up at Moreau when McIver was done. "What about tracking stolen goods through pawn shops?" he asked.

"There wasn't anything on the list that could be pawned, sir. It was all canned food. We had Mrs. Cook go over the house twice. Nothing else is missing."

Freeman rested his chin on his hand and rubbed his jaw as he looked at McIver. "There's absolutely nothing to go on?"

"I've canvassed everyone who has business on the road or who lives uphill or downhill. The best we can hope for from what we have is that someone gets picked up and matches our

THE SPYING MOON

prints. Or the thief breaks into another home and we find a witness."

"Which is not the scenario I would be hoping for."

"We could always try tracking," McIver said.

"Do you think you'd find anything?" Freeman asked.

McIver shook his head. "We could come up empty-handed but it isn't possible to have less to go on than we do now."

"It will only help if the perp left the scene on foot, sir," Moreau said. Part of her felt bad that McIver had been carrying the load of this investigation on his own, but another part of her felt annoyed that this was simply another thing getting in the way of the death inquiry. With Nate Duncan's family so closely involved she couldn't leave him to question people on his own.

"Even if he didn't, it could lead us to the location of his vehicle."

"You might get tire tracks to work with," Freeman added.

"Which may prove just as helpful as the fingerprints, sir," Moreau said.

McIver looked at her. "I know your hands are full, but we have to decide what we're going to do. It won't help us at all if we wait until it rains. Any evidence that might be out there could be destroyed. I heard we just had an experienced officer transfer in."

Freeman nodded his head, slowly at first, then with more conviction. "Constable Bradrick was working out of Cranbrook. He's been with the canine unit for a few years now. He'll know whether or not there's a chance of finding anything. I'll call him."

McIver was silent as they zigzagged around the stacks of boxes and chairs on their way back to the breakroom. Before she could turn down the hallway, he grabbed her arm and pulled her off to an empty space between two desks and a pile of chairs with a few stacks of boxes standing sentry over the nook

92

Moreau and McIver now stood in.

"I would've appreciated some support in there."

"Wow. You're going lecture me on being a team player?"

She watched as a flicker of annoyance was pushed aside by a tinge of regret as he blew out a deep breath. "You think because you're a woman who's Aboriginal you can use affirmative action to get you any job you want and we have to like it?"

"Only a racist assumes the reason someone got a job is because of their race. Did it ever occur to you it has nothing to do with that?"

"You going to tell me you earned it?"

"If you think that's the reason I'm here, McIver, that's your bias and your problem."

"Pretty fresh from training. A few months working in the Saskatoon area. What qualifies you to be part of this task force?"

"If you're so concerned about it why don't you ask Freeman?"

"I'm asking you."

She slid around him and started walking back to the hallway until she felt his hand grasp her right shoulder. Moreau winced from the pressure on the bruises as she spun around and yanked her arm free.

"You've got a bit of a temper," he told her.

"Only when I'm being manhandled by a jerk who has no reason for touching me," she said.

"Maybe you're just extra sensitive."

"You're the one who runs hot and cold, McIver. Maybe it's your time of the month."

He straightened up to his full height then. "Just remember I came to you and asked you myself."

"You've already made up your mind about me, so all you're doing is wasting my time and yours."

Moreau spun back around and as she walked through the stacks of cardboard boxes she elbowed one and sent it crashing down into the opening as she stomped away.

When she reached the breakroom, Duncan set a large Maglite

THE SPYING MOON

and batteries down on the table, along with a few bottles of water.

"What's the flashlight for?" she asked.

"I'm going back tonight?"

"Why?"

"To test a theory."

She sank down into a chair. "What aren't you telling me?"

He glanced at McIver, who had just stalked into the room and, after seeing Duncan, turned his gaze from Moreau and headed for the fridge. "Look, it's no big deal. I just want to trace Randy's steps and see if Mrs. Griffin's story holds."

Moreau stared at him. "That's all?"

He shrugged. "I'll be leaving at quarter past seven."

"Is that an invitation?"

"Suit yourself. If you want to come you can meet me here, but I won't wait around."

She leaned back in her chair and watched Duncan walk out of the room. Saunders entered, approached her and asked how the case was going. She responded casually, and offered little substantive information. From the corner of her eye she could see McIver watching her. Just how far would Duncan go to follow up on a hunch? She thought about her own instincts telling her to get out to the mountains. There was something about the location where George's truck had been towed from that was nagging at her. Despite her brief replies, Saunders kept talking about things of no interest to her. Why was McIver so interested in the discussion? Why was Saunders suddenly being so friendly?

Why had she, a rookie, been called up for this task force? She acted like she knew more than McIver did when he questioned her, but she'd never been certain of the reason for Freeman's interest in her.

He'd contacted her.

He'd asked to put her name in for consideration.

He'd wanted her there, and even when she chose a different post he'd pulled strings to force her to Maple River.

Why?

94

Chapter 11

Moreau left the station after Nate Duncan did. She wanted to get a look at the file on the break and enter case, but had to wait until Saunders and McIver left. McIver's tray was empty so she searched through the box she'd discovered stashed in one of the lower kitchen cupboards with his name on it, but it wasn't there.

After idling for ten minutes while crews had traffic stopped so they could trim trees she decided it was time to start using her GPS or buy a map. Once the app found an alternate route home she wound her way through the streets until she was on the sloping road just outside of town where the rental cabins were.

When she'd left that morning she'd realized hers was the farthest out from the office. As she drove past the cabin closest to the one she occupied she thought she recognized one of the vehicles in the driveway.

A man walked out the door

Nate Duncan.

Her nearest neighbor.

He held the door open and a woman followed, stopped and kissed his cheek, and then went to the car. The sight of the woman leaving Duncan's cabin had been enough to prompt Moreau to give her a second look. The woman seemed familiar and then, as Moreau saw her face under the glow of the one, lone streetlight afforded to the road, she recognized her.

What was Alyssa Everett doing at Duncan's? Before Moreau

THE SPYING MOON

let that thought run wild she chastised herself. Duncan had lived in the town for most of his life and it wasn't surprising that he still has friends there.

But Alyssa's bearing was odd, and Moreau thought about the exchange between Duncan and Alyssa at the office.

As she parked and stepped out into the crisp night she thought about Duncan. Even with the growing darkness she had the impression the angles of his face were drawn into harder lines than usual as he'd held the door.

Moreau went inside and told herself it was time to put her coworkers from her mind. She pulled out her phone and checked it, but there were no new messages, so she tried to concentrate on the crime scene reports from Friday night. Typed terminology blurred on the page, and Moreau finally tossed the file and decided to make some tea. From her kitchen window a light through the trees caught her attention.

Duncan. She heard an engine start and watched red taillights crawl in her general direction as he backed out of his parking space. They stopped, pulled away and disappeared into the night. She glanced at the clock and considered whether he'd felt forced to invite her to test his theory, or if he really wanted to include her as his partner in the investigation, and whether that mattered. Moreau grabbed her keys and coat and headed for the door.

Moreau pulled her ocean blue jeep in behind Duncan's blue Rodeo. She cut the engine and got out.

"I was beginning to wonder if you were coming."

"It's seven-fourteen, Duncan." She walked around and got into the passenger seat.

Duncan parked at the base of Holt Hill moments later. They got out of the vehicle and he grabbed a pack that he slung on his back before he directed them to walk to the far side of the road,

96

as far away from Mrs. Griffin's self-installed light as physically possible. Once they had covered the length of the garage the light registered their presence. They looked at the simple white bungalow. Mrs. Griffin stood at the window and watched them.

"Well, I guess her story holds," Moreau said.

Duncan turned to look around him and shone the flashlight he'd brought.

Even in the fading twilight Moreau could see the shimmer of the fence along the thick brush on this side of the street. There was no ditch. The gravel met the dense underbrush which ran in a strip about a foot wide before the fence snaked through the thick line of trees. It wasn't even possible to see into the Holt property in some places.

"Now we can be certain that there is no way Arnold and Doug could have come down that hill without the light going on."

Duncan nodded. He began walking up the road to the top of Holt Hill.

Moreau paused. "Look."

A gap in the brush allowed a clear view of the fence marking the Holt property. On the other side of the fence there was a man, positioning a stake.

They watched as he lifted a sledgehammer and drove the stake in with one forceful blow.

The man looked up then, his weathered face covered with lines that marked the years he'd seen. His cold, blue eyes stared out forcefully, even through the dusky sky, illuminated by the flashlight in Duncan's hand.

Duncan turned to look at Moreau. "Come on," he said.

She hesitated as Duncan started to walk again. The man said nothing, although his eyes betrayed a hint of amusement as lines formed around them.

He winked at Moreau. She turned her flashlight away from him and followed her partner.

They trudged up the hill in silence. Moreau hadn't gotten

THE SPYING MOON

used to the mountain darkness. When the sun dipped down below the horizon it was as though the world had shut its lights off. The long dusk on the Prairies wasn't to be found in the Rockies. Here, the darkness was a physical force that closed in and cut off everyone and everything.

Holt Hill was extremely steep in some places, and the loose gravel could cause a fall if one was careless. The muscles in Moreau's legs burned in protest from the lack of consistent exercise over the past few days.

Duncan took the pack off his shoulder, removed a water bottle, and passed it to Moreau. She thanked him and drank silently.

"It definitely isn't a quick trip up," she murmured. Duncan collected the bottles and put them back in the pack.

He led them to the alcove where Sammy had died. Moreau watched as Duncan stood and stared at the picnic table. When he didn't move she started surveying the scene again. She pointed her flashlight at the earth and began walking the perimeter and carefully scrutinized every inch of ground and brush.

"Crime scene techs have combed this place. I doubt there's anything left to find." Duncan's voice cut through the quiet.

"You weren't worried about leaving Saunders to handle the scene last night?"

"The techs still know their stuff," Duncan said.

She continued her search for a moment before she glanced up at him. He stood in the same spot, though his gaze had turned to follow her movements.

"I never really had a chance to walk out the scene."

"There are pockets like this all over the property and footpaths." Duncan nodded at a tiny gap in the bushes a few feet beyond the strand of tape that still fluttered between the trees before moving back to the picnic table.

"What are you thinking?" she asked. She met Duncan's gaze and he didn't avert his eyes, though he stared at her blankly and betrayed none of his thoughts.

"Well?" She tucked her hair back behind her ears as she moved toward him. "Don't tell me you're just lost in a daydream. What gives?"

"How could any police officer honestly mistake you for a reporter?"

She groaned. "I didn't know you'd heard that."

"I did. You handled McIver perfectly."

"Apparently he was willing to trade favors."

Duncan's face showed his distaste. "Doesn't that bother you?"

Moreau tilted her head back to look up at the blanket of black above them. "If you let it get to you, you won't get far. Besides, if I worked in the city I'd get it from perps all the time."

"That still doesn't make it acceptable, especially from cops."

Her gaze left the heavens and she looked at him. "The boys can't push me the way they can haze another guy. Is it any different than taking a rookie out to the bar and getting him sauced, not to mention what can follow after he's too drunk to know better?"

Duncan's eye twitched. He didn't respond but he looked away from her.

"I don't buy it, anyway."

"Excuse me?" Duncan turned back and met her gaze.

"That may have been the last thought that went through your mind but it definitely wasn't part of the convoy that was passing through when you first walked over here. You've been holding out on me." About a lot of things, but she decided not to poke him with that bit of truth. "Don't think I don't notice."

He turned his focus to his watch. When he looked back up his face was composed. "Ready?"

She uncrossed her arms and marched past him. Moreau wondered what was lurking behind those bright blue eyes but there was only one thing she felt certain about. Nate Duncan wasn't going to tell her a damn thing he didn't want to.

Chapter 12

The streets were unusually quiet as Moreau drove into Maple River. She'd noted most businesses stayed closed or opened late on Sundays and guessed that was why she didn't find herself detoured by roadwork for the first time since she'd arrived in town.

As she waited for the red light to change she tapped her thumb on the steering wheel. Duncan would be attending the service at the Petersen's church. It wasn't a necessity, but he'd felt it might be a good idea for at least one of them to be there.

She'd offered to go with him. He'd been ambivalent about whether she trudged up Holt Hill with him Saturday night, but he was emphatic about going to church Sunday morning alone.

"I can't stop you from going, but I think it's a mistake for us to both go. It'll make it more official. I just want to observe."

That meant she had her chance to check out Mining Road #2. She flipped her turn signal to the opposite direction and drove away from the station; her jeep bumped along the twisting street that led out of town, into the mountains.

It wasn't long before Google Maps only service was to annoy her. She thought about renaming it McIver as she pulled over and grabbed the map book she'd broken down and bought. Once she identified her location she tossed the book into the front passenger seat and pulled back out onto the road. A pothole swallowed her front tire and the suspension protested with a groan.

Maple River had to be a magnet for mechanics.

Ten minutes had passed since she'd last seen a driveway or house and the trail narrowed even more, until it was barely a lane and a half; if she met oncoming traffic she'd have to pull into the ditch to let them pass.

Judging from the height and health of the grass on the shoulder of the road she suspected running into oncoming traffic wasn't much of an issue.

Which brought her back to her original concern. It wasn't surprising that George's truck had broken down from driving on these rough roads, but what she was curious about was why he'd been out here. She glanced at the map. There was nothing ahead except a mine and a dead end where she'd have to turn around and retrace her steps.

A blur of brown flashed across the corner of her eye and she looked up in time to hit the brakes and watch a deer dash across the road and disappear into the woods on her left.

That prompted her to think about what Duncan had said, about the wildlife. Hunting? George didn't really strike her as the type, but it was a possibility. She'd have to check and see what was in season, and if he had a license.

Which reminded her that they still had to check up on the drug theft.

She continued down the road, followed the curve sharply to the right and braked again.

A barricade blocked her path. Road Closed was posted in the center of a chain that was linked from tree to tree and stretched across the trail. Moreau got out of her jeep.

The sign was standard issue and had official language from the district's government along the bottom, complete with a number to call with questions or concerns. It covered a padlock. She considered picking it, but looked ahead. The thick maze of trees that threatened to swallow the trail she'd followed thinned out and the scorched earth was dotted with charred stumps. A half-burned tree lay across the road not twenty feet from where

THE SPYING MOON

she stood, and a sign that read Beware Falling Trees had been tamped into an ash-filled ditch.

The mechanic she'd spoken to had said George's vehicle had been towed in from the far side of the fire, closer to the mines.

Moreau returned to her vehicle, shut it off, grabbed her keys and a backpack with water and basic supplies that rested on the floor in front of the passenger seat. She'd had the good sense to pack it after the hike up Holt Hill. She shut the door and used the key fob to lock the jeep as she walked away.

Once she dipped under the chain she studied the second sign. An effort had been made, but the lettering was crude and hand-drawn. Although the paper had been laminated to a piece of cardboard, water was starting to seep in and a stain was growing above the *B*.

The tree that rested across the road was charred superficially in the middle of the upper side. It reminded her of the way some Aboriginals made canoes; by burning out the upper part of a felled tree. She retrieved her phone and snapped a picture before she walked to the end of the tree and studied the cut.

A clean line had severed the tree from its stump, which was nowhere in sight. She snapped another picture.

There was no way that tree had come down on its own, and she knew it hadn't crawled on its branches to throw itself across the road. Where had it come from? As she ran her hand along the base of the tree she noted no blackened bark and snapped more pictures.

Someone had taken that tree down deliberately.

It could have been a parks crew, but as she walked along the other side of the tree, studied the burn pattern in what was left of the foliage around her and snapped more photos, her doubts grew.

Which meant what, exactly? George's truck had been towed from past this point, which meant that the tree had still been standing when he'd left with his vehicle.

Assuming he'd ridden back to town with the tow truck driver.

From the far side of the tree it was clear that the warning sign was meant to deter people for some reason other than the threat of falling trees. The tallest stump couldn't have been more than four feet and was well off the road. From left to right all that remained of that once-lush section of forest was a field of charred flowers, shrubs and grass before the burnt trees farther off the road; further down the hill, to her left, unburnt limbs and shafts had been stacked and tethered for retrieval.

The crews that had cleaned up the remnants of the fire had already been through, and a tie taped to the chains on the piles of wood was dated two days after George's truck had been towed.

Gray clouds hung over the mountainside without moving, and no hint of wind disturbed the leaves that remained on the trees that had survived the fire. Other than the deer that had crossed her path on the road she'd seen no signs of life and she heard none now; there were no birds chirping or squirrels foraging.

It was too quiet, even for a wooded area on a mountainside out of town. To the trained ear the forest was always alive with the sounds of animals. She knew that from her long walks in the woods in Muskoka. When she'd been young her mother had tried to teach her to listen to the forest; after her mother disappeared she took those walks alone, trying to hold on to the memory of her mother.

Here, in this burnt-out area, from where she stood near the lumber stacks, there was nothing but silence.

Her phone beeped and Moreau felt her heart leap into her throat. She took a breath and turned off the alarm.

In an hour she had to meet McIver at the station.

She turned and looked down the road, toward the mine. Searching further would have to wait; she hadn't counted on having to make part of the trip on foot. As she trudged back up the hill she paused long enough to photograph the homemade 'Beware' sign before she noticed she wasn't alone. On the far side of the burned area, in the center of the road, a coyote stood

THE SPYING MOON

watching her. She stared back and wondered why he kept turning up wherever she did, then chastised herself for thinking it was the same coyote that had made Duncan slam on the brakes on Friday night. She turned away and walked to her jeep, thankful she'd brought a towel and change of shoes and wouldn't be forced to wear soot-covered sneakers into the squad room.

As she turned her vehicle around and drove back she noted a clearing she'd missed on her way in. It was accessible heading west back to town, but the trees before and after the gap blended together so that you'd miss the spot heading east toward the mine if you weren't looking for it. She pulled off into the recess and got out of the vehicle.

Piles of broken tree limbs had been tossed near the far end of the alcove, furthest from the road. Moreau knelt and looked through the gaps in the wood to see if they concealed anything.

Something snapped behind her and she turned, stood up and reached for her gun. Her hand pushed her jacket back as she wrapped her fingers around her weapon's grip. The stillness had returned. She wasn't far from where she'd seen the deer, but she would have expected more of a scuffle or rustle of leaves as an animal moved through the woods.

As she scanned the bush around her she realized another trick of the lines of the trees. They concealed a path about nine feet from where she stood. She inched closer, hand still on her gun, although she hadn't removed it from its holster.

A few feet down the path it veered sharply toward the direction of the mine. Although she hadn't been there, she knew from the map book that past the burned-out section of forest the road twisted down the mountain until it reached the mine, and if the angle of this path held, it basically formed the other side of a triangle.

There was no sign of recent footprints on the path, so she scanned the woods on either side.

Behind a tree, about five feet to her left, she could make out a strip of camouflage. She realized she was in the woods alone and there could be hunters in the area, but she also knew they wouldn't hide behind a tree.

Unless they were doing something illegal.

"Move out slowly with your hands above your head."

Her fingers gripped the handle of her gun as she spoke. No response.

"I'm an armed RCMP officer. Move out slowly. Hands above your head."

A few feet behind her there was a crunch and she started to turn as she caught a flash of movement in front of her from the corner of her eye. She spun back in the direction of the camouflage and pulled out her gun, but the figure was already winding through the trees and almost out of sight. Moreau raced into the woods, jumped over a fallen tree and zigzagged through the foliage.

The dark-haired figure paused and glanced back. Was that a grin? In adrenaline-charged situations the mind had a way of picking up on or filling in details that the naked eye would normally miss. She darted under a branch and up to the crest of the hill the man had stood on when he'd smiled at her, but when she reached that spot she turned in all directions as she breathed deeply.

He'd vanished, without so much as a shoeprint left for her to trace.

Chapter 13

Moreau watched as McIver explained to Mabel Cook for the third time what they were going to do before he squeezed his hands into fists.

"Look, you don't have to be here, you don't have to do anything, as long as you're fine with us starting from your property. Okay?"

The corners of her mouth twisted. "Make sure you clean up any dog shit yourselves," she said as she marched to her cabin and slammed the door shut behind her.

Constable Brian Bradrick was below average height but he made up for it with a healthy frame, a full head of dark brown hair, green eyes and an easy smile. "Ever considered taking the Dale Carnegie course, Levi?"

"*How to Win Friends and Influence People* is for politicians and managers. I haven't got time for that crap." He glanced up at the sky. "We have to get moving."

Moreau had already noted the dark clouds thickening above them.

"Not that we have much of a chance anyway," Saunders muttered as he followed McIver and Bradrick around to the side of the house where the blackberry bushes were.

Freeman's orders had perplexed Moreau and pleased McIver. Saunders hadn't participated in the investigation, but he was directed to accompany them while tracking. She presumed Alec Chmar was working—if you could call it that—by himself on the

106

drug investigation. Nothing had been added to the bulletin board in the breakroom and she hadn't seen him since Friday night.

Duncan hadn't returned from the church service before they left, so she sent a text to let him know where she was.

"Now we'll see what Tony can find."

"Tony? That's great," Saunders said. Bradrick twisted his head back and looked at him.

"You named your dog after the cat on the cereal box?" McIver asked.

Bradrick's pinched eyes and frown could have made Mabel Cook wilt. "It's short for Remington."

"As in Steele?" Saunders said.

"Tony comes from a long line of police service dogs and was sired by a veteran named Remington. He was the only male in Remington's last litter, if you must know."

"Geez, all right. Relax."

"We need to get going," McIver said.

Bradrick shook his head. "It looks like it's going to rain. If you'd been on time we wouldn't have to rush this."

McIver gave Moreau a look. "Take it up with the woman. She was late."

Moreau bit back the urge to point out it had only been by two minutes, and that was because she'd been stuck waiting for a train.

Bradrick began a perimeter search and walked Tony over the area between the point of entry to the cabin and the edge of the woods.

"Didn't you bring that item from evidence for a scent trace?" Saunders asked.

Bradrick glanced at him. "First of all, they didn't leave anything behind. And we don't work that way. Evidence can be contaminated a dozen times over by crime scene techs and handlers. We look for a general scent trail."

"Is that as effective?" Saunders frowned at McIver, who

THE SPYING MOON

shrugged.

"How do you think the dogs get trained to find avalanche victims or survivors from a mudslide? We don't even have their names usually, let alone something they've touched. The dogs are trained to find specific scents. If there's a trail out here—"

Tony froze with his nose to the ground for a moment and then he started moving away from the Cook home, into the woods. "He'll find it."

Bradrick sprinted after his dog; McIver, Scott and Moreau followed. It wasn't long before the terrain became difficult. The ground was both rocky and treed; in some places the brush was so thick they needed both of their hands to push back enough branches to get through.

"This guy wasn't going for the path of least resistance was he?" Saunders said after he took a branch in the face.

"This is actually a pretty typical route to take," Bradrick told him between deep breaths. He hopped over a fallen tree as he followed his dog, who led them on a determined path without wavering. "There used to be a trail network through here that dates back to rum-running days. There are still remnants that run all through the woods right down to the border. The Holt family was famous for exporting illegal goods back then."

"You know a lot about the local history," McIver said.

"My family roots go back to Constable Lawson," Bradrick said as he ducked under a large branch. Tony was ahead of them, but in their line of sight.

"Wasn't he the police officer that was murdered by some gangster?" Scott asked.

"Yes. The only woman hanged in Alberta's history was convicted for killing Lawson along with Emperor Pic, the bootlegging kingpin back in those days."

Tony stopped. For the first time since they had left Mabel Cook's property he looked uncertain. He seemed to be picking up a trail in two directions, but after a moment he put his nose back to the ground and moved forward.

Within ten minutes they faced a wall of rock. Tony moved in one direction and then the other, again and again.

"What's going on?" McIver asked.

"He's picking up a few trails. He's trying to decide which direction, just like before."

"Or there could have been kids out here climbing the rocks and Tony's picking up their scent?" Scott asked.

Bradrick nodded. "It's possible. But he'll follow the same scent he's been tracking from the house, if he can. The perp could have run back and forth to try to throw off trackers deliberately and then climbed the rock."

That sounded pretty sophisticated for a perp who'd committed a break and enter to steal food. Moreau wondered how likely it was that the thief had given any thought to being caught or how to prevent the cops from catching him.

Still, Brian Bradrick had shown he was thorough and didn't underestimate the criminals he was chasing. That meant he was more likely to uncover any evidence there was to find.

McIver ran his fingers through his hair and watched as Tony went in one direction and then the other. "I don't think our guy is that good, Brian. This would be a tough climb without gear, carrying stolen goods. Let's try going east. There's nothing in the other direction except the old mines. It should only be about two kilometers at most in the other direction to the road."

As though he agreed, Tony turned in that direction and began running.

Moreau noted the mention of the mines and almost wished the dog had headed in that direction instead.

"What are you thinking?" Saunders asked as they jogged after Tony.

"That I'm not hiking into the middle of nowhere with no supplies after trudging through this bloody forest," McIver said. "It would take an hour or more to reach the old mines if we ran the whole way and we still might not find anything."

"Wasn't that where Willmott was when he got hurt?" Saun-

THE SPYING MOON

ders asked.

Moreau wondered again if Phil Willmott's accident was near where George's truck had broken down.

Before McIver could answer, Bradrick slowed his pace.

"Good call," Bradrick said. Beside him, they could see Tony's ears perk up, his rigid back indicating his full attention was focused on something just ahead. The rock cut had leveled off and the sound of rushing water cut through the forest before they could see the stream.

McIver pushed his way around Bradrick and froze. Moreau stopped beside him. She hadn't indulged any false hopes about getting a solid lead from tracking and had hoped that after this exercise Freeman would let her focus solely on the Petersen inquiry, but there was no chance of that now.

Not twenty feet from where they stood was the unmistakable form of a body, slumped in the river.

"I'll call it in," Bradrick said quietly.

Moreau nodded at him as she marched toward the victim. Time had not been kind and neither had the animals. Something had picked at a gaping hole from the chest. An eyeball dangled from its socket. The lower wound had also been at least a source of investigation, with bits of what appeared to be intestines strung out of the torn flesh, trailing into the water. Dried blood had crusted the tattered shirt and made it stiff and hard, but what had oozed down his side and from his chest had long since washed over the rocks and been carried away downstream.

She turned to see that McIver was right behind her. He followed her gaze back to Saunders, who leaned against a tree, face a pasty white.

"You handled Sammy Petersen blowing his brains out and this is bugging you?" McIver said.

There was no sympathy, no understanding in the tone whatsoever. Saunders lower lip quivered slightly as he glared at McIver. "Did you see this?"

"Hell, the chick saw it and didn't flinch."

110

"Yeah, well her people used to scalp ours."

Moreau felt her jaw drop open. She hadn't expected that from Saunders. He was probably pissed she'd put him in his place after more than one attempt on his part to get her to socialize with him the day before. When he'd put his hand on her knee she'd made it clear that he'd better remove it or he wouldn't be able to use it for a week.

"Fine. Stay there and cry like a baby."

McIver turned and looked Moreau in the eye. She had no idea what he was thinking, but his irritation seemed to be fully focused on Saunders and, for once, have nothing to do with her.

Chapter 14

Moreau returned to the station, dragged herself down the hall and paused to lean against a mountain of boxes that were as unsteady as she felt.

The justification for the task force had felt a little thin, but within three days they'd found two deceased males, and at least one of them was directly tied to the drug trade.

Not long after her arrival in town.

Not long after Nate Duncan's, either.

When she made it to the breakroom she saw that Duncan was at the table, with piles of files surrounding him. She watched him write notes on a pad of paper, and then place a file on a stack. He flipped the next file open, made more notes, and put it on a different mound of paperwork.

What files could he be reading, or was it something that didn't relate to their case?

Moreau noted his mouth formed a hard line, almost as though he had reached an undesirable conclusion about whatever he was researching.

She forced herself into the room and went straight for the fridge. As soon as she turned around and opened the bottled water, Freeman approached them.

"Can I see you both in my office?"

It wasn't a request. Moreau glanced at Duncan, who shrugged as he grabbed his notepad. They navigated the narrowing hallways with the stacks of boxes casting shadows over

112

what little floor space could be seen and entered his office. Freeman shut the door behind them.

"Have a seat," he said as he walked around his desk and got comfortable in his chair. They complied.

Moreau realized that for the first time, Freeman's desk wasn't hemmed in by cardboard. Some of the boxes had been removed from his workspace.

"I understand the Petersen funeral is Tuesday," the sergeant said.

"That's right, sir. It's at two o'clock," Moreau said. "They wanted students to be able to go. The school's having an early dismissal. It was posted on their Facebook page."

"I expect you're both planning to attend?" he asked. "I'll be there as well. I'm anticipating a heavy press presence, with local politicians who want to use the family's tragedy for their own political agendas. Uniformed officers will handle any issues that could arise and our media liaison will be there as well. Neither of you will need to worry about crowd control."

Moreau nodded. "Thank you, sir."

Freeman leaned back in his chair. He looked like he was getting comfortable. "How's your investigation going?"

Moreau shook her head. "Well...we haven't been able to fully disprove or confirm the statements from George, Arnold, Doug or Randy. Randy's latest statement seems to hold, if you consider the corroboration from Mary Jensen, Kenny Jensen and Wanda Griffin. However, we have some room for doubt about Mrs. Griffin's statement."

"What's the problem?" Freeman leaned back in his chair and gave her his full attention.

"She says Randy Jensen was the only person who came down the hill Friday night between seven and the time the police went up after the gunshot was reported. It wasn't possible to stay on the public road and get up or down that hill without triggering her light. It wasn't even possible to get past the light if you walked right up against the fence on the far side. There is no way

THE SPYING MOON

someone came down that hill and failed to set off the sensor."

Freeman scratched his head. "Interesting. How important is Mrs. Griffin's statement?"

"Her statement suggests that Arnold and Doug were up on the hill when Sammy died," Duncan said.

Freeman said, "But they weren't on the hill when the first police officers arrived."

"Randy Jensen says he lied about leaving with George, Arnold and Doug because George was afraid nobody would believe him," Moreau said. "George wasn't even on the hill, and his whereabouts are unaccounted for. I don't trust either of them."

"As long as we can't disprove their claims we don't have anything," Duncan said. "All we know is that someone was on that hill after Sammy died and they managed to come down without being seen. Since we know Doug and Arnold were up there that makes them the obvious suspects."

"What about Kenny Jensen?"

"He admitted he came down through Abe Holt's property. Mary and Randy both put him at home at the time Sammy died. He's the only one I'm convinced had nothing to do with Sammy's death," Moreau said. "He was furious when he found out Randy lied for George, and Randy has the bruises to prove it." So did she, but she wasn't about to share that fact.

"We can't clearly demonstrate that they're lying about not being there when Sammy died and we also don't know they had anything to do with his death. For now, I guess we have to set Mrs. Griffin's statement aside and assume that she didn't see Arnold and Doug come down the hill," Freeman said. "But they could have been there when Sammy died."

"If they weren't, they left within minutes of his death," Duncan said.

"Or..." Moreau paused. She thought about the alcove in the woods and the hidden trail. What had Duncan said about the Holt property? "Or they knew a hiding place where they could stay until the police left."

114

Freeman turned to look at Duncan. "Was that the only hangout up there?"

Duncan stared back at him. "I never participated in the hill parties when I lived here."

"But you are related to Abe Holt."

"And I wasn't allowed to set foot on his property." Duncan sighed. "I didn't break all the rules, you know."

Freeman frowned. "That's unfortunate. I've heard stories about the trails and hide-outs Duncan has on his land and I always wondered if they were true."

Moreau looked from Freeman to Duncan as her brow wrinkled with unasked questions. Clearly the sergeant was aware of Duncan's familial connection to the Jensens and Abe Holt, and it was starting to sound like that was part of the reason he'd wanted Nate Duncan transferred back to Maple River, whether Duncan liked it or not.

"Oh, they're true. There are other places up there some of the kids go to, but off-hand I couldn't tell you where all of the spots are."

Freeman nodded, his lips pressed together in grudging acceptance. "And with his dogs, nobody could sneak through his property without trouble."

"Except Kenny."

Moreau looked at Duncan. "How do you know that?"

"He always had a way with those dogs. If there was one person who could get down through the fenced yards, it would be Kenny. Anyone else would have to go through with Abe."

"So we can explain how he went down through the Holt property and why Mrs. Griffin didn't see him," Moreau said. "If anyone else went down that way, Abe Holt had some reason for helping them."

"Interesting," Freeman said. "Do you have anything else to go on?"

Moreau shook her head. "Not unless we can track the source of the drugs. We still need to follow up on the gun. The slug

THE SPYING MOON

that was recovered doesn't match anything on file in British Columbia."

Freeman glanced at Moreau. "And now you have a definite murder on your plate."

"McIver and Saunders can handle that if necessary."

Freeman frowned. "I'm not ready to pull you off that entirely yet."

"With respect, sir—"

He held up a hand to stop her. "I want a report on my desk Wednesday at noon about the status of the investigation into Sammy Petersen's death and what, if anything, is still pending. That's our next step. You have just over two days to cover as much ground as you can between now and then. If we don't have anything more definitive to go on at that point, we'll make a call then."

They both nodded. Moreau gripped the arms of her chair with her hands as though she was about to propel her body off the seat but Duncan hesitated.

"We've been reviewing some of the other cases," he began. Freeman's fingers stopped drumming on the arm of his chair as he looked at Duncan.

We have? Moreau thought about the stacks of paper in the breakroom that Duncan had been looking through when she'd returned.

"Has anyone looked into the drug-bust dates?"

Freeman's brow filled with wrinkles. "Chmar's supposed to be working on that. Why?"

"It looks like there might be a pattern."

So that was what Duncan was working on.

Freeman leaned forward and rested his arms on his desk. "What did you find?"

After they left Freeman's office, Moreau turned her attention to the drug cases and went over them one by one. She had to admit that even she might not have picked up on the hint of a pattern between the busts from a cursory review.

There was a clear timetable. The first arrests were three months apart, followed by a narrowing of the gap to two months and then six-week intervals. If the arrests were directly linked to shipments, then the volume of drugs being smuggled in had doubled over the past eighteen months.

The most recent arrest had happened a month after the previous one. Duncan had also reviewed the province's drug data and correlated new shipments hitting the streets. Each arrest occurred two or three days before a new batch of drugs appeared on the streets in Cranbrook, Revelstoke, Vernon, Kelowna, Creston, or Nelson. Maple River was feeding the cities of the BC interior. That was clear because the initial arrests for small possession charges formed a horseshoe around Maple River. The police focused their efforts in that area and turned up empty; the first overdose deaths always popped up dozens of kilometers away and never in the same city twice so far.

Classic misdirection. The police were looking in one region while the drugs were moving through another.

Duncan's theory was enough to make Freeman hopeful, if his reaction was any indication. He had been quick to note, if this was correct and the pattern held, that another shipment could be coming in Thursday.

That could be good for their drug investigation; however, she had two dead bodies and a break and enter case still on her plate.

Moreau wasn't certain she could help with the drug case, but she hadn't seen Alec Chmar in two days and she was sure that he couldn't handle it on his own.

She glanced at her watch. Since her return to the station she hadn't seen McIver. He'd been happy to leave her in the cold while he worked the break and enter, and she suspected he'd be just as happy to shut her out of the murder investigation now. Moreau packed her things and walked to her jeep briskly,

THE SPYING MOON

thankful that at last she could escape to the sanctity of her cabin and put the day behind her. Get to a space outside of work, forget the sight of organs oozing from a bullet hole that's been torn open by animals foraging for easy food.

She squeezed her eyes shut for a second, thought about the look on Saunder's face when he'd seen the body in the woods, then willed it from her mind.

"Oh, I'm sorry," she said as she stopped just short of colliding with another person who had been moving at an equally rapid pace. Her eyes focused on the face. "Ms. Everett. I didn't see you."

"That's okay," Alyssa Everett said as she looked away. "I was in a hurry."

"Well, I won't keep you."

Alyssa coughed. "I'm sorry. I just have to get a prescription filled," she said as she walked out the door.

She didn't wait to hold it for Moreau.

Moreau paused before she exited the building and walked to her jeep to give Alyssa some space. Alyssa was already halfway across the parking lot by the time Moreau reached her vehicle, but Moreau could make out a figure in the Taurus waiting for her.

Alyssa got in the car and the interior light highlighted the face of Alec Chmar.

Chapter 15

Moreau arrived home, slipped her shoes off outside before entering, and was aware that she heard Duncan's SUV pull up to his cabin as she reached for the handle.

Her front door was open.

She set her bags down on the porch, slipped her shoes back on and eased herself down the steps as she grabbed her gun.

All the tired muscles were at attention then, ready to act on command.

Her cell phone was in her jacket pocket, but talking meant sound. She glanced over her shoulder at Duncan's cabin and saw a faint shadow against the curtains of the living room as the lights came on inside his home.

A tiny thud from inside her cabin prompted her to turn back and face the door. What would she do if she was the one that had broken in and the occupant came home and stood outside the front door?

She kept facing the entrance as she moved in a straight line to her left side, where she had view of the ground floor bedroom window. Only the man's neck and head were in her room; the rest hung from his grip on the ledge, the camouflage jacket hanging loosely over the jeans he wore. She moved toward him, her weapon gripped firmly in her hand, and stopped eight feet back from his position. In the forest she'd judged him to be approximately six feet tall and she knew he could move fast, so she wasn't taking any chances.

THE SPYING MOON

"Let yourself down slowly and keep your hands in the air."

He dropped to the ground almost silently, and bent his knees on impact. With his hands raised above his head, he turned around.

"You're making a mistake," he said.

"This is my cabin and you're the one who was in it without my permission. How's that my mistake?"

"It's not what you think."

She reached into her pocket with her left hand and pulled out her ID. "RCMP. Constable Moreau."

That easy smile she'd detected when she'd chased him earlier was back. "I did not break in."

"You just happened to come along and find the door had been forced and decided to take a look and you thought that you'd climb out the bedroom window instead of leaving through the same doorway that someone else left open?"

"Yes."

The hint of a grin that lingered on his face was starting to annoy her. "Let's say I believe you. That doesn't explain what you're doing out here, by my cabin, to begin with."

The smile faded. Dark-eyed with a gaze neither vacuous nor casual, she felt like he could see right inside her, to the depths of her soul. He had the stealth and intelligence of a wolf. To others, wolves might seem sneaky and deadly; generations of Caucasian children had been raised to think that because fairytales and myths perpetrated misinformation about the animals through movies and books. Moreau knew otherwise. They were powerful and intelligent; they howled because they wanted you to stay away from them, and given a choice they'd rather avoid a confrontation with a man. To be like a wolf was to be strong of body and spirit, capable of taking down your prey.

Given what she'd observed in their two brief encounters she had no doubt this man was a skilled hunter, a tracker, and that he didn't take chances like breaking into someone's cabin without a good reason. She wondered if he was from one of the local

120

tribes.

"We can stand here all night," she said.

"Or I can leave."

"Not until I get some answers."

"Would you believe me if I said I was concerned about the occupant's safety?"

"I'm fine."

"I see that now."

"And that doesn't explain what you were doing out here."

His face was blank as he studied her. "It is a coincidence," he finally said.

Moreau laughed. "Twelve hours ago I was chasing you in the woods and now I find you sneaking around my home." She tilted her head to the side. "Coincidence? Really?"

The hint of a smile flashed across his face again. "Would you believe I was thirsty?"

"This isn't a bar."

He didn't flinch. "I didn't expect you to resort to stereotypes."

She chewed on her lower lip. In that moment she'd taken a page from McIver's playbook to try to push this man off balance, and all she'd done was cheapen herself in the process.

"And I would think that having a gun pointed at you by a cop would make you take this seriously. My partner is in the next cabin and all I have to do is make a call, so don't think you're walking away from this."

She put her ID back in her pocket and fished out her phone.

"I did not break in."

"So you said." She flipped her thumb across the screen to pull up the home page, which wasn't as easy to do with her left hand, but she wasn't about to put down the gun. "Why were you here?"

"I was curious about you."

Finally, something that resembled truth. She held her thumb above the phone icon and paused. "How did you know who I was?"

THE SPYING MOON

"I've answered one of your questions. Perhaps you'll answer one of mine."

"When I break into your home and you stop me at gunpoint you can feel free to ask anything you want."

His expression sobered. "The person who broke in is still inside. When I heard your vehicle I thought it best I exit and come around to assist you to avoid any misunderstandings."

There was no hint of deception in his expression but logic challenged her from concluding that he spoke the truth, although the way he spoke felt honest.

She tapped on the camera app and snapped a photo of him. He winced as he squinted and flinched. His body twisted back as though he was responding to something off to her right.

"Look out—"

Moreau turned too late. Something dark and sharp crashed down on her head and was followed by a flash of light. Fat fingers gripped her right hand and tilted it up so the gun pointed at the sky as she squeezed the trigger. She managed to stick her phone back in her pocket and reached up to grab at her assailant. Her fingers closed on denim-covered muscle as blood seeped down her forehead and into her eyes. Moreau scrambled blindly, her fingers searching for hair or skin she could claw. The bruises across her chest screamed in protest from the pressure against them as he put his weight on her and pushed her down. A spray of dirt flew into her face as something banged against the back of her head and more footsteps faded into darkness.

Sounds had surged from all directions during the attack, but she could isolate some of them and somehow felt she knew exactly what they were. Duncan's door opened. Footsteps came toward her and others ran away from the cabin. Her right ear reverberated with the echo of the gunshot and she wondered how she could hear anything else at all.

Moreau sat up. She swiped her left jacket sleeve across her forehead and tried to clear her eyes. Beneath the skin of her right

122

wrist she was bruised and although she still held the gun, her arm had been sapped of its strength.

Sirens sang in the distance. They grew louder as blue and red lights broke through the black night sky.

Duncan knelt before her. "They got away."

Chapter 16

Alec Chmar kicked Saunder's foot under the table. "You going to make some coffee or just try willing it into existence?"

"If I had that kind of power maybe I could do something about your mouth."

"I can think of some other things around here that could be willed out of existence." Chmar tipped his head toward Duncan as he walked into the room.

McIver leaned back against the counter and looked at Moreau, who sat at the far end of the table as she watched the exchanges between Chmar and Saunders and longed for ice and acetaminophen.

"Get her to make the coffee," McIver said.

Duncan marched toward the kitchenette and positioned himself between McIver and Moreau. "Make it yourself."

"Just because her white mama went slumming and she's got Native blood doesn't mean she should get special treatment."

Moreau felt her blood chill and her whole body froze.

"You assume just because she's a woman that she doesn't have a right to be here."

"You're in a real mood today, aren't you? Since when do you stand up for women instead of hitting them?"

So McIver knew about that old assault charge, the one that had led to Duncan's departure from Maple River all those years ago. His questionable personal history that had come up when she'd researched the team.

124

She knew he'd been charged. Moreau also knew the charges had been dropped.

What she hadn't known was that it involved hitting a woman and she wondered how McIver knew more about it than she did.

Duncan's hands clenched into fists and Moreau could see the fire spreading through his skin, up the back of his neck and into his face.

"Or maybe you prefer to be the only one to get a shot in. I guess we don't have to ask if you like it rough." McIver smirked as he nodded at Moreau. "Must be glad you've got a partner who plays that way but if she's anything like her mama I doubt you're wild enough for her."

"Your remarks about Constable Moreau are unfounded and inappropriate."

"Wow, big words, Nate. You're awfully defensive of your little Indian." McIver stood up straight. "You getting chummy with your neighbor?"

"I'm addressing the sexist, bigoted shit coming out of your mouth and that's it."

Chmar and Saunders both snorted. McIver's eyes darkened.

"Or maybe you want her to think you're her hero. Whenever someone does something that hurts her feelings you're right there to come to her rescue."

"The only thing I want is for Moreau to be treated like part of this team. She isn't the staff waitress so make your own damn coffee if you want it." Duncan bit his lip for a split second, his face taut with rage. "And don't you ever talk about her in such a degrading way again or—"

"Or what? You might decide to take a swing at a man for a change?"

"You just don't know when to quit, do you?"

"What's wrong, Nate? She doesn't fit in with the family image?"

"I'm here to do my job, not find a date."

"That's good, because you two are about as opposite as it

THE SPYING MOON

gets. Moreau's so far removed from her emotions they're in a different postal code, but you're so in touch with your feelings you need to get a room."

"Better to be aware of your feelings than to not have any."

Moreau swallowed. She hated to see McIver get the better of him, but she hadn't asked Duncan to defend her. It was noble but it betrayed the fact that Duncan thought she needed to be protected.

She didn't. She could take care of herself. She just couldn't think of a damn thing she could say that wouldn't make things worse and if she moved nothing would stop her from wiping the smug smile off McIver's face herself.

A small group of officers had gathered at the breakroom door and Freeman pushed his way through them. "We can take this into my office," he said. "Or you can both drop it now."

The hard edges of their expressions faded and the tension retreated behind masks of compliance.

Freeman wasn't finished.

"I'll have reprimands in both of your files if I see you two come to blows. Nobody is untouchable and don't either of you forget it."

McIver turned away and made the coffee. It was then that Duncan looked over to see the crowd at the door. He blinked and turned around to look at Moreau.

"Do you all need engraved invitations?" Freeman said to the crowd outside the room.

They disappeared back down the hallway without a word.

Moreau told Duncan she had a lead but once they were in the vehicle it took her a minute to stop shaking before she turned to face him. "What the hell was that about?"

Duncan opened his mouth to answer and then shut it without saying a word.

"I can take care of myself, Duncan. I don't need you to fight

126

my battles for me."

"Look, I know that. But it's not easy to stand by and do nothing." He fidgeted with his keys. "It shouldn't be easy. It isn't right."

"I-I get that. Really. But I don't want people to feel like they have to run to my rescue. I want to be treated like everyone else."

"But they're being—"

She cut him off. "It's my problem, not yours."

"Yeah, well, he made it about more than you in a hurry and you know it."

Moreau folded her arms across her chest. "Maybe it's time you told me why you left this town."

Duncan stared straight out over the steering wheel without responding.

"You either trust me, or you don't," she said.

When she'd learned Duncan was related to Abe Holt she'd suspect he'd been tangled up in the family business and left to get away. There'd been something about an assault, but no details had been offered, so it didn't undermine her theory.

What McIver had said suggested otherwise.

Mary Jensen was one of Abe's two much younger sisters, which meant that Duncan's mother was Monica Duncan, who seemed to be keeping a very low profile. From what Moreau had learned she still lived in Maple River, but she was the one member of the family Moreau hadn't seen since her arrival.

His voice was low and steady when he finally spoke. "The way the town told it, I beat a woman."

There had been rumors of a temper, and from time to time— like when McIver harassed him—she'd seen evidence of it, but everything she'd observed on the job told her Duncan was good police. He was thorough, honest in his dealings with everyone, and he'd been able to keep his emotions in check even when provoked.

"I don't want to hear what the town said. I want to know

THE SPYING MOON

what really happened."

He turned and stared at her. "Do you really think I would do something like that?"

Moreau realized it was possible he was defending her to improve his own reputation with women, but as his blue-eyed stare cut into her she had the same feeling she'd had when the stranger had stared at her the night before, like he could see inside her. The stranger had offered a lot of simplistic smartass remarks until she'd heard something that struck her as truth. Nate Duncan's words also had an air of honesty to them that her gut told her to trust.

"No."

"Then that's all that matters. You believe me, or you don't."

There was a certain amount of logic to that, and she nodded. "Okay."

"Fine. Then tell me about this hunch of yours."

"I went out to—"

A rap on the glass behind her caught her attention. She saw Duncan scowl as she turned to find McIver on the other side of the vehicle door. She pushed the button so the window would go down.

"We have a call to follow up with the crime scene techs and autopsy for the body in the woods."

Moreau stared McIver in the eye. Framed by a blue sky on a clear fall day he seemed as pleasant as the weather, mere minutes after almost coming to blows with her partner.

Mere minutes after saying lies about her mother that had hurt worse than anything she'd ever heard anyone say before, and there were no shortage of insults for Native kids who ended up in foster care.

"Look, I know you're busy closing this case, but Freeman—"

Ordered him to include her. The only reason he was letting her know.

"You should go," Duncan said.

Moreau looked at him. "You're sure?"

128

He nodded. "I've got a few last leads to check up on and I can do that while you follow up on the murder."

She opened the door and started to step out as McIver backed away, but then turned around, reached over and squeezed Duncan's arm. "Thank you."

He looked at her hand and then her face, offered a curt nod, and after she slid out of the SUV and shut the door he drove away.

Moreau was sandwiched between McIver and the mess of filing that lined the wall of the dim room in the basement of the station. More metal desks held an increasing number of computers and steel shelves had been added that were already jammed full with boxes that overflowed with papers and sealed bags.

"The reno," Benji said. "We're crammed in like sardines."

She'd already heard his explanation, but the space was worse than it had been on Saturday when she was there with Duncan. Moreau hadn't thought it was possible. At this rate, someday they would take a call to their own station and have to work together to dig Benji out from under an avalanche of evidence.

"Tell us what you've got and we're out of your hair," McIver said.

"What we've got isn't much." Benji used one of his chubby fingers to push his glasses up on his nose.

"You're the one who called us down here," McIver said.

"The report is in." Benji swiveled on his seat and pulled a folder from an overflowing tray beside his computer. "There just isn't much to go on. We had to eliminate police from the scene and that damaged some of the possible evidence we did recover, so there are a lot of blanks that—"

McIver grabbed the folder and leafed through it. "Look, I don't give a crap about the technicalities. I want something to work with here. A killer walked at least a mile, if not more, through the forest and you're telling me we've got nothing.

THE SPYING MOON

Bullshit."

"We were working the Petersen case and had to pull that to prioritize this. It's all we have."

"Not good enough."

Benji shrugged. "Maybe you'll have better luck with the autopsy."

"From a guy who was shot from about ten feet away? What the hell do you think? That he reached out and scratched his killer as he was going down? The kid wasn't Gumby!"

"We haven't got anything so far."

"Then get your ass off Pokemon Go and check everything again." McIver tossed the file down on the keyboard. "Now."

Benji glanced at Moreau before he nodded at McIver. "Of course," he said.

As she followed McIver out the door, Moreau heard a string of Korean slip from Benji's mouth.

Levi McIver didn't have a friend in the building, but at least he dished out his brand of bias with equal opportunity.

The death of Sammy Petersen offered Moreau one blessing: her first time in autopsy seeing a dead body was not with Levi McIver. She was prepared for the sterile room of white walls and cold steel, as well as the cynical humor Creaser served the law enforcement officers.

"Donut holes today," Creaser said as they walked in. "Seemed fitting."

McIver glanced at Moreau, who kept her face straight but thought she saw a flicker of surprise in McIver's eyes.

Creaser looked at her and frowned. "You don't approve?"

"Aren't Life Savers the only candy with a hole in the middle?" She walked over and pointed at the box. "And aren't these actually Timbits?"

The coroner popped one into his mouth and then pointed at her. "Ummm hmmmmm. I'll have to remember that."

130

He led the way to the body. This time, she was certain McIver's eyes had widened when she spoke.

"I guess we'll call this good news and not great news." Creaser washed his hands, grabbed a pair of gloves and walked over to the table where their victim lay. "As you can see, cause of death was a gunshot wound to the abdomen. However, he was shot in the back first. In the shoulder."

Creaser snapped the gloves onto his hands and lifted the left shoulder a few inches. It was enough to see the entry wound.

Moreau looked at the man's chest.

"Was there an exit wound?"

Creaser set the shoulder back down gently. "That's the good news. The bullet was recovered and has been sent for testing."

"And the not-so-great news?" McIver asked.

"Well, you're getting ahead of things. Time of death was approximately seven days ago. There was a fair bit of damage to the abdomen because of rats. Interesting that they're the creatures that got to him, but I guess it's lucky for us. A larger predator would have done far more damage."

"He was killed last Monday." Before Sammy Petersen. Before the break-in at Mabel Cook's cabin.

Creaser nodded, and lifted the victim's right hand. "The water submersion has made it impossible to get reliable prints. We've sent the dental x-rays for comparison, but his teeth don't show signs of fillings or braces or that the wisdom teeth were extracted."

"Which means we have next to nothing to go on to identify him," Moreau said as she glanced at McIver. "Not-so-good news indeed."

"The DNA database could get a hit." Creaser shrugged. "But there's evidence of a less-than-ideal lifestyle. The report highlights my findings that suggest he was living on the street for some time."

Creaser held out the file to Moreau, but McIver intercepted it.

"I doubt we'll get a hit off missing persons then," he said.

THE SPYING MOON

Moreau shrugged. "You never know. What about drugs?"

"Not for me, thanks, kicked that years ago."

There was a gleam in Creaser's eyes that made her wonder about his joke. He looked like just the right kind of smart crazy to have dabbled with illicit substances in his youth.

"Right," Creaser said when neither of them responded. "It's in the file. Track marks between the toes and up the arms and plenty of other evidence to suggest he was a regular. It'll take a few more weeks to get test results back from his blood samples, though."

Things had moved so quickly for a well-liked local boy just a few days earlier.

Almost as though he could read her mind, Creaser said, "I called in favors for Sammy. A lot of favors. I know that might seem unfair, but he was a good kid and his parents deserve better."

Moreau wondered if the John Doe on the table also had good parents out there, still hopeful, still praying that they'd see their son again someday.

"There is one other thing of interest." Creaser led them to another table, where John Doe's personal effects were bagged. "Soot on the shoes. Trace is coming to get them."

Moreau thought of her own footwear, still in the back of her jeep. Did that mean he'd been coming from the old mines? She tried to summon a mental image of the map she'd used the day before. Mabel Cook's cabin was further up the mountain slope, but the road twisted down toward another road, and they'd tracked through the woods at least a mile, maybe two. They'd found him in the river...

Not that far from the burn site.

She turned and studied what was left of the victim's face. "Any chance of reconstruction?"

"I have someone I can call. Freeman has to sign off on it, though."

"It may be our only way to ID him," Moreau said.

132

Creaser walked back around the corner to his desk and they followed. He extracted a paper from one of his trays and handed it to McIver. "Get Freeman to sign, or provide a damn good forgery."

McIver smiled. "That could be arranged."

Moreau snatched the paper from his hand and walked out into the hall.

"Touchy," McIver said as he followed her.

She led the way to the ballistics lab silently.

Greg's room remained the anomaly in the current construction phase. Moreau guessed nobody wanted to take the chance that a stack of boxes would fall down on someone who worked with loaded guns. With a file folder in his hands, Greg stood facing the door and offered a small greeting smile when they entered. He extended the folder before he spoke.

"It's a match," he said.

"Match to what?" McIver reached for the file, but Greg pulled his hand back and then extended it to Moreau.

She flipped it open and sucked in a sharp breath.

"A match to the bullet recovered from the scene of Sammy Petersen's death."

"The same gun that Sammy used to commit suicide was used to kill our victim," McIver said.

Moreau didn't correct him. "Was this the bullet that entered through the shoulder?" she asked Greg.

He nodded. "It was the only bullet recovered. The others were, ah—" he pushed his black-framed glasses up on his nose, "—eaten, presumably."

"Is there a reason you know what's in the autopsy report when you work in ballistics?" McIver asked.

"I wanted to be certain I had everything ready for your report, so I asked." The corners of Greg's mouth turned down. "Creaser was happy to show me the body."

McIver laughed. "I bet he was."

Chapter 17

Moreau offered a bright smile to the cashier working at the customer service desk at the local Canadian Tire. It was quiet, and, fortunately, the only other cashier open at the moment was three rows down.

"You guys sell hunting licenses, right?"

The cashier was a young man with thick brown hair, a lanky frame and he'd retained an adolescent smattering of acne across his face. When he smiled back she could see he was also afflicted with braces on his teeth, and not the most up-to-date fashionable kind. *Jeff* was printed on his name tag.

"Yes. It's open season for some types of deer and elk right now, but it isn't cougar season yet."

Moreau wasn't sure how to take that statement, so she reached into her pocket and pulled out her ID, although she kept it on the counter and made sure her voice was low.

"Oh, Officer, I'm, um...." The rest of the lad's face went as red as his zits.

"It's okay." She pocketed her ID. "I'm working on a case at the moment, and it would really help if I knew if one suspect had a hunting license."

"We don't keep all the records here. At the end of the shift they get filed in the offices."

"That's okay. Do you work fulltime?"

He nodded.

"Then maybe you'd remember, but—" she glanced around

her and then leaned forward a little and smiled, "—I'd like to keep this quiet. I'm sure it's nothing and I don't want anyone getting the wrong idea. You know how it is. Talk in a small town."

The look in his eyes told her she'd hit the nail on the head. "Yeah, sure."

"Do you know George Jacobs?"

Just the name made Jeff's eyes widen as his smile fell from his face. Bingo.

"I can see that you do. Any chance you remember if he or one of his friends bought a hunting license recently?"

Jeff shook his head. "No, they don't hunt."

"You're sure?"

"I've worked here for three years. Community college classes at night, cashier during the day."

"Good for you."

"He's never been in to buy a license when I've been here."

"Anywhere else in town he might go?"

"Not really. He'd have to be a lodge member to buy through them, so until they finish the Walmart on the outskirts of town most people come to us."

"Right. Thanks, Jeff."

She walked outside. It wasn't a certainty, but it was likely that he didn't have a hunting license. As she slid into the driver's seat of her jeep her phone buzzed.

A call from a 403 area code number.

"Constable Moreau," she said.

"This is Constable Savage, from Okotoks."

"Yes, I'd been hoping to video conference with you, actually."

"What have you got?"

"You had a theft not too long ago? Some guns?"

Savage got quiet, so Moreau continued.

"We have a gun here that matches the list of weapons that were stolen, but the serial number has been so damaged we can't raise it. I was wondering if you could take a look and determine if it's possible it came from the shop that was robbed."

THE SPYING MOON

"And you want me to do this via Skype?"

"Our sergeant won't spring for us to head your way."

"How'd you recover the weapon?"

"It was planted on the body of a teenage boy."

"That one that shot himself in the head?"

When good kids die, news traveled. "Allegedly."

There was a short pause. "And this gun was planted on him?"

"Yes."

"You mean it wasn't the gun he used to kill himself?"

It was Moreau's turn to stay silent. The idea of lying to other officers didn't sit right with her, but all she had to do was think about Laura Petersen to understand Freeman's reason for discretion. The family didn't need more drama right now. Answers weren't going to bring their son back, and if the speculation was public knowledge it would prompt more gossip that would lead to more pain.

"Not suicide?"

Moreau sighed. "I can't confirm or deny that."

"A suspected homicide and your boss doesn't want you chasing every angle on the gun?"

"I'm not just on this case. I'm working a guaranteed homicide right now, too."

"The body in the woods."

Constable Savage was informed.

"Are we the only ones who have crime in Western Canada right now?" Moreau asked her.

"Just doing my homework. You have two bodies, possibly one of my missing guns and a sergeant who won't spring for a flight? Does that sum it up?"

McIver's face flashed through Moreau's mind but she pushed it aside. "For the most part."

"Can you send me pictures of the gun?"

Moreau got Savage's email address and after she ended the call she pulled up the report on the gun with the images in her work email and forwarded them to Savage.

Chapter 18

When Moreau returned to the station she saw Duncan walking toward the front doors.

"Wait up."

He stopped and turned around.

"Constable Savage from Okotoks called," she told him. "They're going to review the photos of the gun and see what they think."

"It would be nice to match it."

Checking boxes. That's all that would really be, at least as far as the Petersen case went.

It would open up a whole new avenue of investigation as they tried to trace the gun and determine how a weapon stolen from Alberta had ended up almost eight hundred kilometers away.

"I hope we can close this case," Moreau said. "I want to be able to go to that family and tell them what really happened to their son. I don't know how his parents could live with it if they thought he killed himself."

The left eyebrow twitched in sync with the quirk of Duncan's mouth. "I don't know if it makes any difference to them, in a way. Sammy's gone and nothing is going to change that."

"Don't you think they would get some peace knowing why?"

"Not if it was a suicide. Then they would have to live with the blame."

Moreau frowned. "I would have expected you to be the one to play it straight, not sugar-coat the truth to spare someone's

THE SPYING MOON

feelings."

"All I'm saying is that we may never be able to give them ab-
solute truth. And the longer they think it's a suicide the more
questions they'll have about why we kept them in the dark if
Sammy's death is ruled a homicide."

"Constable Moreau."

The voice startled her, and she turned around as she tried to
place it.

Seth Gorden.

She walked toward him to put a bit of distance between
Gorden and Duncan. "If you think I'm going to answer any
questions you have about this case, my partner or his family—"

"It's your family I wanted to ask you about, actually."

She stared at him. What on earth could he possibly know
about her family, or think was relevant for his newspaper?

"Your mother's one of the missing women, isn't she?"

Behind her she thought she heard the intake of breath from
Duncan.

"I don't see how that's any of your business."

"Rookie cop gets assigned to a new task force and she's motivated by her mother's disappearance from years ago? Are you
even concerned about crime in Maple River or are you more
interested in finding out what happened to your mother?"

She opened her mouth but no words came out.

"That's the truth, isn't it? You were heading for Burns Lake
before you were reassigned at the last minute."

"Whether I want to be here or not is none of your business."

"It is if it means you aren't doing your job."

She felt Duncan's hand on her arm. "Let's go."

"But—"

"This guy is just leaving," Duncan said. He didn't make the
mistake of stepping between her and Gorden, but he maintained
contact with her arm without grabbing her or forcing her into
the station.

Moreau turned around and led the way into the breakroom,

her mind filled with the sound of war drums. She dumped a half a pot of coffee down the sink and reached onto the shelves for a new filter.

"You really don't have to do that, you know. You hardly even drink the stuff."

She glared at him. "Duncan—"

He put his hands up and turned away to retrieve his juice from the fridge.

For several minutes they were both silent. Duncan looked like he was pretending to read a file at the table, and she leaned back against the counter, her fingers gripping it so tight they turned purple.

"You have to pick and choose your battles," she finally said. "If they think they can push me around, it's a false sense of power. I only make it because their coffee smells like shit that's been pureed and poured through a strainer. I don't know what they do to it."

Duncan started to laugh. Moreau could see it was a deep, hearty laugh that tightened the abs. His amusement was contagious and she laughed too. All the stress of the past few days seemed to dissipate.

Freeman and McIver walked in just as Moreau wiped the tears from her eyes. If either wondered what was so funny, they didn't ask.

"I want to see you in my office, K. C.," Freeman said. He turned and walked away without waiting for her.

Once Freeman was far enough away that he couldn't hear them, Duncan said, "Reverse discrimination, Moreau. Don't be poking fun at how men make coffee."

She rolled her eyes. "Any more of this PC bull and we won't even be able to refer to people by their genders."

"Then nobody will be able to use any bathroom."

"Hey, this isn't the U.S."

Moreau walked down the hall to Freeman's office. She was either getting used to the haphazard stacks of boxes or there

THE SPYING MOON

were fewer of them. The space didn't seem as closed in as it had before.

When he waved her into the office Freeman pointed at a chair. "Have a seat," he said.

She complied and waited as he got up and closed the door, which she'd left open deliberately. Whether the sergeant shut it or not would tell her how serious this chat would be.

"I haven't had a chance to talk to you about the incident at your cabin."

"I'm sure you've seen the report."

"It's what the report doesn't say that concerns me."

Moreau studied Freeman's gaze. It was firm and confident, but the eyes also showed concern. "I'm fine," she said.

He stared back with a look in his eye that suggested he didn't quite believe her. "This man you stopped outside your bedroom window, had you seen him before?"

What would her boss say if she shared the hunch that had led to her encounter with the man the day before?

He seemed to take her hesitation as affirmation. "Why isn't that in the report?"

"I went out to the mines Sunday morning. Well, near there."

Freeman frowned. "And you saw him there?"

"Near there."

"What were you doing out there?"

"George Jacobs had his truck towed from past the burn zone."

"What does that have to do with the Sammy Petersen case?"

Moreau paused. Before she could settle on the safest response, Freeman continued.

"You went by yourself?"

She nodded.

"And you saw this same man?"

Moreau paused. "I pursued him in the woods."

"Sunday morning?"

"Sunday morning."

"Before you were out tracking with Bradrick, Saunders and McIver?"

She nodded.

"And where was Duncan?"

"He went to the Petersen's church to observe."

"And you didn't go with him."

"He felt it would seem too official. Duncan said he wanted to observe informally."

Freeman looked away, the ends of his fingers pressed together to form a teepee with his hands that he seemed to be studying. After a few seconds he looked up and nodded. "Did you find anything?"

Moreau had a split second to decide whether to tell her boss everything, or try to put an end to his inquiry. She fished her cell phone from her pocket.

"Someone cut a tree down and blocked the road." She held up her phone to show him the picture and then scrolled to another one. "This happened after the cutting crew was out there, and after George's truck was towed."

Freeman took her phone and studied the images. "Which is interesting, but what does it have to do with your case?"

"Maybe nothing. That's why I haven't said anything. But George knows more than he's telling, and I recognized the name of the road he was towed from. It's where Phil Willmott's accident was."

Freeman looked up, his thumb on the screen of her phone. "And you think there's some connection between Sammy's death, Phil's accident, and George Jacobs?"

Moreau considered that. "I don't know, but I still wanted to check it out. When I was driving back I saw a cut-out in the trees where you could pull off and there was a path that led down in the direction of the mines. That man startled me in the woods."

"And you chased him, but he got away."

"That's correct."

THE SPYING MOON

"Which means it wasn't a coincidence that he ended up at your house." Freeman looked back at the screen as he flicked through images. "This is him?"

He held up the phone, which displayed the photo of the tall Aboriginal man in the camouflage jacket that she'd tried to detain, twice, and failed.

Moreau nodded.

"Do you know who he is?"

"No, sir. I haven't looked into it further. With Sammy Petersen and our John Doe—"

"And you haven't mentioned this to the team investigating the break-in."

"I'd rather follow up on it myself."

"Why?"

"We know he wasn't the one who assaulted me. Maybe he was telling me the truth."

Freeman gave her a sharp smile. "Since that wasn't in the report, I'm not sure what he said."

"That he was curious about me after our encounter in the woods. That he came to my cabin to find out more about me." She paused as she recalled the look in his eye and the man's slightly irritating smile. "That he saw my cabin had been broken into and went inside to check it out."

"And he was hanging outside your bedroom window because…"

"He heard me return and thought it would be best to try to exit the house and come around to inform me that there was an intruder."

Freeman nodded. "There's another place that rents cabins a few miles further out of town and there's a house in town we can use. We just happened to have the lease from when Phil was staying where you are now, so it was convenient, but we can move you."

"I'm not worried about this man."

"But whoever it was that struck you could come back."

Freeman scrolled to the next photo.

Phil Willmott had stayed in her cabin. That was the vaguely undefined fact that had been gnawing at her and trying to surface. What if the break-in had nothing to do with her?

"And when were you going to tell me about this?" Freeman held up her phone and she saw a photo from after she'd been grabbed by the second assailant.

"I...I didn't even know I took that, sir." Her recollection of the attack flashed through her mind. After she'd been struck there'd been a flash of light. "I just remember putting my phone in my pocket and trying to grab him."

Freeman scratched his head. "This puts me in an awkward position, Moreau."

She stared at the photo and then shook her head. "No. It doesn't. Don't do anything."

His eyes narrowed. "You're telling me that I should just sit here twiddling my thumbs when one of my officers assaults another member of this team?"

"Don't you think there's a leak?" she said. "Willmott gets injured. Someone breaks into my cabin, which just happens to be where he was staying before the accident. That someone is a member of this team." She held the phone back up for Freeman. "And right now, Alec Chmar thinks he got away with it. We know he assaulted me, but he doesn't know we know that."

Freeman rubbed his chin. "So you're saying..."

"Alec isn't going anywhere. We can keep an eye on him." She paused. "If he's the leak, maybe we can use that. Maybe we can set a trap."

"What are you thinking?"

"That it's time to create a new covert task force, and keep the one you have in the dark."

"Spread false information within the team and see if our traffickers slip up?"

"Something like that."

Freeman seemed to be processing that. "I'd just like to think

THE SPYING MOON

that a man under my command isn't that stupid," he said.

"I'd like to think that he isn't corrupt."

"That goes without saying, Moreau."

"We have another problem. The bullet removed from the John Doe matches the bullet extracted from Sammy Petersen."

"Does McIver know?"

"That they match? Yes. But I haven't had a chance to tell Duncan yet."

"Does McIver know you're looking at Sammy's death as a possible murder?"

She shook her head. "Not as far as I know."

Freeman leaned back in his chair and scratched his head. It was a tough call to make, and part of her was glad that he was the one who would be responsible for whichever direction things went in. McIver had taken an interest in the Petersen investigation from the start and Duncan didn't trust him.

"Your impressions of McIver and Duncan?" Freeman asked.

"They're both thorough, sir."

"Speak candidly, Moreau."

"I'm inclined to trust Nate Duncan. He wasn't here when Willmott was injured. I suspect you brought him in because he knows the town, would help catch people off-guard, and there was no reason to think he'd be involved in the local drug trade. By all accounts he hasn't been back here in years."

"What about McIver?"

"He puts on a front here. Acts like a jerk, but outside this building he's professional and astute."

"And what does that tell you?"

"That there's more to McIver than meets the eye. I just haven't decided if that's a good thing or a bad thing."

Freeman nodded slowly. "Which is why you're going to keep him out of the loop on the Petersen inquiry."

"Sir?"

"You're the only one who knows everything about the two cases." His eyebrows arched. "Three, if we count the drugs. We may suspect Alec Chmar of being the leak but we need to be certain."

Freeman fidgeted with a pen on his table as he spoke. There was something about the lines in his face that told Moreau he was holding back.

"Do you have a reason to suspect McIver?"

The sergeant raised his head and looked her straight in the eye. "He was Phil Willmott's partner. If there was one person on the team I didn't suspect, it was Levi, but I can't afford to rely on my gut. I never wanted Alec Chmar on this team. Scott Saunders either. They were hand-me-downs assigned to me by the former sergeant. I didn't want them, but I didn't think Chmar would be capable of this." He gestured at her. "Levi's been here for a while, and he was here when Phil was injured. He has to be considered a suspect."

"There is something you need to know, sir." She took a breath. "McIver was asking questions about our case."

"It's not unusual for a cop to ask another cop about their investigation."

She shook her head. "No, sir. He was asking potential witnesses. Mrs. Griffin."

Freeman straightened in his chair. "She confirmed him by name?"

"No, sir. She didn't like him, so she wouldn't take his card."

"Then how do you know it was McIver?"

"Mrs. Griffin called him McIdiot."

A smile flickered across Freeman's face. "That's hardly conclusive proof, Moreau."

"I could go back with a photo array."

Freeman's mouth twisted before he nodded. "Keep Duncan out of it."

"And what about the investigations, sir?"

The sergeant seemed to consider the options and finally tossed up his hands. "What do you and Duncan have left to cover?"

145

THE SPYING MOON

"We want to check Sammy Petersen's locker but we won't have access until tomorrow."

Freeman glanced at a calendar that was now visible on his desk. "You know you're a cop when you work Thanksgiving Monday and forget it's a holiday."

"No, sir, that's how you know you aren't married."

He offered her a thin smile. "Don't tell Duncan any more than you have to. For now, let's try to keep things quiet."

She got up to leave. "You're sure?"

"If McIver's mismanaging investigations you'll know about it. If Duncan's staying closer to the family business than anyone thinks you have the best chance of finding out. Duncan's got a temper. McIver likes to push his buttons, and I don't need that getting in the way of either investigation."

She put her hand on the doorknob when Freeman spoke again.

"Moreau."

"Yes, sir."

"Nate plays the outsider, but he wants to belong. Make him feel trusted. Tell him I suspect McIver. Let him think he's earned your trust."

She nodded and exited Freeman's office. In the few days she'd been in Maple River she'd already slipped between the dividing lines within the team. The situation with McIver meant that she was going to have to keep everyone at arm's length until she understood why McIver was sneaking around and getting involved in cases that had nothing to do with him.

Moreau found Duncan in the breakroom. McIver leaned against the counter, a mug in his hand.

"Good coffee. You should make it all the time, Casey. It's actually drinkable."

She ignored his failed attempt at using her given name. "You're a smart boy, McIver. I'm sure you could figure it out if you put your mind to it."

"Why waste my time when we have you here?"

146

Moreau bit her lower lip, looked at Duncan and tipped her head toward the door. He got up without a word and followed her.

"Are you going to tell me where we're going, or are you driving?" he asked once they were outside.

"Anywhere. Lunch." She glanced at her watch. "Or I guess we could call this dinner. But we can't talk here."

Wrinkles spread across Duncan's brow, but he got into the SUV without a word.

He opted for a drive-thru and drove to a local park.

"This can't be good," he said once he'd cut the engine and passed her the food she'd ordered.

"It isn't great," she said. "There's a link between our case and the murder McIver's on."

"The body in the woods? Vagrant youth, regular drug user. How does he connect to Sammy Petersen?"

"He was killed with a bullet fired from the same gun used to put a hole in Sammy's body."

"So our case is linked to McIver's."

"Except he doesn't know we're investigating a suspected homicide. He thinks it's a suicide."

"And Freeman wants it to stay that way?"

Moreau nodded. "He wants me to put up a wall between the cases. I'm sorry."

Duncan's eyes narrowed. "For doing your job? Or because you suspect I'm corrupt?" Half his mouth tugged into a smile. "Wait. You think I'm incompetent?"

She grinned. "No, no and definitely no. Because he's ordered me not to tell you anything about the other case if I don't have to. It's not because of you, Nate."

He studied her before he popped a fry into his mouth. She'd used his first name for the first time, deliberately. And she could tell he was smart enough to see through that action.

"It's McIver. He's got doubts."

"Something like that."

THE SPYING MOON

"Are you working two murders, a break-in, and trying out as an internal affairs officer now?"

She hadn't thought about how this order might seem to someone else. The ease with which she accepted directions to inform on a member of the team surprised her and she turned her attention to her burger so she could avoid Duncan's gaze.

"I get it," Duncan said. "He's been an ass and you're trying to do your job. If he's dirty he shouldn't be protected by other officers."

Even as the words came out of Duncan's mouth she knew he was correct about not protecting corrupt cops, and she also knew deep down McIver didn't feel right for what Freeman suspected him of doing. He was too good when he actually did his job.

"Who's left to canvas about George's route?"

Duncan grabbed his notepad from the center console and flipped through it. "Nobody. I did find witnesses for the latter half of their walk down, but after eleven-thirty."

"Which is much later than they said."

"And they didn't come down Holt Hill. It runs a straight path through Maple River to the border, but the witnesses I found put them three blocks east. They would have had to veer back west to go to George's house, so it doesn't make much sense that they would have come down Holt Hill, walked over three blocks out of their way, and then turned back."

"Unless they were up to something."

"Mrs. Griffin didn't see them, though. And neither did anyone else who was anywhere along Holt Hill. They first appeared at the base of the hill, but on Spruce Road."

"That suggests what?" she asked.

"That they came through the Holt property."

"I thought you said Kenny was the only one who could handle those dogs."

"He is. Other than Abe Holt himself."

She chewed her lower lip as she looked at him.

148

Duncan stared back for a second before he shook his head and turned the key in the ignition.

Abe Holt's compound was comparable to a fortress. The chain link fence that surrounded the property met at a tall gate that hosted signs warning trespassers they would be shot.

Moreau glanced at Duncan, who shut the Rodeo off and stepped outside the vehicle. "Not part of the local Welcome Wagon, is he?" she asked as she got out and closed her door.

Duncan gave a curt shake of his head as he pulled out his phone and pressed buttons on the screen until he finally put it to his ear.

"Constable Duncan. We need to speak with you on official police business."

Whatever was said on the other end of the line caused Duncan's face to darken, and he clicked the phone off without another word.

The wizened face of Abe Holt appeared about ten minutes later. He walked down the hill, flanked by dogs who were calm and content with him, but bristled and snarled when they saw the strangers at the gate. Mutts, but with the look of Pit Bull and Rottweiler in the mix.

"You be pokin' yer nose in where it don't belong."

"We're investigating the death of Sammy Petersen."

"Kid tops himself by my property. What's it to do with me?"

Duncan glared at his uncle. "It's my job to investigate whatever crimes happen here. Sammy Petersen died on the border of your property, his body filled with illegal drugs. If you think I'm going to back off because you might be involved I'd say the elevator doesn't go all the way to the top."

The old man's lip curled. "I'm sharp as ever, boy. You let me get my hands on you and you'll find that out sure enough."

Duncan ignored the threat. "Then you'll recall letting some local boys pass through your property on Friday night."

THE SPYING MOON

"What I recollect or don't is no business of yours."

"This is a police investigation."

The beady blue eyes seemed to get even smaller. "You can't get a warrant for my memory."

"But I can get one for your property. Just think. Two or three dozen officers combing every inch of your acreage. I can't imagine what they might find."

Abe walked over to the fence and pointed a finger at Duncan. "Just because you have a badge don't mean I have to take that shit from you, boy."

He turned and stomped back up the hill. The dogs snapped at Duncan and Moreau one last time before they followed him.

Duncan's fists were clenched, his face as red as a vine-ripened tomato.

"It could have been worse," Moreau said.

His jaw dropped open as he looked at her.

"He could have let the dogs out."

Duncan smiled as his face faded to its normal color. "Where does this leave us?"

"Any banks or ATMs we might be able to use to verify the timeline for their hike down the hill?"

He shook his head. "I checked everywhere along that path. There's nothing we can use except eyewitness testimony."

Moreau considered that. It wasn't as good as video footage but it was better than nothing. "We'd need a warrant to completely retrace their steps and prove one of them could have fired the gun."

"It seems thin. I'm not convinced a judge would sign off on it yet. And it still doesn't put a needle in their hands."

"Which leaves us with Jim Petersen and Sammy's camera."

"Jim was out of town Saturday until the funeral," Duncan said. "Working."

"What kind of work does he do that takes him out of town?"

"He's in management with one of the construction crews. Oversees projects between here and Kelowna and as far west as

Abbotsford. I did confirm with his boss—" Duncan flipped through his notepad again, "—that he's off for the next three days."

"He works out of town regularly, and travels between several different communities in the interior." Moreau's eyes widened.

Interesting.

Chapter 19

They decided to talk to Freeman about the possibility of a warrant but he almost crashed into them as they turned to go down the hall. McIver was right behind him.

"You won't believe this, Casey" McIver said.

Moreau ignored him. "Sir—"

Freeman shook his head. "You need to go with McIver," he told her.

She glanced at Duncan.

"Sir—" he said.

Freeman pointed at Moreau. "You. With McIver. Now." He pointed at Duncan. "You work on whatever's left to cover for your report."

Moreau glanced at Duncan and turned to follow McIver.

One step forward, three back. It was the way the entire case had been.

"You aren't going to believe this," McIver said as she followed him outside to the same unmarked SUV he usually drove. "Someone tried to break into Mabel Cook's house again."

"Tried?"

"She has him standing in a corner with a loaded rifle pointed at his backside. Let's hope Mabel Cook's intruder is a repeat performer."

When they arrived at the cabin Moreau followed McIver up the steps to the open door. He knocked and announced their arrival.

"In here."

When they stepped inside Moreau watched a genuine smile spread across McIver's face. The feisty fifty-plus firecracker had her rifle in her hands, trained on a young male she had made stand facing the corner.

Moreau loosened her grip on her own weapon, which was still holstered. "It's all right, Mrs. Cook. You can put your gun down."

Mabel Cook glared at her but the muscles in her face relaxed. It was like freeing Jell-O from a mold. Mrs. Cook put her gun down and moved back.

McIver approached the youth, directed him to spread out his arms, and searched him for weapons. The young man was thin with scruffy brown hair that poked out in all directions and he wore an oversized pea green coat that looked familiar.

It wasn't until McIver cuffed him and turned him around that Moreau recognized him. His eyes widened when he saw her, and McIver turned and looked at Moreau.

"You know him?"

"No."

McIver looked back at the youth. "You know her."

"I've just seen her before, okay. Once."

McIver fished into the pockets of the coat and came up empty until he pulled his hand out of the last compartment with a standard issue RCMP business card in it.

He read the card and whistled. "Nate Duncan."

McIver led the young man out to the vehicle. Crime scene techs arrived with Saunders, who said Freeman had sent him to handle the scene so that they could question the suspect.

It never seemed to bother him that he was everyone's clean-up crewman and never lead on a case of his own.

Moreau had expected McIver to let a string of profanities fly when he saw Duncan's card. Instead, McIver was calm as he loaded the young man in the back of the SUV and he said nothing on the entire drive back to the station.

THE SPYING MOON

Once there, he pulled up to the curb and told Moreau to park the vehicle and meet him in interrogation as he got out and collected the prisoner. She had just slid into the driver's seat when McIver disappeared in the front door with their suspect.

It didn't take long to park the vehicle, but before she entered the building her phone buzzed.

Casey, have Alec with me. U can go back 2 other case.

She sucked a sharp breath between her teeth as she slid her phone into her pocket. Interrogation was at the end of a long, gray corridor that appeared to swallow what little light there was coming from old, uncovered bulbs that were browned on the sides of their spheres, spaced at least fifteen feet apart, and flickered as though power was in short supply. Shadows swelled around the edges of the hallway. It wasn't hard to imagine how someone under arrest felt walking down this path, as the only hint of natural light quickly disappeared behind them and darkness closed in.

The hallway emptied into another corridor that looked much the same. Doors lined the wall. Blackness swallowed the edges of the floor here as well, and it was easy to believe in the possibility of a rodent or cockroach scurrying along the concrete, safe in the shadows.

Outside the first door the light flicked from green to red.

They'd just gone inside.

Moreau went to the room beside that one, where she could observe. She held the door so that it closed quietly. The gray paint must have been on sale, and only one dim bulb failed to brighten the small but surprisingly empty space she entered. With all the shuffling of boxes and furniture, Moreau had assumed the interrogation wing had been required to do double duty as well. Once inside, she had a clear view of the holding room.

The young man sat at the table; his leg vibrated as he glanced from Chmar to McIver to the mirror that gave Moreau visual access to the room. Blond hair so dirty it looked brown, torn

clothes that hung off of him even as he sat and the oversized pea
coat that appeared to be at least four sizes too big. The perp
looked at the floor and finally slumped against the table.

McIver sat down.

And Alec Chmar...Chmar faded into the corner of the room
farthest from the table.

"Let's start with your name."

The young man looked up, licked his lips and then mashed
them together.

"You want, I can call your buddy here." McIver tossed
Duncan's card on the table.

The man shook his head back and forth.

"Then give me your name."

"Ch-Ch-Chuck Turner."

"Now, that wasn't so hard, was it? We're going to get along
just fine."

Moreau had to hand it to McIver. He kept his voice smooth
and bordered on being almost friendly, yet employed a firm
tone and let Chuck know he was boss.

"It looks like you're going to be enjoying our hospitality for
a while."

Chuck kept his gaze down.

"Of course, there's a way you could get out a bit quicker,
maybe make a deal with no time at all."

"All you got me on is trespassing."

"You were found on private property, illegally."

Chuck looked up. "Yeah, but you didn't find any goods on
me, did ya? All you got is trespassing. With that crazy, ol' bitch
how d'ya know that she didn't pull out that gun and force me
into her place? You got no proof I did anything. Her word
against mine."

McIver stood up and leaned across the table. "We're trying
to help you out of this mess. Look at you. Covered in dirt. If
you had patches on your clothes it would be an improvement. I
could probably squeeze you through the eye of a needle with

THE SPYING MOON

room to spare and you couldn't stop your leg from shaking if your life depended on it. Where are you sleeping? The streets? One of the parks?"

Chuck shrugged. "I got a place."

"Yeah? Has it got a roof?"

"I ain't tellin' you nothin'. You wanna charge me, whatevs. Don't I get a phone call or a lawyer or somethin'?"

The door to the observation room opened and Freeman entered. His eyes widened when he saw Moreau.

"Is he getting anything from this kid?"

She shook his head. "I don't think he will. He knows there isn't much of a charge here, not enough to scare him."

"Why are you in here, Constable?"

She pulled out her phone and showed him the text. Freeman's mouth twisted and he looked like he was about to growl.

"I saw this guy the other day," Moreau said. "McIver found Duncan's card in his pocket and he wasn't too happy about that."

"What were you and Nate talking to him for?"

Moreau shook her head. "Not me. Just Duncan. Sounded like he knew him from some other case."

"And McIver decided he wanted to keep you out of interrogation because of that?"

"McIver hasn't wanted me on this case from day one, so this is no surprise. It's just an excuse."

On the other side of the one-way window, McIver had produced a photo from the folder on the table. "Know him?"

Chuck didn't even look at it and shrugged.

"I asked if you know him."

"Whatever that's about is nothing to do with me."

"Really?" McIver stood up and walked around the table. He held the photo up an inch from Chuck's face.

"Oh my God, man, I don't want to see that." Chuck turned away from McIver and gagged. For a second Moreau thought he was going to puke.

156

"Yeah? Better to see it than to be it. I can take you down to autopsy and show you what it's like to lay on a steel slab while some stranger slices through your rotting skin."

There was no warning gag this time. Chuck spewed chunks onto the floor.

McIver walked back around the table and sat down. "Now that you've got that out of your system, are you ready to tell me who he is?"

Chuck had a string of vomit hanging from his lips and his skin had turned a pasty white. He wiped his mouth on the sleeve of his coat and gave McIver a look that was best described as sour. Moreau wondered if he was going to projectile vomit across the table right into McIver's face.

She'd consider paying money to see that.

If he had been on the verge of getting sick again, it passed. The hoods over his eyes retracted and the lines of his face softened.

"Looks like Rich, okay?"

"Rich who?"

"Robinson, Robson. Something like that."

"How do you know him?"

"We hang together."

"At this place you've got?"

Chuck nodded.

"But not this past week or so."

"I ain't seen him in..." Chuck look confused. "What day is it?"

"Monday."

"Like a week or so. Maybe Sunday or something."

"And you weren't worried?"

"I came into town looking for him. Nobody'd seen him."

"So you're telling me that you didn't kill him?"

Chuck shook his head vigorously. "Whatever happened to him, that's...that's not right. But it wasn't me."

"Were you there when it happened?"

THE SPYING MOON

"I told you I didn't know where he was. I hadn't seen him in days."

"So you say."

"It's the truth. He left to, uh, he had stuff to do. That's all I know. He never came back."

"How do you know Nate Duncan?"

"Busted me with an ounce of weed. Said he was going to send me up."

McIver leaned back in his chair and folded his arms across his chest. "But he didn't?"

"I gave him the name of the dealer."

"You snitched."

"I made a deal, man, that's it. When they bagged Eddie he skated on some technicality. Figured me for it and put the word out I was dead if I hit his streets again."

"That was Vancouver?"

Moreau knew Duncan had been working in the Vancouver area before his transfer, and when he'd seen Chuck on the streets Chuck had seemed surprised to see Duncan here.

"Yeah."

"I bet you were glad to see Nate the other day."

"Fucking kidding me? He finds out I'm here he'll be up my ass about—"

"About what?"

Chuck's eyes got wide, as though it had just dawned on him that talking about Nate Duncan might not be a good thing. "Nothing."

"Sounded like you were going to say something to me."

Chuck pressed his lips together and shook his head.

McIver tried waiting him out. Chuck stayed silent.

"I can go get Nate right now if that's what it'll take."

Moreau wondered how much it hurt McIver to say those words. She'd also received a text from Duncan and knew McIver wouldn't find him easily; he was working on statements from the eyewitnesses for George, Arnold and Doug's move-

158

ments from Friday night. The only computers available in the station were tucked away in a space harder to find than the alcove at the crest of Holt Hill.

Chuck flipped his hands over and held them up an inch off the table before he put his head down on the steel surface and closed his eyes.

"Sir," Moreau said. "Any chance of getting Abe Holt's call records for the night of Sammy's death or a search warrant for his property?"

"Based on?"

She told him about the possibility that George, Doug and Arnold had come down through the Holt property after the gun that was used to disfigure Sammy's corpse was fired.

"Sounds possible. I'll make some calls." Freeman knocked on the glass. Chmar emerged from the shadows and walked out the door, followed by McIver. The sergeant was already back in the hall. Moreau stayed where she was, but could hear clearly, even through the closed door.

"My office, McIver. Now. Alec, have him taken to a cell."

Moreau watched Chmar return to the room, lean in close to Chuck, grab his left arm and say something in his ear. She couldn't hear a word, but Chuck's eyes went from hooded to wide and, while she hadn't thought it possible, even more color drained from his face. Alec removed Chuck from the room

She listened for the click as the door shut and then counted to twenty before she exited.

As she walked back to the main part of the station Moreau was stopped by Dr. Creaser.

"I didn't expect to see you here," she said.

He waved a file at her. "I was looking for you."

"Should we go find Duncan?"

Creaser shook his head. "Already checked the breakroom. I was told Duncan's gone for the day and McIver is still in Freeman's office."

She glanced at her watch, what some considered an unneces-

THE SPYING MOON

sary relic that she wouldn't abandon. It was waterproof and had outlasted more than a few cell phones in her lifetime already. "Okay. What do you have?"

He opened his mouth to answer, but the whirring of a power tool cut through the air and prevented him from speaking.

She pointed to the door and led him outside.

"The next phase of the renovation," he said as they followed the sidewalk away from the main entrance.

"Freeman actually has space to spare in his office now," she said as she recalled how much more room there'd been when she'd talked to him earlier.

"I hear your conference room is supposed to be ready tomorrow. You won't be winding your way around stacks of boxes anymore, but you'll be deaf. They're jackhammering through the concrete at the far end for new plumbing."

"We might need to move our workspace down with you."

"I'm afraid I've had too many deceased lately to have room for the living."

She couldn't argue with him on that point. A climbing accident had brought in two more bodies since the weekend, which was almost as bad for the local tourist trade as the murders.

"I made a few calls. There were drugs in Doe's system. Not as potent as Sammy Petersen's, but they're from the same batch."

He handed her the file and she read the report. "The drugs in Doe's system were from the same supply as the drugs found in Sammy, but the drugs in Doe's system had been cut."

Creaser nodded and his shaggy white hair bobbed up and down with his head. "The drugs Doe had were ready for distribution."

"But Doe died before Sammy Petersen did."

"I don't know what it means, Constable, but I felt bad for pushing the results for Sammy, particularly given the gun link between the cases. Whoever gave the drugs to Sammy had access to the uncut batch before it ever made its way to Doe's hands."

160

"Freeman told me to keep the link between the cases quiet."
She sighed as she weighed Freeman's words to her from earlier.
"It's probably best that McIver not know about the tox results
yet, either."

Creaser grunted. "The politics are your problem. My col-
league is going to finish a proper report in a few days and send
it over. At that point, there won't be anything I can do to keep
McIver from knowing about the results. What you do with this
advanced copy," he pointed to the file, "is up to you."

She watched him open the door and disappear into the hallway.

There was some tenuous connection between Sammy Petersen's death and the murder of John Doe, but what? And how
did George Jacobs fit into the picture?

Her phone buzzed with a text from Duncan.

*Interviewed Jimmy. He got back early so I met him for cof-
fee. Said he hadn't talked to Sammy the week before he died.*

She slid the phone back into her pocket and walked across
the parking lot to her jeep. That left the video camera. They
couldn't get into the school because of the holiday and that was
out of their control.

Like it or not, searching Sammy's locker would have to wait.

Chapter 20

Moreau wound her way through the alleys and side streets of Maple River. Every day she'd taken a different route to the station, as long as she wasn't detoured. The two real seasons of Canada for drivers: snowplow and road construction.

She'd been making a point of driving different routes home, too, so that she could learn all of the streets.

The air had the cool tint of fall mingled in with the smell of pumpkin and cinnamon that wafted out of the grocer's bakery as she drove by. It wouldn't be long before winter weather arrived. She'd seen it already, near Jasper on her drive through the mountains.

They'd have snow there before long, which meant she didn't have much time left to get back out to the mines.

She stopped at a red light and tapped her thumb on the steering wheel. A glance left told her she was by the Petersen family church. The sign out front declared "Jesus Christ is Lord of the Country."

In red spray paint someone had written "Then can he pay for a skateboard park?" overtop of it.

Below that, someone had used blue spray paint to write "Washington state has one."

She was less than a mile from the border. The omission of U.S. cops and cases from their investigation reeked of oversight or ignorance. At no point had anyone mentioned reaching out to officers working the area on the other side of 49th parallel.

Freeman's team had been looking at the cases in British Columbia with no consideration of the fact that Maple River was a border town, and had a steady influx of U.S. traffic.

Moreau glanced at her watch. When the light turned green she made a left and drove away from her cabin and Maple River.

After idling for twenty minutes by a group of construction workers, who chatted by the side of the road with no tools in hand while one held up a stop sign, Moreau honked at them. They barely glanced at her and kept talking.

She put her vehicle in park, grabbed her ID and got out.

One of the men stopped talking long enough to look stern as he marched toward her. "Whoa, there, you need to get back in your vehicle or we'll call the—"

Her ID was right in front of him when he stopped.

"I don't care if you guys want to chat all night, but I'm on my way to interview someone about a murder."

"Right. Of course. Sorry." He clicked on his radio and asked a few questions. "Go on through," he said when he was finished.

After that she was able to make good time on the highway.

When she arrived at the hospital she purchased a gift basket from the shop, went to reception and asked to be directed to Phil Willmott's room.

Phil was propped up in bed. He had a graphic novel across his lap, and his head was still wrapped in a bandage.

She held out her ID. "Kendall Moreau," she said as she set the gift basket down on a nightstand by his bed. "I'm working in Maple River now."

"And you came all this way to bring me goodies." His words dripped with sarcasm, but he grinned when he added, "Not that I don't appreciate it."

She smiled. If Willmott was this astute injured she imagined he was sharp as a hawk's talon on the job.

He reached for the basket and helped himself to a chocolate. When he held out the basket toward her she shook her head.

"Hospitals aren't like they were. I've got mint green walls

THE SPYING MOON

and a blue blanket instead of everything being white on white."
He gestured at the nearest wall. "Even framed pictures of coyotes. But the food's still shit."

She glanced at the picture. A group of coyotes circled one in
the center, presumably the leader. He stared out with authority
and reminded her of the print in her cabin. It seemed an odd
decorative choice for a hospital. "You've been here a while. I'm
sure you're looking forward to a juicy steak and baked potato."

"Now that's just cruel." Phil set the basket back down.
"What can I do for you, Constable?"

"I was out by the mines the other day."

He didn't flinch. "Where I had my accident."

"If that's what you want to call it."

Phil looked down at his hands and picked at his bedding
aimlessly. When he lifted his head his mouth had settled into a
hard line, although there was an apology in the downturned
corners of his eyes. "I can't tell you anything."

"Can't? Or won't?"

"Both."

"You remember what happened."

"It doesn't matter, Constable Moreau. I'm sorry you drove
all this way with your questions, but I'm not supposed to—"

"I got you rotisserie chicken, mashed potatoes and gravy."

The words came from behind Moreau and she turned around
as McIver walked in, looked up and stopped.

"Casey."

"It's Moreau," she said with a bit more force than she'd intended.

McIver's eyes darkened. "What are you doing here?"

"I could ask you the same thing. Freeman didn't rip you a
new asshole for the stunt you pulled this afternoon?"

"You could have told me how you knew Chuck before questioning but you held out."

"I don't know him. Duncan talked to him for less than a minute in the middle of our investigation and I wasn't introduced."

164

"And you didn't think you should mention that when we arrested him?"

"You didn't even give me a chance, McIver. You've been shutting me out of this investigation from the beginning. This was just an excuse to keep me from talking to Chuck Turner."

"Why would I want to do that, Moreau? What reason could I possibly have for giving a shit one way or the other about whether you talk to him?"

She scrambled for a retort and settled on the first thing that came to mind. "Maybe you needed me to make you coffee instead."

Phil Willmott started to laugh, and voiced his amusement loud and long. Moreau glanced at him and he finally stopped with a grin.

"Look, if you two want to bicker that's fine, but can I have my chicken, Levi? All I've had to eat today are the chocolates Moreau brought me. One thing that hasn't improved in hospitals is the food."

McIver glanced at Moreau before he nodded, and Moreau took the opportunity to thank Willmott for his time, hand him her card with cell phone number printed on the back and make her exit. She paused at the door.

"At least let me know when you're coming back," Moreau said. "They've got me staying in your old place until then."

She didn't wait for a reply, but thought as she turned away from them that she saw the color drain from Willmott's face.

A few hours later Moreau was armed with another gift basket when she walked into the lab and handed it to Benji.

"Peace offering," she said. Halfway back to Maple River she'd called the station and had them phone Benji with instructions to meet her at the lab at nine-thirty. It was nine-fifty when she rushed through the door. "Got held up by roadwork."

He nodded, took the basket and set it down on an empty desk

THE SPYING MOON

and pushed his glasses up his nose, which she recalled seemed to be a nervous tick from when McIver had chewed him out.

She glanced around. A lot of the boxes and tables were gone.

"I was hoping you might have something for me on the Petersen case."

Benji nodded. He lifted the basket up off the tray he'd set it on and rifled through papers until he pulled one out. "We couldn't match the prints from the cigarette butt to anything on the hill."

Moreau frowned. "Really?"

"There's no evidence of him being on that hill."

She took the papers from him. "What about the evidence Nate Duncan brought in?"

"The chewing gum? We got DNA from that and prints. Lucky for us the person chewing it didn't just spit it out. We did get a preliminary match from the fingerprints to some beer cans found at the scene. Doug Terry."

"He has a record?" She wondered why his prints wouldn't have turned up without the DNA.

"Printed when he volunteered at the border patrol as part of a school internship program. Those prints aren't in the criminal database but they were attached to his file in the DNA database." Benji turned back to the tray and dug out another paper. "Nate told me to give this straight to him when I had it."

"I'm assuming you have a file copy on your computer," she said.

He nodded.

"Email it to him. If you don't tell him you let me have a sneak peek, I won't."

Benji paused. "There's something else. It's on the second page of that first report I gave you. We matched the first set of DNA to vomit found at the scene."

"You found vomit? Other than Scott Saunder's?"

"Yes, well, we did. A few feet away, near the trees."

An image of Chuck Turner gagging and puking in the interrogation room earlier passed through her mind. Vomit suggested

166

shock, a visceral reaction to what had happened on the hill that night. George Jacobs didn't strike her as the type of guy who'd toss his cookies over a few beers, and with nothing to prove who else had been on the hill that night he no longer seemed like a plausible suspect.

Maybe he'd just been careful.

"And Miss, uh, Constable Moreau? There was no trace of alcohol in the vomit."

Curious. "Thanks, Benji. I really appreciate it." She started to turn to leave when he spoke again.

"And on page three…"

She flipped to the last page and started reading.

The techs had been thorough. Each bit of liquid left in any bottle or can had its temperature listed. Some of the cans with Doug Terry's fingerprints and a few sets of unidentified prints were much warmer than other ones with the same prints.

Suggesting Doug and presumably Arnold had been on that hill when Sammy died, and much later.

Unless someone had gone to the trouble of planting those cans when they put a gun to Sammy's head.

There were other cans that had no prints. Those cans were amongst the coolest ones recovered.

"There were marks on the ground that looked like a cooler had been there," Benji said. "But we didn't recover it from the scene."

"And you're sure about the temperatures?"

Benji nodded and adjusted his glasses again. "The prints that we connected to the gum you brought in are on containers that were opened approximately an hour before we got there."

"Well after the time of death but before Sammy was shot." She looked up at Benji. The bookends may have been there, but why would they kill Sammy? George was the type of guy who seemed like he'd take a life just because it suited him, well on his way to being a tough guy without remorse. Doug and Arnold hadn't come across that way. "Anything else?"

THE SPYING MOON

He shook his head.

"There's one other thing I'm curious about. There was soot on the shoes of Rich. Our John Doe. Can you see if it's a match to anything recovered from Phil Willmott when he was attacked?"

Benji's mouth opened and then he cleared his throat. "Yes, of course. I'll check."

"How long will that take?"

"I can email you the results as soon as I have them."

"Thanks again."

She left the lab, folded the reports and slid them into the pocket on the inside of her coat.

When she arrived home Moreau felt a sense of relief. Her door was closed and there were no signs it had been tampered with.

That was one of the things that didn't make sense about the break-in. It was amateur. Without a picture accidentally snapped on her phone to prove it, she never would have believed that a cop would have been so sloppy.

Unless that was the plan. He intended to make it appear like your standard issue break and enter. Like an imitation of the break-in at Mabel Cook's, perhaps.

Alec Chmar may be sharper than she thought.

She entered cautiously and kept her shoes on as she eased herself into the dark room. Nothing disrupted the quiet, but she wasn't taking any chances.

Instead of switching the living room light on, Moreau used her flashlight instead. The strong beam focused in on one object or area at a time as she slowly surveyed her main living space. A check of the vents showed they were clear. She lay down on the floor and inspected the bottom of the couch, chair and coffee table. Nothing out of the ordinary.

The TV was a flatscreen that was wall-mounted, and she shone the light behind it but found nothing unusual there, either.

She opened each kitchen cupboard one by one. The top and bottom of every shelf was checked. She removed each drawer and inspected all sides. There was nothing out of place below or above her microwave, and all that moving the fridge revealed was a number of cobwebs and that her right shoulder was still sore.

The bathroom and bedroom on the main floor yielded no answers.

She slowly climbed to the loft. It was almost its own room. The stairs led up from the side of the house behind the kitchen, and once you were halfway up the stairs you had no view into the main level at all. A window on the front side of the house looked down over the porch and driveway, while the window on the other side of the room was surrounded by trees.

After she checked the beds, nightstands and vents, Moreau sat on the carpet in the middle of the space and wondered if it was possible that Alec Chmar had found whatever he was looking for. Other than the door, the cabin had seemed undisturbed when they'd had her check it after the assault. There hadn't been much to look through because there wasn't much she'd brought with her.

If he had located whatever he was looking for he should be buying lottery tickets to have found it so fast without disrupting anything else in the house, or he already knew where it was, and that didn't make sense. There had been days the cabin had sat empty between Phil's accident and her arrival. Why wait until someone else was living there?

Unless you hadn't expected it. You thought you had time to get in before Phil returned to duty.

And why assault her? Unless he thought that would prompt Freeman to relocate her.

She reached for one of the lamp stands and turned it on. The lights by the beds were short and stout. The bases were solid, made as one whole piece and when she lifted them the weight proved they'd be better used as defensive weapons than for storage.

On a small desk by the window on the back wall there was a taller lamp that looked like a metal canister that had been spray

THE SPYING MOON

painted a dull gold. Moreau walked over to it and picked it up.

The bottom detached. She unscrewed it and felt the paper pressed against the inside of the lamp's cylinder. Her fingers tugged the large brown envelope out of the space.

She reattached the lamp's bottom and returned it to its spot on the desk. After she turned off the light by the bed, Moreau waited for her eyes to adjust.

A light from the window on the front side of the house caught her attention and she inched her way to the window, careful to stay just to the side of it where she couldn't be seen.

A vehicle had pulled over near the end of her driveway.

With luck, if they'd seen the flashlight upstairs they'd think she was on her cell phone.

She carefully worked her way toward the stairs with her flashlight in one hand and the envelope in the other.

From partway down the stairs she could see the front door. Although the main level rooms were swallowed in the shadows of darkness, she could just see enough of the key shapes to know if something moved.

After a few minutes of waiting, she crept down the rest of the steps and through the kitchen. Once she was in the bathroom she slowly shut the door and locked it. Moreau closed the window drapes, stepped into the bathtub and pulled the shower curtain along the length of the tub before she sat down and turned on her flashlight.

The envelope contained pictures. One showed George and his bookends out at the old mines. Another showed Doug and Arnold passing backpacks to some guys who looked like they were homeless. There were lots of trees but nothing to prove the exact location that she could see. The men getting the packs had their backs turned to the camera. She didn't recognize the one who was at the end. The one in the middle might be their John Doe. He looked like he was the right height.

At the end of the row, all you could see was the arm of a coat reaching toward Arnold.

The arm of a pea green coat that looked like Chuck Turner's.

Moreau flipped to the next photo, which showed a couple in a heated exchange. Alec and Alyssa, who had her finger pointed at Alec and a scowl on her face. They sat in a car, and there was a passenger in the backseat whose face was partially concealed by Alyssa.

The next picture was an image of a computer screen. A girl was pushed down on a bed and appeared to be trying to break free from the boy who held her arms down. He wasn't overtop of her, but behind her head, and looked down at her so he wasn't facing the camera. One of her legs kicked up, but the other was held by a hand that led to a person off screen. Beside that hand and closer to the lens of the camera was another male. Trim, muscular, with dark hair, no shirt. He was unbuckling his pants.

The girl on the bed looked like the girl in the car with Alyssa and Alec.

Notes followed the photos. The first one was a list of sites, including the mines outside of town. She didn't recognize the other locations, but none of them were in Maple River.

The next note had only two words written on it with a question mark.

Sammy Petersen?

Had Willmott questioned if Sammy was involved with the drugs, or if he'd been involved with the assault on the girl?

She took pictures of all of the items she found and emailed them to her private account. Then she removed the reports Benji had given her and did the same thing with them.

Moreau tucked the photos back inside the envelope, folded it in half and slid it into the inside pocket of her coat.

After she turned off the flashlight she opened the shower curtain and then the drapes. It only took a moment for her to slide the window open, shimmy out and drop down to the ground.

Once she reached the end of the house, Moreau peeked around the side. The vehicle was still there.

THE SPYING MOON

She didn't recognize the pick-up truck near the end of her driveway, and she also didn't think anyone was in it, unless they were lying across the front seats. One lone streetlight between her cabin and Duncan's was enough to be certain of that.

Whoever it was, they were on the move.

Moreau turned and slid behind a tree near the back corner of the cabin. She moved around it until she could see both ends of her rental home, and reached for her gun.

A soft snap near the front corner of the structure on the side closest to her betrayed the shadow of a figure as it eased its way around the corner and scanned the woods. Moreau pressed herself as close to the tree as she could and peered out with one eye as the person moved in her direction. Their hands were pulled around in front of them, and a tiny glint of light on steel suggested they held a gun.

The closer they got, the more they blended into shadow because the reach of the streetlight helped less. As the person turned the corner she inched her way around the other side of the tree and came up behind them.

"I'm armed and I'm an RCMP constable with the Maple River detachment." When they didn't respond, she said, "Do you understand me?"

"Yes."

A male voice, which fit her impression of the shadowy figure.

"Raise your hands slowly."

The hands reached skyward.

"Set your gun down on the ground nice and slow."

The man bent down, left hand still in the air as his right hand dropped the weapon.

"Now stand back up." Moreau took a few steps backwards. "Turn around and take two steps toward me."

The figure complied. As the man walked in her direction, Moreau turned her the flashlight on and shone it in the face of Scott Saunders.

He moved a hand to shield his eyes. "Can you drop the gun

now?"

"You're trespassing."

"I wanted to make sure you were okay."

"By sneaking around my cabin in the middle of night with a gun in your hand?"

"Look—" He started to lower his arms.

Moreau gestured upward with her gun. "Keep your hands where I can see them."

"Look, Moreau, I know I blew it the other day, but really."

"Take four steps down to your right."

He did. Once he was halfway along that wall she told him to turn around and put his hands against the cabin.

"I'm going to search you." She set her flashlight down on the ground. "Anything you want me to know about before I find it?"

"Thought you already said no to that."

Wise ass. "Don't make me add a sexual harassment charge, Saunders."

Saunders exhaled. "Fine. No."

She patted him down cautiously. Once she was certain his only weapon lay behind her home she told him to turn around.

Moreau pulled out her cuffs and tossed them to him. "Put them on," she said as she grabbed her phone from her pocket.

He stared at her for a second and she straightened her aim with her gun.

"Fine."

Once he was cuffed she led him around front and removed her spare cuffs from the glove compartment of her jeep. She used them to secure him to her vehicle's mirror and went back around the cabin to retrieve his weapon.

Her call to the station took less than a minute and although she kept a wide berth as she returned to the front of her cabin there were no surprises. Saunders was right where she left him.

"How did you know where I lived?" she asked.

"It wasn't hard. There was a police report."

THE SPYING MOON

"And you just thought that instead of calling me or texting you'd drop by unannounced?"

"If I'd called would you have answered?"

"That isn't the point, is it? We'll never know because you decided to trespass instead."

"You're a bit of a bitch, you know?"

"Really? You guys have been princes and gentlemen."

"Christ, Moreau, I know Levi was an ass to you but he didn't know you were a cop."

"Reporters wander the station unchecked all the time, do they?"

Saunders shook his head. "You've got all the answers, don't you?"

"Nope. I'd like to know who hurt Phil Willmott, and who killed John Doe and I'd definitely like to know what happened to Sammy Petersen. If you ask me, I'm a little short on answers these days."

"You're really going to make people we work with come out here and arrest me?"

"No, Scott. I'm not making them do that. You're the one who's made that happen. When you decided to come onto my property with a gun in your hand and were sneaking around my cabin, you made choices that have consequences. I'm not responsible for that."

"It's a wonder you didn't shoot that guy who was in your bedroom the other day. I guess Indians get special treatment from you."

"I don't give a shit if he's brown, white or green with yellow stripes, Constable Saunders. I haven't shot you, have I? And you're the only one who's come to my home with a weapon drawn that I know about."

He didn't respond.

Moreau stood silently and wondered if she was overreacting, but she didn't put her gun away until officers arrived at the scene to take her statement.

174

Chapter 21

Maple River High was located a handful of blocks from the center of town, within walking distance of coffee shops and convenience stores that tempted students away from school grounds for caffeine and cigarettes. It was an odd building, the front entrance a flat edge between two long walls that veered away at angles out from that center point, and had been built into the side of a hill, with a large flat area for parking that flanked a garden with benches that embraced a rock mosaic of the school mascot.

A coyote. She thought about Randy's jersey. The Maple River Tricksters.

On the other side of the garden there was a wide sidewalk that led to the main doors.

They didn't have to be buzzed in.

The foyer was wide and spacious and led in three distinct directions. To the right there was a hallway, and slightly left of center was another hallway that represented the two main arms of the school. Immediately to their left there was a glass door beside a large window that offered a clear view of the school's office, and beyond the receptionist's desk there were more doors.

In the entrance area a large television monitor was perched on the wall between the two hallways, and a rolling display of school announcements and pictures of students flashed over the screen.

Moreau followed Duncan into the office, where they signed

THE SPYING MOON

themselves in and the receptionist pointed them in the direction of Sammy Petersen's locker. She was a thin, tall woman with gray hair and an easy smile. "I'll have someone from maintenance meet you there," she said as she picked up a radio.

Duncan thanked her and led the way, empty box in hand.

For Moreau, the memories of school after school blurred together as they walked past the orange lockers that lined the halls. Although the walls were freshly painted a lemon yellow and the floor sparkled beneath them, the lockers gave away the fact that the building was old.

A remnant of the seventies.

They'd arrived early enough for the school to be open but not filled with students and they passed nothing but empty classrooms that were dark and closed lockers before reaching their destination.

A man with dark hair, blank eyes and no smile stood at the locker. He wore blue overalls and held bolt cutters in hands that were weathered and worn. Moreau knew it was Sammy's locker even without his presence. Already a few candles and flowers circled Sammy's piece of real estate within the school grounds, and someone had gone to a Build-a-Bear or something like it and made a stuffed puppy with a video camera secured in the left paw.

Duncan exchanged a few words with the maintenance man, who snapped the lock. He reached for it and Moreau held up her hand.

"Thanks, but we need it. Evidence," she said.

The blank eyes asked no questions and he turned without a word and walked away.

"I'm surprised administration doesn't want to be here for this," Moreau said as she pulled a pair of gloves from her pocket. After she grabbed a bag from her other pocket she removed the lock and sealed it in the plastic.

"Evidence of what?" Duncan asked as he set down the empty box he'd been carrying and moved the makeshift memorial

176

away from the bottom of the door. Once he opened the locker he pulled out his cell phone and snapped a photo.

"We'll want to have it dusted for prints, just to be sure," Moreau said. She began rifling through the contents on the shelf at the top of the locker.

A textbook. A notebook. A pencil case.

"If it was here, it's gone," she said.

On cue, the crime scene techs they'd requested arrived. Instead of dusting the locker door on site they removed it, and within minutes they'd filled the box Duncan had carried in. Moreau poked her head inside and pulled out her flashlight so that she could scrutinize the bottom of the shelf.

No sign anything had been taped there. No evidence of a secret he'd concealed that may have gotten him killed.

No indication of anything out of the ordinary at all.

She shut her flashlight off, pulled her head out and shook it. The techs disappeared with all the items they'd bagged and tagged, and Duncan bent down and pushed the memorial back where they'd found it as Moreau removed her gloves.

Duncan snapped another photo of the memorial.

"There must be some kids on the property already," he said as he looked at the screen of his phone. Just after seven.

Classes started at 7:50 a.m.

Instead of leading Moreau back to the exit he continued down the hall and turned right where it intersected with another hallway. A large set of double doors on the right side were propped open, and the room was filled with light.

Inside a few girls in cheerleader uniforms stood near bleachers, whispering and giggling, cell phones in hand instead of pom poms.

"Perhaps you should take the lead here," Duncan said in a voice that was barely above a whisper.

She didn't ask him why, but pulled her ID out of her pocket.

"Constables Moreau and Duncan," she said as she approached them. There were three girls. One had a long, blonde ponytail.

THE SPYING MOON

Another had short, dark curls. The tallest of the three, in the center, had straight brown hair that hung down over her shoulders.

"Oh my gosh, are you here about Sammy?" she said.

Small towns. Big gossip.

"Just wondering if you could tell us anything about him. Did you know him at all?"

Three girls drew in breaths and paused as they exchanged glances.

"Not really. He was, like, really into video stuff." The shortest girl, with the dark curls, offered.

"And he used to hang out with that huss…" The girl with the ponytail let her voice trail off. "This girl who's a bit…you know." She widened her eyes and gave Moreau a look, as though it should be obvious what she meant.

"No, I don't know."

The girl leaned closer and lowered her voice. "I heard she, you know, did it with some guys."

"And that's when Sammy dumped her." The brunette offered this information.

"No," the blonde said. "She dumped him. Because he—" The girl glanced at Moreau and shrugged.

"I heard—" Curly said.

Moreau held up her hand. "Thanks, ladies. Any of you know this girl's name?"

The blonde exhaled and scrunched up her face. "Emily?"

"It's Ellie," the brunette said.

"Whatever."

"Thanks for your time." Moreau fished cards out of her pocket. "If you remember anything helpful or hear anything odd please give me a call."

"Are you, like, sticking around then?" the one with the dark curls asked.

"You mean the school?"

"Maple River."

178

An odd question. "This is where I work," Moreau said.

She wondered about the girl's remark as she followed Duncan back to the hallway and down the hall to the point where it connected to the other arm. He turned right, to head back to the lobby.

A few more students had trickled in since they'd arrived, and about ten feet ahead of them there was a slender girl with long, auburn hair that waved its way down her back. She stood at her locker, looking down as though there was something at the bottom of it that had her attention.

When she lifted her head to study the contents of the upper shelf her hair fell back from her face. The defined lines of a strong jawbone were evident.

Duncan gasped.

"Kelly," he said as he quickened his pace.

She turned to look at him and within a second several emotions registered on her face. Surprise. Shock. Fear.

"You can't be here," she said.

"We're here about Sammy."

"I have nothing to do with that."

Duncan stopped. "Kelly, it's me. You've sent me two cards, every year, with no address."

Kelly spun her head to look over both shoulders. "That's a secret, Nate. I'm not supposed to talk to you."

"Because of Mom. You're going to let her control your life?"

"You're the one that got out, Nate. I've been stuck here. You don't know..." The look that came into her eyes was regret and sadness and anger mixed into one. "I was never supposed to talk to you, from the day you went away."

"You've been living with Uncle Abe?"

Duncan's voice registered shock. It was part question, part accusation, although that didn't seem to be directed at the girl Moreau realized now must be his sister.

"They couldn't put you somewhere better?" he asked.

Kelly slammed her locker door shut, spun on her heel and

THE SPYING MOON

started walking away from them, toward the lobby.

"Wait," Duncan said as he trotted forward and grabbed her arm.

She spun herself free. "I can't talk to you."

"You were there the night Sammy died."

"I had nothing to do with that. I don't go to those parties." She sounded shocked, like she was offended her brother would suggest such a thing.

"No, I mean, you were at Abe's property. You know if anyone else was there, and what they were talking about."

"You."

"Me?"

"I heard you were back. You've been back for days and the only reason I'm seeing you now is because you're here about a case."

"Kelly, I didn't even know where you were."

"And you couldn't guess? Or ask Kenny when you were talking to him?" Kelly spun on her heel. "Your old girlfriend sure knew you were back."

"Al...Why would you say that?"

Kelly turned and looked at Duncan. "Because the night Sammy died. At the house, talking to Uncle Abe? She was there."

Duncan stepped forward but his sister clammed her mouth shut into a hard line that told Moreau she had nothing more to say. Kelly turned on her heel and disappeared down the hall.

Moreau had to speed-walk to catch up to Duncan.

"I should have known," he said.

"None of this is your fault," she told him, although she still wasn't completely sure what "this" was.

"They blame me, Moreau."

"You're here now. Whatever happened, you'll get a chance to work it out. Part of her was happy to see you."

"And another part was scared."

"Just because she thinks she'll get in trouble from your mom.

180

Kids her age start to think for themselves. She'll come around."

"No. She won't be able to. If she's living with Abe—" He shook his head as he walked through the parking lot.

"You'll reach her. You'll find a way."

Duncan stopped and spun around. "You don't know what it's like to be ripped from your family and sent away to live with strangers and have your family blame you for it. You don't know anything about this." He turned, opened the Rodeo door and started the vehicle, leaving Moreau to stand in the middle of the parking lot as he backed out and drove away.

Chapter 22

Freeman was standing outside his office and as soon as Moreau entered he jerked his head toward his door.

Alyssa Everett wasn't even in yet. Moreau walked past her empty desk and entered Freeman's office. He shut the door behind her and this time he didn't ask her to sit down.

"Mind telling me why I have one of my officers in a cell next to Chuck Turner?"

"I'm sure you've read the report."

He picked up the folder on his desk and gave her a look. "I just wanted to be certain there wasn't anything missing this time."

She didn't flinch. "All I know is in there. He showed up at my house with a gun and offered no explanation for his presence."

"But he didn't touch you."

She shook her head.

"How am I supposed to manage a drug investigation when I have one of my officers I know is guilty of assault and another who's in a jail cell?"

"With better police?"

His eyes widened but there was no hint of a smile on his face. The look he gave Moreau reminded her of a cartoon character who's so mad smoke is about to come out of his ears.

"You and Duncan found a pattern in the drug busts. The times are narrowing." He set an eleven-by-seventeen page down on his desk. Dates were highlighted. Everything they'd discussed was laid out on paper.

"Another shipment could pass through as soon as Thursday. We need a proactive way of assessing possible candidates for importing."

"What intrigues me is the secondary source points for distribution." Moreau grabbed the folded map on the edge of Freeman's desk and spread it out on top of the timeline. "We have shipments to Cranbrook, Nelson, and anywhere else within a four hundred-kilometer radius in BC. The drugs that have been picked up all trace to the same source material, and the earliest arrests are never where the drugs hit the streets. They're all closer to Maple River. The source point for distribution is always varied, with no recognizable pattern. It makes me think we should be looking for someone who travels different routes who can move in and out of town without attracting attention, and who does it often enough that nobody would be suspicious about their trips."

"Like a truck driver." Freeman nodded. "They could be a local, which would explain why the drugs hit the streets in this area first, and then vary their secondary distribution point depending on their trucking routes. Nobody would question why they were coming and going from town because it's part of their job."

"You were the point person on the Saskatoon taxi bust," Freeman said.

Moreau's mouth opened and it took her a second to find the right answer. "You knew about that, sir?"

"I have clearance for that level of classified material, Moreau."

Classified because of who had been involved. Public officials. Established criminals who would stop at nothing to exact revenge.

"That's why you wanted me here."

"You broke the taxi case. How did you catch on?"

"Just tracing movement, sir."

"You're being modest."

THE SPYING MOON

"What we need to do is find a way to correlate trucks coming into Maple River within a three-day window preceding the delivery of the drugs here and then compare that against trucks going out within three days of the secondary source. If we can find a link, we might be able to find the one who's moving the goods," Moreau said.

"I have concerns about asking shipping companies for their records or even trying to get the information from the weigh scales," Freeman said. "Too many people who could talk. People still believe the best about their friends and neighbors when the chips are down. There's always a chance they'll tip them off, deliberately or otherwise."

"If they're able to vary the drop points and still distribute the same product over the region then they have an exhaustive network. The only way we're going to kill the snake is if we can cut off the head. Otherwise, it will just shed its skin, get rid of whoever is expendable, and pop up somewhere else later."

"Agreed." Freeman sat down. "But we need a way to do this and fast. We don't have much time. What I'm proposing is random stops and searches of trucks along the highway. Safety inspections. It's the only way I can think of to justify stopping those trucks." He paused. "I can't pull you and Duncan off of your case to handle it. I can't use Scott if he's under arrest and I don't want to use Alec, since we know he assaulted you. That leaves me with McIver on his own."

"Brian Bradrick."

"Bradrick?"

"He's got a trained police dog. Wouldn't it make sense?"

"We pull them over for random safety checks. Brian Bradrick and his dog just happen to be there." Freeman nodded slowly.

"The truth is, sir, that they could be ready to move now. A random arrest always occurs a few days before the drugs hit the street."

"I'll pull a few men assigned to this. We'll be ready to start stops tomorrow morning."

"And none of them will know why they're really there?"

"Bradrick will. I'll put him in charge. If you clear your case or if something breaks you and Nate can back him up."

Moreau paused. With so many unanswered questions it felt like they were still grasping at straws. "Did you know that Sammy's brother works in construction? He travels all over the region for work."

Freeman rubbed his chin as he processed that. "You think he's involved?"

"I haven't got a clue who's involved, sir. It was just something Duncan and I found interesting."

"What was your read from talking to him?"

"Duncan did that alone, sir. I was busy with McIver."

He nodded. "I guess I can't fault you for that, Moreau. Considering the Petersens just lost a son I wouldn't want to get ahead of myself looking at Jimmy without cause."

"We don't have that, sir."

"So there's nothing else you're holding back?"

Should she tell him about what she'd found in her cabin? The real reason she believed Chmar and Saunders had been there? He had his hands full. Duncan and Moreau were supposed to bolster the numbers after losing Willmott; with Chmar and Saunders sidelined, McIver working a murder and Duncan and Moreau focused on Sammy's death he'd been left without the team he'd fought so hard to build.

"Nothing that will help right now," she said. "And what about Saunders, sir?"

"He can be charged with trespassing. Reckless endangerment if you want to go wild."

"I think it might be time to take a closer look at him, sir. See if there's anything that connects him to the drugs."

"Didn't you think Alec was good for that?"

"All I know is that Alec and Scott both turned up at my place without invitations. I'm wondering if they're looking for

THE SPYING MOON

something Phil had found."

A shadow passed across Freeman's eyes. "That would be very serious."

"You'll have to handle Chmar. He's going to wonder why Saunders is in a cell."

"He's off today. Called out sick."

Moreau nodded. "One less thing to worry about." She glanced at the clock that she could now see on Freeman's wall and wondered if Duncan had calmed down yet.

"I'd like to get a look at some phone records." She pulled out her cell and jotted down a number. "George Jacobs has two cell phones."

"Two?"

"Curious, isn't it?" She wrote down the second number. "We do know he asked Randy Jensen to lie for him the night Sammy died. I think we've got grounds for records of the calls Randy, Kenny, Sammy, George, Doug and Arnold were making that night. I'd like to see Abe Holt's incoming and outgoing calls, too. The only way that Doug and Arnold got down through that property was if Abe Holt led them, and that would mean that he knows something about what happened."

"And he'd have to have a reason for protecting those boys."

"Exactly."

"I'll handle it myself, Moreau. We'll get the records and see if anything leads to the Holt property."

Chapter 23

Moreau left Freeman's office and went to the breakroom, out of habit. A notice was posted on the bulletin board, which no longer had the words Task Force taped to the top.

The notice informed everyone that the task force had moved to the conference room, and the breakroom was now available for regular use.

Further proof of that fact was evident from the missing trays at the end of the counter. Moreau walked to the fridge, grabbed a bottled water and turned to leave.

A copy of the *Gazette* sat on the table. It had been left open to a features page inside, and Moreau's eyes widened as she saw her own eyes staring up from the page.

'Crusader Cop?' was printed in bold at the top. The photo of Moreau appeared to have been snapped in front of the station, the day before.

A subheading dished details about Moreau's tragic past as an orphaned girl whose mother had gone missing on the Trail of Tears.

Moreau didn't have to read more to know who had the by-line.

She left the station and began to drive around the town. A train delayed her three minutes and she was detoured six blocks because of roadwork, but she didn't care.

Obstacles on her way to nowhere as she drove in circles until she finally turned down the road that led to her cabin.

THE SPYING MOON

Duncan's Rodeo wasn't parked in front of his cabin.

She pulled in her driveway, stopped the jeep and turned off the engine.

A quick check of her phone told her she'd missed no texts. One new voicemail had been added, from an unknown number.

Her voice again. Telling Moreau tonight was the night.

Moreau did a quick search of the phone number. A payphone outside some bar in a town hundreds of miles away.

The girl wouldn't listen to her, even if Moreau had a way of calling her back. She had to live with the fact that she'd set this in motion, raised the girl's hopes that they'd find the answers together. Moreau's promise hadn't materialized, and neither had Moreau. When the transfer came through it never occurred to her to quit or take personal leave.

Why?

If something happened to that girl...

Moreau pushed that thought from her mind as she got out of the jeep and went to her cabin.

Moreau changed into black pants and a gray shirt. Her wardrobe wasn't exactly overflowing with options, and she realized she may need to stop wearing jeans to work each day and keeping a single pair of pants as her formal clothes. She returned to the station and wondered if she'd be going to the funeral alone. Most of the plastic in the main rooms had been removed, and the walls gleamed with fresh paint that brightened the space. The floor was concrete and barren, but the stacks of boxes and furniture had been removed.

All it needed was carpet and proper furniture and they'd actually have desks to spread out on.

Straight ahead was Freeman's office. To her left was the hall to the breakroom. And to her right was another hall lined with doors. The third one had a sign above it that read Task Force. Just before the open entrance to that space there was a door to the conference room that hung open.

Nate Duncan was inside, straightening his tie.

188

She walked into the room and for a split second their gaze met.

"You ready?" Moreau asked him, turning the focus away from what had happened at the school and putting it back on the case.

Duncan nodded and grabbed his coat.

She doubted most parents imagined what it would be like on the day they'd bury their son because that was something they hoped they'd never have to do, but she was certain the ones who did think about it didn't picture a cloudless sky, the crisp, fall air, or trees filled with golden leaves. Today, the Petersens had to withdraw from their pain and confront the coffin, a physical representation that confirmed this wasn't a nightmare they would wake from; it was reality.

When they lowered their son into the grave ashes would trickle against the bright blue sky instead blending into dismal autumn gray.

At St. James Anglican Church the paint had been scrubbed from the sign and the building looked quiet. Only a few cars were in the parking lot.

It didn't take long for that to change. A media crew from the Kelowna affiliate arrived and moved at a brisk pace as they set up the desired shot for their clips and prepared for the moment of grief they hoped to capture and expose to the watching world. Moreau glanced at Duncan, whose lips curled as he watched the vultures prepare to descend on their prey, ready to exploit the pain of the Petersen family for ratings.

Duncan turned as though he was about to open his door and then twisted in his seat.

Moreau followed his gaze.

Randy Jensen walked down the street. He wore dark black dress pants with a white shirt, black jacket and a somber gray tie. His mouth was in a hard line.

About a block from the church another male appeared from a side street. At first Moreau couldn't tell who the person was.

THE SPYING MOON

Randy pushed past him and the figure turned around. She recognized him from the photos. Jim Petersen.

Jim grabbed Randy and Randy yanked his arm from Jim's grasp. Randy's hands were balled into fists and his face flamed red. Jim backed off and Randy strode to the church.

A group approached Jim. It was George, with the bookends in tow. This time they reminded Moreau more of the walkers the one woman had chained to her in that zombie show. Undead used to ward off the other undead with the scent of their decay.

How much of what they'd learned about Sammy's death was a decoy? Everything about the case felt like smoke and mirrors; nothing was just as it seemed.

George didn't have the same angry look as Randy, but he wasn't the picture of grief either. He fell into step beside Jim and seemed completely focused on whatever Jim Petersen was saying as Arnold and Doug walked behind them.

"Interesting," Moreau said.

"Yes. Very interesting," Duncan echoed.

But what does it mean?

The four of them cut through a gap in the foliage that comprised part of the fence around the church and they lost sight of them.

Duncan and Moreau got out of the vehicle and walked toward the building. Cars had begun to fill the parking spaces. When they got to the other side of the lot they could see to the street in front of St. James. George, uncharacteristically alone, walked away from someone who grabbed his shirt. George twisted his arm to free himself and Kenny Jensen shoved him.

Whatever Kenny said was out of earshot, but George turned. "Maybe you should go home and have a good cry," he said.

The comment only fueled the rage that blazed in Kenny's wide eyes. He lunged at George and knocked him forward.

Moreau grabbed George to stop him and Duncan stepped between them and Kenny.

"This isn't going to help things," Duncan said quietly. Kenny glanced from side to side as though he was still looking for some way to get past his cousin and take another shot at George.

"Son of a bitch," George said. He put his hand on the side of his cheek, which was bleeding.

"You'll live," Moreau said.

He glared at her and stomped across the sidewalk to the church door, yanked it open and disappeared inside.

Moreau turned back to her partner.

Kenny's shoulders sagged. "I'm fine. He's just a jerk."

"I know. And he's likely always going to be a jerk. Are you going to be okay?"

"Yeah." Kenny's gaze was on his toes. He glanced up only long enough to see Duncan step back to let him pass.

As Kenny approached the church door a girl Moreau guessed to be about his age stopped on the sidewalk. She wore black jeans and a long, baggy black sweater with three quarter sleeves that stopped between her elbows and wrists. Her right arm boasted a small tattoo that looked like the number eight. It seemed like Kenny was going to say something to her, but she turned and ran across the grass toward the side street.

"Who was that?" Moreau asked.

"Ellie Everett."

Everett?

Duncan answered her unasked question. "Alyssa's sister."

Kenny watched Ellie disappear and then he shuffled off to the door and went inside.

Ellie Everett. The girl in Willmott's photos? From that video? She hadn't told Duncan about that yet, and she hadn't gotten a good enough look at Ellie to be certain, but there was the picture of the girl in the car with Alec and Alyssa...

"What was that about?" Moreau asked out loud.

"Which part? Kenny and George, or Kenny and Ellie?"

"All of it."

He shook his head. "I don't know."

THE SPYING MOON

"I thought he was friends with George."

Duncan's eyes hooded then, shadowed by dark thoughts he wasn't ready to share just yet. "I don't think so. That's something that's always bothered me about this case."

He didn't elaborate or give her a chance to ask. She could see Freeman across the parking lot, and a growing number of people headed toward the door. She followed Duncan inside.

An hour later they stepped back out into the sunshine.

"Other than the conflicts Kenny and Randy had with George, the funeral didn't give us anything to go on," Duncan said.

"There was Kenny and that girl."

"I'm not sure how Alyssa's sister would fit into this."

Moreau glanced at Duncan as they walked back to the SUV. "But you could ask."

"Or you could."

"You know her."

"Which isn't necessarily a good thing."

"I just—"

"You want me to talk to her, I will. What else?"

Moreau shook her head. "Did you finish your report?"

Duncan nodded. "You?"

"It isn't due until tomorrow."

"I put your name on mine."

An apology? A peace offering? He was watching her, but if there was more he wanted to say he kept it to himself.

She nodded. "Thanks."

The burial at the cemetery was private. Uniforms would be on site to ensure everything went smoothly and had been ordered to report anything unusual.

"I guess we should head back to the station," she said. "Maybe the techs have something for us from the school."

Chapter 24

As Moreau and Duncan approached the front doors of the station, Levi McIver strode across the front lawn and blocked her path.

"We need to talk."

She folded her arms across her chest. "I'm listening."

"Not here."

He reached as though he was going to grab her and she twisted away from him.

"Back off, McIver," Duncan said.

McIver held up his hands. "Fine. Tina's, on Fourth Street. You know it?"

She nodded.

"Meet me there in ten minutes." He glanced at Duncan before he pointed to Moreau. "Just you."

Duncan looked her in the eye and she gave the shortest nod possible as she turned on her heel.

Tina's was the kind of nondescript place you went to for the food and not the décor. Orange booths lined paneled walls. Sunlight trickled through the dingy windows that had lettering boasting everything from pumpkin pie to strawberry milkshakes. Judging from how much text was spread across the glass Moreau figured their entire menu was posted. One table in the center of the room had a sign on it, noting that it was reserved for a local war veteran who frequented the place.

McIver was settled into a booth in the back when she arrived.

THE SPYING MOON

She slid onto the orange vinyl bench and set her bag down beside her.

"I ordered coffee," he said.

"What do you want?"

"Why did you go see Phil yesterday?"

The waitress arrived, set two mugs down and filled them with coffee. "Anything else?" she asked.

McIver paused. "Corned beef on rye with a side of fries."

Moreau hated to admit that sounded good, and she suddenly realized she hadn't eaten a proper meal since the late lunch with Duncan the day before. "Same for me," she said. "With mustard." She slid the coffee toward the waitress. "And just water for me."

"Gotcha," the waitress said as she picked up the mug and took it away.

McIver exhaled and fidgeted with his phone before he tried again. "Look, I don't think it was an accident."

"Don't think what was an accident?"

McIver leaned back in his seat. "This is how it's going to be? I try to talk to you and you shut me out?"

She reached for the glass of water.

"I've been a dick to you and you've got every right to be pissed with me."

She stared at him as she took a drink.

"I—" he looked away, "—I didn't know about your mother."

"It's none of your business."

"You want me to beg for forgiveness? You want me to tell you I'm a heartless ass? Is that what you want to hear?"

"I want to hear the truth, McIver."

"I think Phil was attacked."

"The report says he fell. His injuries are consistent with a blow to the head while he tumbled down an embankment."

"And the blow could have been deliberate. The examination didn't rule that out."

She pulled the wrapper off a straw that had been left on the

194

table and stirred her water. "Why would Freeman let them write up an assault on an officer as an accident?"

"To keep him safe."

Moreau looked at McIver as she processed that.

"Look, just follow me for a minute here. If someone attacked Phil and that was known, that person would lay low. But they'd also think that Phil knew something and might talk. They might try to finish what they started."

"That's reasonable."

"If people start poking around and asking questions about his accident it could put him in danger."

"And by visiting him in the hospital you think I've put him at risk."

McIver sighed. The waitress returned and announced their food as she set down a platter in front of each of them and once she confirmed they didn't need anything else she walked away.

"I don't think so. Not once."

Moreau took a bite of her sandwich before she asked, "And what about your visits?"

"He was my partner, Casey."

"Would you stop calling me that?"

"You strictly on a last name basis with everyone except Nate?"

"He calls me Moreau, too. And my name isn't Casey."

"It's what Freeman called you."

She pulled her bag up from the seat so he could see her initials stitched into the flap. K. C.

A hint of color crept into McIver's cheeks. "Not Casey."

"No."

"I'm sorry."

"The reporter got it wrong?"

"The reporter only called you Constable Moreau. In the part I read, anyway."

Moreau took her bag and put it back on the seat beside her.

They ate in silence for a few minutes.

195

THE SPYING MOON

"I don't think it was an accident, either," she said finally.

McIver looked up at her. "You weren't even here when it happened."

"No, but I've been out near the mines—"

"What were you doing out there?"

"Following a lead."

"You have a lead about Phil's accident?"

"It was a lead about my case."

He frowned. "Sammy Petersen? How could his suicide connect to Phil's accident?"

She watched the realization flicker in McIver's eyes faster than she could turn her attention back to her plate.

"Sammy Petersen wasn't a suicide, was he?"

"Keep your voice down, McIver."

"Levi."

"Whatever. The Petersen investigation isn't your concern."

"To hell it isn't. The bullet that killed our victim was shot from the same gun that killed—" McIver stared at her. "Sammy wasn't killed with the gun, was he?"

Moreau reached for her water.

"You do that every time you're avoiding my questions," McIver said.

"Last time I looked at my food."

"Whatever."

"I'm not going to talk to you about that case, certainly not here. There's a link. That's all you need to know."

"Yeah? We'll see what Freeman has to say about that."

Moreau picked up a napkin and wiped her mouth.

McIver slumped back in his seat. "Freeman ordered you to keep quiet about this."

"Do you want to talk about Phil or not?"

"I want you to stay away from him."

"You're looking into what happened to him, aren't you?"

It was McIver's turn for a distraction. He grabbed his mug and gulped down undiluted black, bitter coffee without complaint.

196

"You are," she said.

"This isn't a one-way street. If you aren't talking to me this conversation is over."

Moreau studied McIver's eyes. The waitress returned and left them their check.

McIver snatched it up.

"I can pay for myself, you know," Moreau said.

He ignored her as he went to the register. She walked outside and paused.

Across the street a man in a camouflage jacket disappeared into a second hand shop. The height looked right and his hair was dark, but she hadn't seen his face.

Fingers grasped her arm and she twisted it to break free of the grip as she turned.

McIver let go. "Look, I just wanted to say—"

"Forget it."

She started walking back to the station. McIver kept pace with her.

"We have to find a way to work together, Moreau."

Moreau stopped and turned. "Is the sudden desire to mend fences because you suspect I have information that you want?" She looked him in the eye. "You said yourself this isn't a one-way street. If you want to work with me you have to level with me. Otherwise, quit wasting my time and yours thinking because you were decent to me for five minutes I'll bare my soul to you. I don't need your acceptance or approval, Levi McIver."

The few people around them on the street glanced at her as they passed by, but nobody said anything.

"I'm trying to apologize, Moreau."

He was like a set of Russian dolls; every one you opened revealed a distinct personality. The similarities were there, but there were subtle differences as well.

There was the Levi McIver who'd been a sexist jerk the night she arrived, the man with an attitude, prepared to dismiss her in less than a heartbeat. Then there were the times he treated her

THE SPYING MOON

almost like she didn't exist. When Freeman had ordered her out to a scene with him, McIver had acted like she was an inconvenience. Then, there was the subtle and overt sexism that he dished out every morning when it was time to make coffee.

On the job, at the scene, however, there was an entirely different Levi McIver that emerged. One she wanted to work with. One who could be an asset to the team. One she practically respected.

Who was the real Levi McIver?

From the corner of her eye, Moreau saw the camouflage jacket again.

It was him. Moreau started to walk back toward Tina's and looked out to the street to see if it was clear to cross when McIver grabbed her left arm.

She spun around and punched him in the face.

When Moreau realized what she'd done, she felt like she was going to throw up. She'd let McIver push her buttons to the point where she owed him an apology.

He let go of her arm and stared at her for a moment before his face broke into a genuine grin.

"Bet that felt good."

It had made her feel sick. "I'm sorry."

"Sure."

"Really. Can you just keep your hands off of me?"

"It's Freeman," McIver said as he held up his phone. "He wants us in his office right away."

Moreau looked back across the street. The Aboriginal man had seen them, and he stared across the road with black eyes directed at McIver. When he adjusted his gaze it met Moreau's.

A van drove by and blocked her view. Once it was out of the way the man was gone. Moreau felt like a flat tire. She turned on her heel and followed McIver to the station and straight into Freeman's office, where there was room to breathe. For the first time since she'd started working in Maple River, Moreau noticed he had a window on the far wall.

198

He held out a sheet of paper that was enclosed in a plastic evidence bag.

McIver held it so that she could read it alongside him.

I shot Rich. I'm sorry.

Signed by Chuck.

"Are we buying this?" McIver asked.

Freeman tossed his hands up as if to say he didn't know. "He's dead."

"Boss," McIver said, "we knew Rich was dead when we found his body."

Freeman shook his head and reached for a folder on the desk. "Richard T. Robeson. He popped up from missing persons with the partial name Chuck gave us."

"And the letter, sir?"

"Chuck's suicide note."

"What? He's dead?"

"That's what I said, McIver."

McIver usually wasn't that slow. Moreau wondered if she'd hit him harder than she thought.

"Who the hell was watching the cells?"

Freeman got quiet. "Why don't you both sit down."

A command. Not a question.

Moreau took the chair closest to the door. McIver sighed, scratched his head and sat down beside her.

"At ten o'clock, Nate Duncan signed in to see Chuck Turner. They spoke for about ten minutes."

Moreau could see the color creeping into McIver's face as his hands squeezed the arms of his chair.

"About what?" he asked.

"We don't know. Nate kept his voice low, they sat on the bed close together and you can't even see their mouths in the video footage."

No chance to lip-read or piece together their exchange.

"Sonofabitch."

Freeman said, "McIver—"

THE SPYING MOON

"This screws my case."

"And if we have a confession from the right guy it just saved taxpayers a lot of money."

"Of all the people working in this department, I'd think you'd want the truth."

"I want nothing less. I know you don't agree with how we've handled Phil's attack, but this isn't the time to question me."

McIver had taken his issues to Freeman? Perhaps he wasn't as far out of line as Moreau had thought. "Respectfully, sir, you saw the look on Chuck's face when he saw that picture. He was genuinely shocked."

McIver's head snapped around as he looked at her. She ignored him, although from the corner of her eye she could see McIver piecing things together.

"A week in a river changes a body, Moreau. It could just be that he didn't expect the physical damage."

"Perhaps, but I'm not sure I like him for it."

McIver had recovered enough to speak. "I agree with Moreau. He knew something. Chuck was scared, but he didn't act guilty."

"Of anything other than breaking into Mabel Cook's home."

"There's a long road from theft to murder," McIver said.

Freeman exhaled. "Well, this technically closes the case."

"Technically," Moreau echoed. She hadn't wanted to work the break-in or murder with McIver, but nothing about the way this had been resolved felt right.

"Levi, I know you've been looking into Phil's accident. Maybe you can tie it together with this. I'll slow down the paperwork to keep Robeson's name active for a few more days, but I'll need you with me on the drug investigation."

"Fair enough."

"Another thing I really need from you is a ruling on Nate. Check into his history with Chuck. Let's make sure he didn't have anything to do with this."

McIver's face darkened, but he nodded. "Understood."

Freeman leaned forward. "I want the truth, McIver. If he's in the clear I want to know."

McIver offered another curt nod.

"Now can you go tell Nate I need him in my office?"

Moreau started to stand up too, but Freeman shook his head. "I need you here."

Once McIver shut the door behind him, Moreau said, "What about Saunders?"

"I found out something interesting. His sister is Councilor Stothers' girlfriend."

The one with the addiction to pain killers? Wasn't that what Moreau had read only a few days ago? "Wasn't he in the cell next to Chuck?"

"He's not talking to us."

"That doesn't mean he didn't say something to Chuck."

"No, but there's something else." He spread out the papers and walked her through the call records.

When they were finished Moreau sank down into a chair wordlessly, and waited for Nate Duncan to arrive.

Chapter 25

Nate Duncan entered a few minutes later and glanced at Moreau.

"Have a seat," Freeman said.

Duncan's eyes narrowed, but he complied.

Freeman extended the letter.

Moreau watched the color drain out of Duncan's face as he read it.

"You like him for this?" Duncan asked.

"McIver and Moreau don't."

Duncan glanced at her. "You think he was set up?"

"There isn't a shred of physical evidence that would stand up in court."

Duncan waved the letter. "Then why this?"

"I'd like to know what you were talking to him about this morning," Freeman said.

Duncan set the letter down on the sergeant's desk. "He was an informant of mine in the city. I went to talk to him about what happened."

"He claimed that the perp he named for you was let go on a technicality and threatened his life."

Duncan nodded. "It wasn't the arrest. There was an incident in the cells. The guy probably bashed his head against the bars himself when he was collared, but he claimed a cop used excessive force."

"And that held up?"

"The cop in question had a sketchy record and there was a

problem with the video recording." Duncan looked from Freeman to Moreau. "Do you think I went to coerce Chuck to confess? Ask him yourself. I didn't talk to him about this case."

"Nate, Chuck's dead," Moreau said.

"He hung himself in his cell," Freeman added.

Duncan processed that. "And you're looking at me. You think I went in there to threaten him."

"Did you?" Freeman asked.

"I already told you what we talked about."

"You came in at six this morning to put things right on an old case?"

"Yes. He was my informant. I had a responsibility."

"Any chance your conversation spooked him?"

"How could it? It has nothing to do with this case. Chuck wasn't even into hardcore street drugs. He was a nobody so low on the ladder that all the dealer did was threaten him. It wasn't even worth his time to take Chuck out."

"How comforting."

"Look, I didn't want it to go down the way that it did. The dealer was an up and comer. He was making moves and connections and increasing his trade. We suspected him of links to distributors in the Seattle area, but when he skated on the charge we couldn't touch him. The bosses were afraid it would look like harassment. If you don't believe me, call them yourself."

"I will."

Duncan paused. "Are we clear here? Or is there something else?"

"I'd like to know about your local family connections."

"You mean you want my family tree?"

"I want to know who you've kept in touch with over the years."

"I get a card from my sister every year on my birthday and Christmas. Otherwise, until I came back to Maple River for this assignment, I hadn't spoken to anyone."

Moreau thought about the exchange earlier, between Duncan

THE SPYING MOON

and his sister. His words rang true.

"You were in touch with your uncle."

"That's bullshit. I never talked to him."

Freeman leaned forward and rested his hands on his desk. "For all I know, you've had a hand in the family business ever since you left, using your position to tip off drug suppliers."

Duncan jumped to his feet. "I've never had anything to do with their dealings."

Freeman stood up, picked up a file, pulled out a piece of paper and tossed it down. He leaned over the desk and braced himself against his arms. "Right there. A call from Abe Holt to your home the day before you reported here."

Duncan swallowed. "Son of a bitch. Since when are my phone records up for scrutiny?"

"I only pulled the call history for the past month and it's Abe's records. Turns out Abe received a call from the Jensen house on the night Sammy died, just after the shot was reported. That could connect him to Sammy's death."

Duncan picked up the report and then looked at Moreau. "You asked for this?"

"Abe Holt's call records. Incoming and outgoing."

Freeman sat down. "What will I find if I go back further? Calls that connect to drug busts and raids?"

"I never spoke to him. He left a message on my machine, that's all. You can see for yourself how short it was."

"What was his message about?"

"He knew I was coming here. I don't know how."

Freeman's eyes narrowed. "You don't expect me to believe that?"

"It's the truth. I don't give a damn whether you believe it or not."

"Maybe you'd better start caring what I think. I never really seriously considered you, because it looked like we had a leak in the department long before your name was put forward to come home, but this raises a lot of questions."

204

"You're so fucking paranoid I'm surprised you haven't listed your shadow as a suspect," Duncan said.

Freeman stood up. "Go home. Stay in town and don't report to the station until I order you to do so. Is that clear?"

Duncan looked Moreau in the eye and held her gaze as he said, "Crystal." He tossed the phone logs onto Freeman's desk, left the office and slammed the door shut.

Moreau stood up and took the report.

"Before you leave—" Freeman pointed a finger at her, "—the judge denied your original request for a search warrant for Abe Holt's place, but I think you have enough to get one now if you prep the paperwork."

She nodded as she gathered the phone records. Freeman's phone rang and he answered it. Moreau turned to leave but he held up his hand and stopped her. He only offered polite acknowledgements to whatever was said on the other end of the line and when he hung up he looked at her.

"It seems the Okotoks department is taking the gun theft very seriously."

"Sir?"

"Constable Savage will arrive tomorrow morning from Okotoks. File for the warrant and then go home and get some sleep. I'll need you to work with Savage on the gun case in the morning."

Chapter 26

Moreau reached the conference room Wednesday morning and found a Native women waiting inside. She was at least four inches taller than Moreau, with a willowy figure, flowing black hair and a wide smile that filled her eyes as soon as she saw Moreau.

"Constable Raina Savage," the woman said as she extended a hand. "I hope you don't mind the intrusion."

"Of course not," Moreau said. She led Savage back down the hall and noticed that the last of the stacks of boxes had been moved out of the area. Alyssa wasn't at her desk so Moreau knocked on Freeman's door and introduced Savage.

"You're going to follow up on the gun, then?" Freeman asked Moreau.

"That's your call, sir."

He studied Savage for a moment. "Sergeant Ryan said I could keep you for a few days. You want to jump in on some of our investigations, Savage?"

"Love to, sir."

"Excellent. Partner up with Moreau. She could use some backup."

"And the," Moreau paused, "other things we talked about, sir?"

Freeman shook his head. "Bradrick and Zadecki will be looking after that. They're pulling uniforms in from Kelowna. You can focus on Petersen. I don't think I have to tell you—"

"The clock's ticking. I know, sir."

Sandra Ruttan

* * *

When they reached Greg's lab, Moreau introduced Savage and explained her connection to the weapon recovered from the scene of Sammy's death. He brought her all the reports to review while he went to evidence to sign it out.

Moreau watched as Savage tucked her long, black hair back behind her ears. It reminded her of her mother pushing her own silky raven mane away from her face. With her height and hair and quick smile, Savage looked more like her mother than she did.

"The measurements of the gun match," Savage said after she examined the data. "Still isn't conclusive."

She'd made herself at home and pulled herself up onto one of the stainless steel tables at the back of the room while she spread out the papers around her. The change in her elevation drew Moreau's attention to the cowboy boots Savage wore under her jeans.

"Calgary plainclothes," Savage said when she noticed Moreau looking at her footwear.

"I thought you were in Okotoks."

"We work with the city police as needed. Cross-jurisdictional cooperation, Moreau. That's the name of the game these days."

"Not here," Moreau said. "We can't even get our team members to work together."

Savage's smile slipped from her face. "Really? That's too bad. Is that why you don't have a partner?"

Before Moreau could decide how to answer that, Greg returned with the gun. Savage hopped off the table and snapped on a pair of gloves.

She handled it expertly, and with care. Greg took no offense when she apologized for her need to measure the piece again, and Savage photographed each step in the process.

After the gun was returned to evidence, Savage and Moreau left the building.

THE SPYING MOON

"Your conclusion?"

"It could be a match."

"Impossible to be certain."

Savage looked at her. "You think this was a waste of my time?"

"No. Not at all. This has just been a crap case from day one. Nothing's added up from the start."

"Well, I'm supposed to jump in with you for a few days, so why don't you lead the way to whatever's next? I'll email my sergeant an update and then you can fill me in."

Moreau parked her jeep and got out. She walked up to the first house, located right across from the Jensen residence, and knocked on the door.

Savage stayed in the vehicle so that she could read the reports Moreau had from the murder and suspicious death. The drive over had given Moreau enough time to fill Savage in on some of the details that weren't in the report, such as the reason she didn't have a partner. Moreau had to admit she wasn't sure she was ready for the energy with which Savage seemed to tackle things, although she appreciated the enthusiasm.

A quirky little man with big glasses opened the door and stared at her. He reminded her of the nerdy guy with the big glasses from the ads for *Trailer Park Boys* back when it had been popular. She put on her least enticing smile and held up her ID.

"Constable Moreau. I'm very sorry to interrupt you," she said.

"Oh, you're good. You have the voice down. Do you want to come in?" he asked, his eyes wide and shiny.

"I'm afraid I'm on police business. I was wondering if you remember the night that Sammy Petersen died."

He frowned. Whether it was from her unwillingness to step inside or from the mention of Sammy's name, she couldn't tell, but his eyes pinched with confusion. Clearly, he wasn't the brightest bulb on the shelf. He leaned against the doorway and smiled with what she interpreted as approval.

And not of her job performance.

She glanced at the jeep. Savage lifted her head and studied them. Moreau considered waving her over.

"Okay," he said.

She turned back to the man. "This is just a formality. We have to make sure we look at every possible angle so that we understand exactly what happened..."

"What does that have to do with this?"

There was a trickle of fear that pitched his tone higher. Moreau had wondered why he hadn't been concerned when he opened the door and found a police officer standing on his front step to begin with.

A car pulled up in the driveway, and a tall woman stepped out, her long legs accentuated by the tight fit of the dress blues associated with TV cops, her narrow waist hugged by a belt that contained handcuffs and other toys, just not the ones real cops used. The woman was a little thicker around the waist than the average stripper, and Moreau guessed that was what you got in a small town. She had blonde hair like Mary Jensen's, and her face betrayed her age and some hard years she'd put in to get to this point in her life.

"Did you see either of the Jensen boys that night?" Moreau asked.

"Huh? Yeah," he said. His gaze was stuck to the gap in the shirt where the woman's chest heaved against the material as she walked toward them.

"Which one and what time?"

He glanced at her with an open mouth for a moment. A tinge of red had crept into his cheeks and she had a pretty good idea now why he'd invited her in. It was a card she could use.

"Um, the young one. He was helping clean out the garage for half the night." He looked past her and stared at the woman who had just bent over to retrieve something from the back seat.

THE SPYING MOON

Moreau snapped her fingers in front of his face and he looked back at her.

"You're sure?"

"Yeah. His mother was out there yelling at him for a few hours. She's either screaming while she gets it or yelling while she gives it, if you know what I mean. Guess it's in the blood." He grinned. She glared back at him. "His brother came home and hung out in the driveway tinkering with that car of his while Mary told the younger one what a gutless sack of crap he was."

"Do you know what time he came home?"

"Geez," he said. He rubbed his forehead. "Well, by the time *Wild Things* came on. I was popping popcorn so I saw him just before the show started."

"Did he go out again?" she asked.

The guy just shrugged. "Not the young one. Older one went out later, but that's all I saw."

She nodded. "Thanks for your time," she said.

Moreau put up her hand before the faux cop, who'd stopped on the sidewalk a few feet away, could say anything. She had more important things to worry about.

As she walked back to the jeep she avoided looking at the passenger side of the vehicle. When she got in Savage flashed her a grin.

"Not a word," Moreau said.

She put the key in the ignition and told her hand to turn it, but instead she leaned forward with her head against the steering wheel and laughed until her eyes blurred from the tears.

Once Moreau and Savage pulled themselves together they finished canvassing the street.

Six houses later she had four more supporting statements that indicated Kenny spent the better part of that fateful Friday night getting an earful from his mother. One was even certain he hadn't gone back out because he could see the lights in Kenny's room, see the boy moving around and he heard loud music for a while before midnight.

"Are you sure?" Moreau had asked him.

He'd scoffed. "Of course I'm sure. I thought about phoning the cops but that seemed like a bloody waste of time."

"What about talking to his mother?"

"Ha! You're new in town, aren't you? She only pays attention to ya if you're servicing her horizontally."

It was enough to persuade her that he wasn't involved in Sammy's death. She went back to her jeep, ready to take the next step.

"This is a bit messy," she told Savage.

"Messier than your partner being suspended?"

Moreau nodded. It was a fact that she'd hated to share with Savage, but felt she had to. She picked up a folder that was tucked between her seat and the console and led the way to Mrs. Griffin's front door. The woman answered her first knock.

"I'm so sorry to intrude, Mrs. Griffin, but I have a few more questions for you."

"Yes, well, that's all right. You can pause the TV now so you don't miss a thing."

Moreau opened the folder. She removed the photo array. "You said that another officer had been here, asking questions about the night Sammy Petersen died."

"That's right."

"Do you think you could identify him?"

Moreau held out the paper and Mrs. Griffin tapped the picture in the middle of the top row. "That's him."

It wasn't the picture Moreau had expected her to pick. "You're positive?"

"Yes."

"Can you sign that for me?"

She passed Mrs. Griffin a pen and watched her put her name and date in the appropriate box. When Mrs. Griffin passed it back to her she handed it to Savage and asked her to sign and initial the box beside Mrs. Griffin's signature.

THE SPYING MOON

"I know you said you only saw Randy Jensen come down the hill Friday night," Moreau said.

"That's the truth and it hasn't changed."

"I was just wondering if you saw anyone down here that he talked to."

She seemed to think about that for a moment. "The only other person I saw that night was a woman."

"Walking up the road?"

"No. I saw her halfway up the hill around ten. I'd gotten up to take my medication. She hadn't walked up the hill."

"So she'd been up on the hill, came partway down and then...?"

"I can't say that for certain. She could have been dropped off by aliens, if you believe in that sort of thing. I never saw her walk down the hill and I didn't see her go back up. She disappeared into the bushes."

"Any chance you could identify her?"

Mrs. Griffin led her to the window and pointed up the hill. "From that distance?"

"You didn't mention this before."

"You asked who I saw walk down the hill. I can only tell you I saw a woman partway up the hill, and I never saw her walk up or down."

"I know you phoned in a report of a gunshot. Do you remember how long it took for a police car to arrive?"

Mrs. Griffin paused. "That night, everything blurred together. You think you'll be a good witness and keep all the facts straight."

"It's okay. Nobody's really prepared for that sort of thing."

"But now that you ask about it, I'd gotten up to shut off the porch light. That's when I saw a police car heading up the hill."

"And that was a few minutes after you'd phoned to report the gunshot?"

"No. It was a few minutes before. I went to bed and that's when I heard it." She shook her head. "I'm sorry. I didn't think of it before because there was nothing odd about a police car driving by on a Friday night and I'd assume you'd know what your people were doing."

"You heard the gunshot, called nine-one-one." Moreau nodded. "Thank you, Mrs. Griffin. I'm going to add that to your statement and come by for you to sign it."

"All right then."

She stepped outside and pushed aside her irritation with Wanda Griffin's technicality. They could have known a few days earlier that a woman had been on the hill not long before the police had arrived.

Before the gunshot had even prompted calls to nine-one-one.

Moreau led the way back to the jeep, tucked the folder with the photo array under her seat and drove into town.

"Care to tell me what I just signed my name to?"

How could Moreau tell Savage that one of her team members had impersonated another team member to get information about her case?

What would the constable think of their team?

"It's a long story," she said.

"Longer than losing your partner at the eleventh hour because he's suspected of involvement in the drug trade?" Savage offered an apologetic smile. "Actually, that was pretty quick. Okay. Tell me when you're ready."

Moreau nodded, and wondered if that moment would ever come.

Chapter 27

She found George and the bookends not far from where she'd first met them. They liked to hang out on the street a few blocks from the school where Arnold and Doug should be. She was stopped at the end of a street that intersected with the road George, Arnold and Doug were on. George's crew was just to the right of her position, and she pulled over and watched in the rearview mirror.

There were two differences from the last time she'd seen them. George was sitting on what Moreau assumed was his own truck, and Nate Duncan had just jumped out of his Rodeo and marched across the pavement toward him.

George exhaled from his last drag on the cigarette when Duncan reached him and hopped off the truck. Moreau put her window down and listened.

"Gee, Nate, did you miss me?"

"Listen to me, you little smartass. Don't play the games. I know the kind of shit you're about, ever since I pulled you off that girl years ago. What was it you used to do? Kicked dogs until one of Abe's took a chunk out of your leg. None of his mutts have liked you since."

George laughed. "So what?"

"So you couldn't have gotten through the Duncan property, not without help. But you were on the hill when the gun went off."

A thin smile danced across George's face. "Yeah? Prove it."

"Oh, I will, George. If it's the last thing I do in this damn town."

George's face froze as he stared at Duncan, and then he smirked. "If you had any evidence at all we wouldn't be standing on a street corner, would we, Nate? Where's that pretty little partner of yours? I bet I could make her see things my way."

Duncan smacked his fist against the hood of George's truck. "You stay away from her. And if you know what's good for you, you'll come in for a talk about what really happened, before we aren't interested in dealing."

"George," Arnold said.

"Shut the fuck up, Arnold. This hasn't got anything to do with you."

"The hell it doesn't," Duncan said as he turned to Doug and Arnold. "If you were on that hill when Sammy died you can be charged. Do yourselves a favor and talk to me now, before it's too late."

Moreau undid her seatbelt. "I think you should stay here," she said to Savage.

Savage looked back at the group and gave a slow nod. "If things get any messier I'm coming to back you up."

"Fair enough."

Moreau got out of her jeep and walked toward Duncan.

The bookends had the deer-in-the-headlights look in their eyes.

"You boys need to head home," she said.

"They bump you down to truancy officer?" George asked.

"Hardly." She glared at Doug and Arnold and snapped her fingers. "Get going. Now. Or I'm taking you in."

They looked at George, who responded with a curt nod and then smiled at Moreau. "Almost makes me wish I was still in school. You could show me what you can do with your cuffs."

"Thought you didn't like half and half."

"Maybe I'm warming up to experimentation. You only live once. Why not go Native? I guess your daddy did."

Duncan lunged forward and grabbed George by the shirt.

THE SPYING MOON

George held his arms out wide.

"You see I'm not doing anything. Not resisting. Nothing," George said.

"Nate. Let him go."

Her partner's grip on George relaxed but he didn't release him.

"You heard me."

Duncan looked at her and let go of George's shirt. He backed away, and Moreau stepped in and put herself between her partner and her suspect.

"Come on," she said to Duncan. "I'll walk you to your vehicle."

"Whipped by a woman, Nate?" George's laughter filled the air as Moreau and Duncan walked away. "How things have changed."

"Don't let him rattle you," Moreau said. "I don't want to have to take you in."

"But you would."

"Nate, what do you want me to do here? When Freeman finds out I saw you talking to George and didn't report it, I'll have to answer for that."

"What do you mean 'when'?"

"I'm not alone." She stepped in front of him and looked him in the eye. "I can't help you at all if I get suspended."

He had that look on his face that he got from time to time, the one that made all the angles harden and protrude, like there was something inside of him fighting to burst through his skin. Then he exhaled and it was gone.

"You think I'm dirty?"

"No."

"But you're going to follow Freeman on this."

"He has to protect the investigation. That comes first. What I think doesn't matter."

"It does to me."

"I see no reason to think you're involved."

"Gee, that's a ringing endorsement."

"Nate—"

216

"Forget it. I'll go." He walked around her and opened the Rodeo door.

"It's not like you haven't been holding out on me. Whatever happened to you here, your past, it's shadowing you everywhere you go and it's getting in the way of this case. You've given McIver, Freeman and the team an excuse not to trust you."

"Good to know where I stand with you, Constable."

She grabbed the door. "Nate, be reasonable. You've kept me in the dark. I don't know what happened to you and I'm not trying to pry into your personal business. I've given you the benefit of the doubt. Everything I've seen on the job tells me you're a good cop. Don't make me think otherwise."

He started the engine. "Thanks for letting this slide."

She let go of the Rodeo door and stepped back. Moreau blew out a breath as he drove away. When she turned around, George was perched on the bumper of his truck.

"I'm surprised you stuck around."

He shrugged. "I've got nowhere else to be."

"Let me tell you a little story, George. Once, there was a boy who died from a drug overdose. And it was no ordinary overdose. He had no track marks and showed no signs of long-term drug use. The cocaine in his system was so pure the volume was lethal all on its own. Add in mixing it with alcohol and the boy didn't stand a chance.

"A few hours later, someone else came along. They saw the boy's body and vomited in the bushes. There's no shame in that. Seeing a dead body for the first time can be quite a shock. After they calmed down they had something to drink. They took out their cell phone and made a call. What happened next could have gone down a few different ways. Someone brought him a gun, or told him where to locate one."

Mrs. Griffin had confirmed a woman, but the cell phone records told her someone else had been there too. Whatever had happened, she was betting George Jacobs knew who had killed Sammy Petersen.

THE SPYING MOON

Moreau watched the cockiness seep out of George's eyes as she stared at him.

"It was bad enough finding a dead body, but now they had to take a gun and stage a suicide. There wasn't much time after pulling the trigger. Get the syringe, grab the cooler and get off the hill. Or, at least, get to a place where the cops wouldn't be able to find them.

"Somewhere like Abe Holt's property. I hear there are lots of places to party."

All the color was gone from George's face by this point. He reached into his pocket and pulled out a pack of smokes. Trembling fingers held a cigarette as he tried to ignite the lighter.

He kept his gaze on his hands like they were the only things that mattered in the world.

When he finally lit the cigarette and drew in a breath he looked up at her. "Cute story. You planning to write mysteries?"

"You know who was on that hill, don't you, George? You called Abe Holt that night."

"Which isn't a crime."

"This is your chance to come clean. Tell me what happened so that I can clear you."

He stared at her for a moment without the cocky grin or the look of disdain. Moreau was beginning to think he might just take her up on her offer until he stood straight, flicked the cigarette onto the street, walked to his truck door, got in and drove away.

Moreau returned to the jeep.

"Your suspect is that racist peckerhead?" Savage said.

Moreau shook her head. "Suspected of defiling a body, but if Sammy was murdered I don't think it was George Jacobs who killed him."

"Too bad. I'd like to drop his name to some guys doing time who'd be happy to show him a whole different interpretation of going Native than the one he was thinking of."

Chapter 28

When Moreau walked into the lab, she wondered why the only tech she ever saw working was Benji.

"I thought there were a bunch of you jammed in here," she said.

"There were. They moved into their new labs."

"And you drew the short straw and got left with the storage room?"

"It's not as bad as it was."

She looked around. It was true. The other desks had been moved out, along with several bookshelves and the boxes of overflowing papers that they held. Benji's desk was in the same place, near the door, but he had a long workstation set up in the center of the room, surrounded by stations with computers and other equipment.

"This is Constable Savage," she said. "I know you haven't had much time—"

He led her to the table in the center and slid a file folder to her. "The report on the soot. The chemical composition is consistent."

"Is there any way to conclusively prove it's from the same area? Or could one be from a campfire and the other from a forest fire?"

"There are some distinctions. With a campfire you would get a concentration of a type of wood, typically the same. A forest fire can have multiple species intermixed. Environmental factors

THE SPYING MOON

such as the ozone can affect the results. However, in this case, it's not just the soot that suggests the same source; there was animal feces mixed in with the soot."

"And it's a match?"

"Preliminary findings show that shoes from both sources stepped in bear scat and I can tell you that the same diet was present in both samples. It will take a lot longer to absolutely prove that the source of the soot and scat is the same, but every indication from the findings we have so far suggests that they are."

"This would hold up in court?"

Benji pushed his glasses up his nose and nodded, which caused them to slide back down. "What you have now is a probable match on two items. With only one match it would be a reasonable conclusion, but with two it's highly likely."

"Wouldn't a lawyer argue bears all eat the same thing, so it doesn't mean anything?"

"Exact same contents with the same rate of decay. The results will prove what we already know; the two men walked in the same area around the same time."

Rich Robeson had been out near the mines. There was a good chance Chuck Turner had been with him. Had they known who had attacked Phil?

"Now, the picture you sent me. It would have been better with the original," Benji said as he led Moreau and Savage to one of the computers. "But I was able to get a lot off of it."

He pulled it up on the screen. Enlarged and enhanced, the facial features were more pronounced.

"Do you think we have enough here for facial recognition?"

"Of the girl, yes. I got a copy of the yearbook from Sammy's school." Benji pulled it out and flipped to a page.

Moreau looked at the picture he tapped. Ellie Everett.

The name of the girl the cheerleaders had mentioned.

The same girl who'd been at the funeral, arguing with Kenny.

The sister of Alyssa.

"We'll see what we can do about the assailants. I do have something else with the girl that might interest you."

He zoomed in on section of the picture revealing the part of her left wrist that wasn't covered by the person holding her down. She had a small tattoo of an infinity symbol with the letter E in one loop and S in the other.

"That's excellent, Benji."

He flashed her a smile and said, "I'm not done yet."

After he minimized the photo he pulled up another one. This wrist was splattered with blood, but boasted the same tattoo.

"Do we have a source on this?"

Benji nodded. "Sammy Petersen."

"How was that missed in autopsy?"

"It's in the report," Benji said. "But you already had an ID. It wasn't the most pertinent detail."

Moreau nodded, but still felt sloppy for not making the connection before Benji did. It made sense that it hadn't seemed crucial when they were reviewing the preliminary findings with Creaser, but it certainly seemed relevant now. That's why you could never dismiss information out of hand. Context affected relevance, and in this context this tattoo was significant.

"The other thing that might help you is that the photo is of an image back here." Benji tapped a few more buttons on the keyboard and shifted the focus of the picture.

"That's a URL," Moreau said.

Benji nodded. "What you actually have is a photo of a screenshot, and when you analyze the photo it's clear that it isn't even of your primary source." He pointed to an area around the central screen. "This photo is of a video of a video. I was going to pull it up when you called."

He didn't wait for an invitation. A private video channel filled the screen, with a request for a password.

"Invitation only," Benji said.

"Whose account is it? Can you tell?"

She watched Benji push more buttons and unlock screens she

THE SPYING MOON

didn't even know existed. "Sapet," he said. "That's all I've got for now."

"Do you think you can crack the password?"

"We have someone who's better with computers than I am. Maybe."

"Can I get copies of the enhanced photos?"

"Already printed," he said as he reached for a file beside the computer. "I should get you your own tray."

She turned around to leave and then paused.

"Have you tried pulling this video up on Sammy Petersen's computer?"

Benji shook his head and slid his chair down to another desk where the computer had been sitting since it had been recovered from the Petersen home.

"We've gone over his machine and haven't found anything that seems to relate to his death."

"I'm just wondering if he has passwords saved in there."

Benji nodded. He keyed in the URL and was denied access.

"What about another site where he might have stored his videos? Did you find a file or anything?" Moreau asked.

Benji started checking popular sites for saving private photos and videos. On his third try he went straight to a mailbox.

"Bingo."

Moreau and Savage hovered over his shoulders as they watched him pull up a video.

"This is your second source," Benji said. "It's video of a video."

The girl was carried in kicking and screaming. She grunted as she twisted her body and cried for help before she started calling for Sammy.

There was movement from the outer edges of the screen as hands reached in to hold her down. She lurched up off the bed and twisted her head.

Benji hit pause.

"Can you get a picture of that?" Moreau asked.

222

He nodded as he hit a few keys and the printer whirred as Benji let the video continue playing.

The shirtless figure in the foreground who was undoing his pants in the still image Moreau had found entered and proceeded to strip down to his socks before he crawled on top of Ellie Everett.

Benji paused the video again and printed another still. "Seems to be the best angle we have so far," he said. Moreau nodded and they watched the rest of the video and listened to Ellie's screams as the boy raped her.

When the video was over Benji hit stop and they were quiet for a moment.

"You have anyone you want me to run it against?"

"Try George Jacobs and Randy Jensen."

"I'll go through the other videos on this site and see what we come up with, too," Benji said.

"Thanks," Moreau said. "Call me if you find anything."

He nodded and Moreau glanced up at Savage as they walked out of the lab.

"Possible motive for his murder," Savage said.

It felt bittersweet. Nate Duncan would want to know, and she couldn't even tell him. Add in the fact that they'd uncovered yet another crime and she wondered just how far this investigation could spiral.

Moreau started at the end of Kenny's street and worked her way back, checking down alleys as she went.

After five blocks of zigzagging they found him walking alone. Moreau wondered how she hadn't noticed the family resemblance between Kenny and Nate the first night she'd met him. All the angles of his face followed the same lines as Duncan's and his hair flopped the same way.

Kenny's walk was one major difference. While Duncan strode with purpose and perhaps a bit of defiance, his cousin

THE SPYING MOON

sauntered and slouched. He was adrift, without direction in life, or perhaps it was the result of losing the anchor of his best friend.

She pulled alongside him and pushed the button to put the passenger-side window down. "Can we talk?"

He looked at her and shrugged.

"Hop in."

Kenny glanced into the backseat where Savage sat. "Where's Nate?"

"Busy. This won't take long. We'll drive you home."

He shrugged again and got in.

"I wanted to talk to you about Sammy."

"Figured as much."

"All the kids we talked to at the school and the funeral said the same thing. Nice. Quiet. A film buff. But it's all superficial. They didn't know him like you did. What are we missing?"

He looked at her. "He wasn't into drugs."

"We know that, Kenny." She tried to keep her voice soft. "He seemed like he was a good kid."

"Sammy didn't deserve this."

"You're right."

When Kenny stayed silent she pulled out the photos of the assault. "Do you know who this is?"

His eyes widened as he looked at the images Benji had printed for her. "What the hell is this?"

"What happened to this girl...Sammy found out about it."

Kenny tapped the shirtless image in the photo that was moving toward the girl as he undid his pants. "That's—"

"Do you know who that is?"

His cheekbones sharpened. "That's just sick."

"Was Ellie his girlfriend?"

Kenny swallowed, dropped the photo on the dashboard and said, "I have to go." He grabbed his bag and opened the door.

"I know you have no reason to trust me, but I'm trying to find out who else was on the hill the night Sammy died. A woman."

224

Kenny turned and looked at her.

"You went down through Abe Holt's property. I'm not talking about Kelly. Someone else. Someone who doesn't live there."

He turned away and got out of the jeep.

"Kenny, we want the same thing here."

He slammed the door and said, "I doubt that." She watched him run down the street, back in the direction he'd come from.

Savage moved back to the front seat. "That went well."

Moreau made a face at her and didn't comment. After being detoured for paving, delayed by more tree trimming and stopped by a deer that dashed out in front of her, Moreau finally reached the dump that was on the dirt road leading out the other side of town.

Once she'd located the dump supervisor she introduced herself and Constable Savage, explained why they were there, and was pointed in the right direction.

"You're lucky," Willie, the man who claimed authority over the dump, told her. "Pick-up was this morning. It's all in a fresh pile."

One thing she'd learned at the Depot, where RCMP officers trained, was to come prepared. She had a kit in the back of her jeep, along with a pair of coveralls that she pulled on over her clothes and a set of work boots that she replaced the sneakers with. She had extra pants for Savage, although she apologized for not having footwear.

"It's okay. Cowboy boots are pretty solid," Savage said.

Once Moreau secured her jacket and locked the vehicle, they took the kit to the section of landfill that the staff had pointed her to.

It was a longshot, but the fact that George had called Abe Holt hounded her. Why him? There were other calls, too, from an unlisted number. She couldn't pursue those without more information and what she did know was that George had been talking to Holt the night Sammy died. Holt was a gruff geezer, the kind of old man who didn't suffer fools lightly and wouldn't

THE SPYING MOON

think the approval of a few young kids would help him recapture his youth. He didn't strike her as the type to associate with many people at all, never mind a bunch of reckless teenagers.

The Holt family hadn't built their reputation and evaded prosecution for years by being sloppy. They ran a tight ship.

Which probably explained why they had so much tension with Nate.

George Jacobs had called Abe Holt's home the night they'd found Sammy's body on the hill. That meant two things. He had Abe's number, and he believed Abe would help him.

The fact that George, Doug and Arnold appeared to have descended the hill through Abe's property demonstrated that George's belief in Abe wasn't misplaced.

"We're looking for a cooler," she told Savage, "and a gun. 9mm. The real gun that was used to shoot Sammy. Plus, we never recovered any of Sammy's video equipment."

They sifted piece after piece of garbage as they looked for anything that identified the Holt family or might connect to the investigation.

They may not have gotten a warrant for Abe's place, but trash was considered public domain. The problem was, Abe was sharp.

But someone else at the property that night wasn't.

"Check it out," Savage said. For someone who'd spent more than an hour sorting garbage she showed far more enthusiasm than Moreau felt.

However, Moreau felt her pulse quicken when she saw the cooler. Savage brought it to a clear spot near the pile they'd been working through.

"You do the honors," she said.

"Thanks." Moreau opened the lid. The cooler still held partially unopened bottles of beer. She moved them aside one by one, and then held up a video camera.

"Nice," Savage said. "That could be Sammy's."

Moreau bagged it and then pulled out a few more cans of beer before she carefully extracted a gun that had been concealed underneath them. "Right make and model."

"Looks like it could be another one of mine," Savage said.

Once they had everything bagged Moreau pulled off her gloves and dug her cell phone out from her pocket. She held her breath until he answered.

"McIver, I need to see you."

"What do you want, Moreau?"

"I'm at the dump."

"And? You know Freeman didn't give me much time to follow up on the Robeson murder, and then there's that other thing."

Clearing Duncan. Or convicting him.

"This is about the case. I found something that could help."

He paused. "Fine. Be right there."

He hung up before she could get another word out.

She'd set the cooler in the back of her vehicle, along with the bagged alcohol and waited for McIver to arrive.

"It's a bit early, isn't it?"

Moreau made a face at him.

"Constable McIver, this is Constable Savage from Okotoks."

Savage reached out and waved a gloved hand. McIver nodded back.

"Explain to me what Okotoks has to do with my murder investigation," McIver said as he turned his gaze from Savage to Moreau.

"The gun recovered with Sammy Petersen's body may have been one of a number of weapons stolen from a shop in Alberta," Savage said.

"Which means you're here about the Petersen case, not the Robeson murder."

Moreau reached into the cooler and extracted the bag with the gun.

McIver whistled.

"It hasn't been tested yet."

THE SPYING MOON

"Where'd you find it?"

"In the cooler."

"Seriously."

"That's where it was. Someone rather carelessly threw the cooler away with the gun in it."

"And it could match one of the other weapons from the robbery I'm working," Savage said. "If they can get a serial number off of this, it could be our first big break in the gun smuggling investigation."

Moreau set the gun back into the cooler. "This just may be the evidence I need to get a search warrant for Abe Holt's place."

"You think he's connected to Sammy's death?"

"I think," she said as the crime scene crew pulled in, "there's a lot I need to tell you."

Chapter 29

When Moreau got out of the shower she heard a knock from the front of the cabin. She scrubbed her wet hair with a towel as she walked to the door wearing her bathrobe.

She'd let Savage use the bathroom first, but didn't see her in the living room.

"I'm not—" she said as she opened the door. Moreau stopped when she saw who was there.

"I'm not who you expected."

"You could say that. Can you give me a minute while I get dressed?"

She left him in the living room and once she was dressed she made sure that she put her gun back in its holster and secured it to her waist before she returned from the bedroom. As she entered her cell phone buzzed. She checked the message, responded, and then set the phone on the coffee table.

"I guess with everything that's happened you can't be too careful."

She shook her head. "What can I do for you?"

He gestured at the room around him and did a three-sixty. "I guess you aren't much for small talk or socialization."

"I've barely been here since I arrived. Can I get you something? Soda? Water." She swallowed. "Coffee?"

He followed her toward the kitchen. "I'll take a Coke."

Moreau handed him a can and grabbed a bottle of Canada Dry for herself. She focused on opening it and took a long drink

THE SPYING MOON

instead of repeating her question.

Duncan jerked his thumb toward the couch and she nodded and followed him there.

"I was accused of assaulting a girl. Accused of rape. The gossip was halfway around town before the cuffs were on."

He couldn't have done that and had a clean record, never mind join the RCMP.

Footsteps bounded up to Moreau's door and it swung open. "I've got enough to feed an army." McIver stopped cold when he saw Duncan on the couch with Moreau.

"We might need it," she said.

He came in, put the bags of food on the coffee table and sat down in the chair across from them. "Thought you were suspended."

"I was just explaining why I left Maple River."

McIver leaned back in the chair. "Glad I didn't miss it."

Duncan looked at Moreau. She didn't flinch as she nodded.

"The girl I was accused of raping, she was high on drugs. She attacked me and I was trying to hold her off. My mother came in and didn't know what she was seeing. At first she blamed me. It took a while for everyone to calm down and get the facts straight. By the time they did, I was black and blue." He took a breath. "Ma did most of the damage. They took the cuffs off me and put them on her. She just got paroled six months ago."

His mom was the one who went to jail but his relatives treated him like an outcast. "Your family blames you?" Moreau asked. She thought about Mary Jensen beating Duncan, how he'd refused to press charges.

Echoes of the past affecting the present.

"The way they see it, me being a cop is the icing on the cake. There was always something wrong with me, and carrying a gun and a badge proves it."

Cold.

"My mother was a big part of their operation. I don't really know the details. They always kept me out of it, but I got the feeling she called a lot of the shots."

"Your own mother." No wonder he hadn't wanted to talk about it.

"Hallmark hasn't got it right about all moms."

"They don't exactly sell cards for the deadbeat parents, do they?" McIver said.

"They're missing a market," Duncan said. "But it was a long time ago, Moreau."

"It's Kendall."

All the angles of Duncan's face softened. "I never wanted to come back here."

"And the girl?"

"She was a juvenile so she was never named publicly."

"Was she charged?"

"No."

Moreau held up the soda bottle and looked at McIver. He nodded. She got up and walked to the fridge.

"Coke, Canada Dry or Orange?"

"Coke, please."

She walked back to the living room, passed McIver a can and looked at Duncan. "Alyssa Everett," she said.

"How did you—"

"Something about the way she talked to you outside Freeman's office that day. There was history." Moreau returned to the kitchen, grabbed plates and utensils, and brought them to the coffee table.

"It was a long time ago."

"She has a history with drugs, and now she works for the RCMP department that's leading the investigation into drug distribution in the area."

"I should have told Freeman."

"Especially since she's involved with Alec Chmar."

Duncan's jaw dropped down as his eyes widened. He hadn't known.

"You think he's involved with the drugs somehow?" McIver

THE SPYING MOON

asked.

She grabbed her phone and brought up the photo. "The other night I got a picture of my attacker."

Duncan looked at the screen and his eyes narrowed before he passed it to McIver.

"Alec Chmar broke into your house, beat you up and he's still walking free?" McIver said.

"If it's any consolation, Scott Saunders is still in a holding cell for sneaking onto my property last night with a gun."

Duncan frowned. "He kept his back turned when I was in there talking to Chuck, but he was in the next cell."

"You don't need to worry about this suspension. Within twenty-four hours you'll be cleared," Moreau said.

"That's a bold statement."

"I'm confident."

"Me too," McIver said. "We think we found the real gun that was used to kill Rich and shoot Sammy."

"Where?"

"In a cooler at the dump," Moreau said.

"Our cooler?"

Moreau thought about the evidence of a cooler on the ground where Sammy had died. "Benji's on it, but the measurements match."

"Is it possible to trace the weapon?" Duncan asked.

McIver said, "We have Constable Savage here from Okotoks, looking into that gun theft."

As though she knew she'd been summoned Savage appeared on the steps, walked through the kitchen and smiled. "Raina," she said.

"This time tomorrow, Nate, drinks are on me." Moreau reached over and squeezed his hand. "But you can't be here now."

"You've got more?"

"What I've got is a need to ensure that everything is handled properly. McIver was in charge of investigating you, and we

232

can't have that compromised."

Duncan frowned. "And you're sure I'll be cleared tomorrow?"

McIver leaned forward in his seat and rested his arms on his legs. "Look, Nate, I had to be sure. I did some digging and I already gave my report to Freeman. Everything about your case with Chuck checked out just like you said. Your phone records proved no contact. Your work schedule had you up to your elbows in cases that had nothing to do with the drug trade here when things were happening. And what you didn't tell Freeman was that you'd saved a recording of the message your uncle left you, which proved he wasn't too happy about the fact that you were coming back here. But if we're coming clean, I need to tell you guys something. I wasn't interested in either of you because I knew you couldn't be the drug leak."

"You're investigating the team?" Moreau asked.

McIver's eyes betrayed the truth before he confirmed this with a nod.

She thought about his attitude, the way he kept everyone around him on edge. "Anyone ever tell you that you can catch more flies with honey?"

"A little on the nose, don't you think? You never suspected."

"But Chmar and Saunders? You didn't just start acting like an ass one day without them questioning it."

"I let them think that Willmott had been keeping me in check. People see what they want to see."

And Chmar and Saunders weren't the most discerning members of the team.

"My history," Duncan said. "That's how you had access."

McIver nodded. "It was a dirty play—"

Duncan's elbows were propped up against his knees, his head in his hands.

McIver glanced at Moreau. She saw nothing in McIver's face to suggest he'd enjoyed any of this, although to say he looked like he regretted it would be a mischaracterization. He'd done what he had to do. Now he hoped for understanding, even if he

THE SPYING MOON

didn't have their acceptance.

"Nate wasn't the only one," McIver said as he studied Moreau's face.

"There was no way I could have been involved," Moreau said.

"It was…" McIver shook his head. "Just this image I was playing up."

She thought about how Freeman had told her to play McIver and Duncan against each other, about how willing she'd been to hold out on the men she was supposed to be working with.

"The thing was, I couldn't figure why Freeman wanted you here."

"Gee, thanks."

"Seriously, Moreau. He tried to get you interested when he was proposing the team. You took a different position hundreds of miles from here, but he went over your head. That didn't strike you as odd?"

It had, but she'd pushed her own questions aside to focus on the job.

"When something doesn't sit right, it's usually because it's wrong."

McIver's words cut through her. Something had been off about her sudden transfer from the start but she'd pushed those doubts aside and trusted in the chain of command. She'd assumed it was because of the Saskatoon taxi case.

"Anyway," McIver said, "these cases would pop up all over the lower mainland and interior. Drugs that were connected by batch, but widely distributed. Every time there was a reasonable lead it came up empty. Eventually, everything tied back to one office."

"Freeman, Chmar, Saunders and Willmott."

"But Freeman wasn't the original sergeant. He was transferred in and left with those officers. That suggested he was in the clear."

"And Willmott?"

"I knew Phil. We'd worked together before. He'd already had his suspicions. When he had his so-called accident I knew he'd gotten close to something."

Duncan raised his head and folded his hands together. "Don't you report to someone above Freeman? Couldn't you go around him to investigate?"

"Not without tipping my hand. Chmar and Saunders would know they were being looked at, and if one of them was the leak we'd be left with nothing."

"The problem is, they aren't the only ones who had access to all of the information," Moreau said. "Administrative reports, warrants. Every bit of paperwork from Freeman's office crossed Alyssa's desk."

"Yeah, but until I knew about what happened with Nate, I didn't know she had a history with drugs. I was ordered to clear the cops first." He paused. "In a way, your transfer broke this case. It made me start looking at Alyssa. It took me a while to get access to your file, but once I did…"

"It's too thin to move on," Moreau said. "Chmar broke into my house and assaulted me. Saunders turned up here with a gun. Alyssa assaulted Duncan years ago when she was high. That makes Chmar and Saunders more likely suspects. We don't have anything current on Alyssa."

"And I'm nowhere close to having something to question either Chmar or Saunders on, other than what's happened to you, Moreau."

"If we're going to bring in a suspected dirty cop it needs to be rock solid," Duncan said. "You can't piss off the whole team with false accusations."

"I didn't point the finger at you, Nate. I never suspected you of doing something to Chuck."

"He was all right, you know? One of those guys you work with that you hope will get out of the life and pull themselves together. I really thought he might stand a chance." He looked up at McIver. "You think you have the right gun?"

THE SPYING MOON

"Greg's working on it," McIver said.

"Without you breathing over his shoulder?" Moreau asked.

"I told him I'd be back after dinner. Since you waved the white flag I figured hearing what you had to say was more important," McIver said.

Duncan frowned. "Aren't you the one who owes her an apology?"

"Hey, I bought her a late lunch and said sorry yesterday."

"Nate—" Moreau noticed that Raina had sunk down into a chair and was quietly taking everything in.

"I know. I have to go." He stood up. "By the way, Kenny never went home tonight. Mary called me to see if I would look for him. Given the circumstances—"

"Given the fact that it hasn't been twenty-four hours..." McIver said.

Duncan nodded. "Nobody will be looking for him. Nice to meet you, Raina." He walked to the door. "Just remember something if you're going after Abe Holt. He's never been sloppy. And if someone he was working with got messy and put him in the hot seat Abe won't let it blow over."

Moreau thought about that as Duncan closed the door behind him. Freeman had brought him in to throw everyone off balance. She scanned the table in front of her, went to the kitchen, and grabbed the last few things they needed to be able to eat. Savage and McIver started filling their plates as she grabbed her folders and walked over to the bulletin board.

It was propped up on a side table at the end of the room, in front of the TV. She started pinning up photos and cards wordlessly, and McIver and Savage ate in silence.

They were almost finished when she sat down. As she dished up food for herself McIver got up and went to study the board, plate still in hand.

Savage followed.

"I see it. A little thin for a judge, though," McIver said. "But I see it."

236

"It feels like it just scratches the surface," Savage added.

"I think this all ties back to Phil," McIver said.

"Chuck and Rich seem to connect, but Sammy?" Moreau set her plate down. "That's where this goes sideways."

"He's connected by the gun."

"It was a rock that did the damage to Phil's head, right?" Savage asked.

McIver nodded. "Either by chance as he rolled down a hill, or by deliberate blow."

"Which would make it a weapon of opportunity," Moreau said. "If it wasn't premeditated what does that suggest? He found something nobody wanted him to know about."

"We searched the area," McIver said. "He rolled down from a ridge. There wasn't anything there except forest."

"How far did they mark the scene?"

"About half a kilometer from where they thought he fell. It was late, we were losing light, and we planned to head back the next day."

"But there was a forest fire."

McIver nodded.

"And the spot where Phil fell?"

"Burned to a crisp."

"Let's say Phil found something or someone out there and they attacked him." Moreau paused. "Why? What could they be doing that would be worth attempted murder of a police officer?"

"The other thing that Sammy and Rich do have in common," Savage said. "What if it connects to the drugs?"

Moreau looked at McIver. "He had that picture of Jacobs and his lackeys. Taken near the old mines."

"You went out there because Jacobs' truck was towed from the area?"

She nodded.

"And what did you find?"

"What you've seen." She gestured at the photos. "Someone

THE SPYING MOON

cut down a tree and put up a bogus sign to try to keep people out of the area."

"Why would they do that unless they have something to hide?"

"I need to get back out there."

McIver nodded. "Yeah, you haven't got enough here."

"Well, I had to go running through the woods after a dog so I didn't have a whole lot of time."

McIver grinned. "I'll pick you up at daybreak."

"I don't need a babysitter."

"This is my case, too."

"Isn't Freeman expecting a report from you?"

"I already gave it to him and cleared Duncan." McIver's phone beeped and he pulled it out of his coat pocket. "Text from Greg. They got a hit."

"From the gun?"

"And they matched the bullets from Sammy and Rich to a robbery in Similkameen, Washington."

Chapter 30

Once McIver left, Moreau started clearing plates and food in an attempt to return the living room to the sterile look it had possessed when she'd moved in.

The only thing left out of place was the bulletin board, perched by the far wall, which she continued to glance at as she scraped the remnants of food left on plates into the garbage and rinsed the dishes.

Savage collected the soda cans and dropped them in the recycling bin by the fridge. She leaned against the kitchen counter.

"You know many tribes have references to the coyote in their mythology," Savage said. "Some believe he was a god. A trickster."

"Is that like a naughty god?"

Savage made a face. Moreau had already noticed she had a way of raising her eyebrows and tilting her head just a touch that made Moreau feel like Savage had a strong opinion of whatever had been said. This time, her opinion wasn't favorable.

Moreau glanced at Savage and offered a small shrug as an apology before she turned to look at the single picture in the entire cabin, of a coyote in a field of fireweed, staring straight out into the eyes of the photographer who'd captured his likeness.

Like the coyote who'd stared her down in the hours after Sammy Petersen's death.

"I never realized coyotes had any special significance," she said.

239

THE SPYING MOON

Raina looked puzzled. "You don't know much about your ancestry, do you?"

Moreau didn't know anything. She'd been shut off from that side of her life since the day her mother had disappeared. "There's a lot of misinformation out there. Names that are supposed to be Native that aren't."

"Well, I can't speak for all tribes," Savage said. "But there is a story about some tribes believing in the spying moon."

"Like the moon sees all?"

"Not the moon."

Moreau set the last plate in the dishwasher, closed it and looked at Savage. "The spying moon wasn't a moon at all?"

Savage smiled. "The way some tell it this was before there was a moon. Others say that when the moon disappeared, Coyote volunteered to take his place. From far above the earth he could see everything. He spied on everyone and tattled on them for their bad deeds."

"In this case," Savage said, "Willmott was seeing pieces of everything, but he wasn't ready to tell yet. We need to know what else he saw."

"He can't talk."

"Can't?" Savage asked. "Or won't?"

Moreau didn't have an answer for that. "To me, this case is like a hidden picture. Tilt it one way and you see an old man's face. Shift it another way and you see a young woman. Things don't come into focus with more facts."

"That's just because we don't have all the information yet."

Moreau couldn't deny that they were missing information, but there was something more. It was like they had the pieces from different puzzles. Maybe they were trying too hard to make this fit with their other investigation.

In her dreams that night all the pictures on her bulletin board had been scattered and torn. A coyote hovered high over the earth and stared down at her as she tried to find everything and put it back together. She felt her heart hammering against her chest as she tried to breathe, overcome by the sense that no matter how hard she looked she was still missing something.

It was almost a relief to rise before dawn and toss the covers aside. She yawned as she walked from her jeep to the station in the early morning calm.

The pace of the week had begun to take its toll, and the little sleep she'd gotten the night before hadn't helped either. Her body longed to rest but her mind was on fire with the questions that still needed answers.

McIver waited by the front door as she approached, but before she could reach him, George Jacobs ran across the parking lot.

Moreau stopped walking as Jacobs approached her.

"You aren't going to leave it alone," he said.

"What? Sammy's death? Drugs? The murder? The meaning of life?"

"This isn't funny."

"What won't I leave alone, George?"

"All of it. I need to talk to you."

"You had your chance, so unless you've got some serious information about one of these cases, you're wasting my time."

"Is confessing enough? I did it. I killed Rich."

Moreau looked at McIver, who'd started to approach them. "Why?"

"He was a putz. A little snitch."

"Yeah, George? What did you think he was going to talk about?"

George's eyes bugged out of his head and his cheeks paled. "Nothing. I'm full of shit. Never went home from the bar last night."

"Which is funny, because you aren't nineteen and can't legally drink."

"Christ. I fucked up, all right? I fucked this whole thing up."

George started to cry. His skin covered the colors of the Canadian flag within seconds as it puckered up like a raisin and fat tears rolled down his cheeks as he grabbed his head with his

THE SPYING MOON

hands and spun around, saying "Oh Christ" over and over again.

"Pull yourself together and go home," McIver said.

George turned around and punched McIver in the jaw with so much force that George took three steps bent over like the Hunchback of Notre-Dame before he could steady himself and stand up straight. McIver reached out just in time for Moreau to steady him so that he didn't fall on his backside.

McIver cuffed George. "Seems a little too convenient, doesn't it? Now we've got to deal with him."

Moreau shook her head. "Have a uniform put him in holding."

"You're sure?"

From day one, Moreau had faced roadblocks. She'd been alienated within the team, put with a partner who was reviled by most in town and just as they started to make progress the case shifted. "I'm tired of unexpected developments getting in the way on this case. Or you can stay back and book him yourself."

"Not a chance in hell," McIver said as he pulled out his phone, called another officer and passed George off to him with instructions to hold him.

The officer, whose name was Michaels, nodded and led George into the building.

"I've been wanting to get him into interrogation since the first day I met him," Moreau said.

"You'll have your chance. Unless—"

"You're not going out there alone, McIver."

"I'd have Raina."

"Don't even dream of trying to get rid of me."

"You're sure that's where you want to be?"

Moreau turned her back on the station door. "George Jacobs can wait. Besides, I'd rather have the chance when we come back armed with something solid to connect him to all of this."

With her back to the door, Moreau ignored the sound of it opening and footsteps trotting up behind her until she heard her name.

242

"Constable Moreau?"

She drew a breath and looked at McIver before she turned around. "Yes?"

It was the same officer who had pointed her to the break-room the night she'd arrived.

Constable Zadecki glanced at her, then McIver. "Can I have a minute?"

Moreau reached over and snatched the keys from McIver's hand. "Don't go anywhere," she told him as Savage winked at her.

She followed Zadecki about twenty feet away. "You sure this can't wait?"

He shook his head. "Look, I just want to come clean about something."

"You told McIver I was a reporter." The words were out of her mouth before she thought better of them.

"What? No. It's about George. George Jacobs."

"What about him?"

"Friday night, the night Sammy Petersen died? George wasn't up there with the other teenagers."

"How do you know that?"

"I was on patrol with Michaels. We saw George getting a little too friendly with a girl. He had her backed up against a wall in an alley."

"Not a working girl?"

"A schoolgirl. Ellie Everett."

Ellie Everett. Interesting.

"When we flashed our lights and sirens she ran off."

"You didn't talk to her?"

"Later. She didn't want to press charges, and she really didn't want her sister to know."

"What time was this?"

"That's the thing. It was just before seven in the evening."

"Which alley?"

"That doesn't matter."

THE SPYING MOON

"It accounts for whether he had enough time to get up to Holt Hill."

Zadecki paused. "That's the thing. We thought he needed to cool down a bit."

Jacobs' name hadn't come up at the station so he didn't mean in a holding cell. "How, exactly, did you think he should do this?"

"We took him for a walk."

A term used by cops who took a disorderly person and dropped them out of town so they'd have to walk it off on their way back into town. It was a practice under scrutiny because a number of Aboriginal men had frozen to death because of cops picking them up when they were drunk and dropping them outside cities in the dead of winter.

"And you were hoping this wouldn't get out at the station."

"Something like that."

"Where did you drop him?"

Zadecki took out his phone, pulled up a map of the area and pointed out the spot. It was far enough that there was no way George was on the hill when Sammy was injected with the drugs, but he could have been there for the gunshot.

All this time they'd assumed George had been escaping into the Holt property. Maybe that's where he'd been coming from.

Something else was bothering Moreau. "You said you were on patrol with Michaels?"

"Yes."

"Wasn't he the one who found Sammy Petersen's body?"

Zadecki nodded.

"But you were here, at the station, weren't you? You were the one who pointed me to the breakroom, and then you came in to tell us about the body."

Zadecki nodded again. "We were supposed to be going off shift. Michaels said he was just going to go grab a burger while I finished up the paperwork. I didn't really think about it. He was pretty pissed with George. I heard George say something about rape before Michaels shut him up."

"Rape? That's it?"

"And a name." He paused. "Sammy. But I didn't hear everything George said."

More pieces to the puzzle. Where had Michaels been when the call reporting a gunshot came in? In a drive-thru in town, or was he already parked on Holt Hill? Mrs. Griffin said a police car had gone up the hill before the gunshot and Michaels had been first on the scene.

Moreau thanked Zadecki and walked over to McIver and Savage. "Let's get out of here before anything else—"

"McIver. Moreau." Freeman's voice called from the station.

"You jinxed it," Savage said.

Freeman hadn't waited for them to even turn around. He closed the gap between them with wide strides.

"We got a call from the high school. Student with a gun."

"Isn't that for the Emergency Response Team?" McIver said.

"The ERT is almost an hour away by air. We don't have time to wait for them." Freeman pointed a finger at Moreau. "It's Kenny Jensen."

Kenny, who never went home the day before. Who couldn't be reported missing, officially, because it hadn't been twenty-four hours.

What was he doing at the school with a gun?

As they drove to the school with Freeman they were briefed. Kenny had at least one hostage in the front lobby. The rest of the building was on lockdown.

When they reached the front parking lot Freeman walked up to the closest cruiser and took their map of the building. "School administration is here and Kenny's here."

"Have they been able to secure the office?" Savage asked.

"Negative," one of the uniformed officers said. "He's too close to the door. They've taken cover in administrative offices in the back and locked those doors. We're in touch with the principal by phone."

THE SPYING MOON

Moreau scanned the school's entrance. She could see the shadow of one figure holding another, one of the arms at an angle that suggested he could be pointing a gun at the other person's head.

"Have you established trust with him?" Freeman asked her.

"I think you have a better chance if you bring Duncan in," Moreau said.

"He's been called."

They waited until Duncan's Rodeo pulled in behind them and he jumped out.

"What's his status?" Duncan asked.

"One hostage we know of," Freeman said.

"Identity?"

"Unknown."

"Weapons?"

"The school's secretary clearly saw one gun. It's not known if he had more."

"Can we make contact?"

The officer who'd answered Savage before shook his head. "We've tried the phone in the office. He isn't answering."

"What about his cell?"

"No answer."

"The school has a media room, right?" Duncan said. "They broadcast the announcements over TV and there's one in the lobby."

"What are you thinking?" Freeman asked.

"If we can hack the feed I could talk to him."

"You could use a megaphone for that."

"I think this is about what happened last Friday. If Kenny thinks he's going to get justice maybe he'll listen."

"How does broadcasting over the school's media system help with that?"

"I'm going to tell him who murdered Sammy Petersen."

246

Chapter 31

Benji was brought to the scene and put in a mobile command center equipped with all the latest technology. Moreau had to admit she was surprised their detachment had this kind of equipment.

"How long will this take?" Freeman asked him.

"Maybe twenty minutes. We need to make sure the system is activated inside the building."

Freeman talked to Benji and gave orders so that they could connect to the school's media feed.

Moreau nodded toward Duncan's vehicle and backed away from the group. Duncan followed.

"Are you sure about this?"

He shook his head, the look of helplessness softening all the lines in his face with uncertainty. "I think it's the only way."

"What if you try calling him? Maybe he isn't answering because he doesn't know the number."

He walked back to the command post and stopped just outside the door. "Do you want me to try his cell before we do this?" he asked Freeman.

"Let's try this first. We're almost ready."

Benji directed Duncan to a seat by a video camera. Duncan went inside and Moreau followed.

"Okay, I think we're ready," Benji said. "You should be live."

"Have we got the principal on the line to confirm?" Freeman asked.

THE SPYING MOON

McIver nodded and passed the phone to Freeman.

"My name is Nate Duncan."

Freeman held the phone to his ear and gave a thumbs up. Duncan continued.

"I grew up in Maple River. I even went to this high school, until I moved away. I'm an RCMP officer, and I've been investigating Sammy Petersen's death."

Everyone in the van sat stone still as Duncan talked. Moreau knew that snipers were in place outside the school. Officers with vests and helmets were armed and ready to advance on command. Another team was feeding a minicam through the roof to try to get a visual on Kenny Jensen, and behind the barricades parents had started to arrive. Between the frantic parents and the school there was a sea of blue uniforms peppered with the turnout gear that firefighters wore. Volunteers that had been called in to help handle crowd control.

Benji pushed buttons on the keyboard and one of the monitors came to life above him. He'd tapped into the school's network.

"It's been a tough week because you've lost a classmate, a good person most of you have known your whole life. For Kenny Jensen, it's been especially tough because he lost his best friend.

"Many of you were led to believe that Sammy Petersen put a gun to his head and killed himself last Friday night. I think the reason we're here today is because of that misunderstanding and I want to set the record straight. Sammy Petersen didn't kill himself. He was murdered."

A cell phone buzzed. Freeman's head swung around as he tried to determine whose it was.

Duncan reached into his pocket and pulled his phone out. He held it up for them to see.

Kenny Jensen.

He put it on speaker and answered.

"Hello, Kenny."

"I want you to bring me the camera so that I can talk to

248

everyone," Kenny said.

"We need to make sure everyone's okay first."

"Everyone's not okay. Sammy's dead. How can everyone be okay?"

"Have you been injured?"

"What? You mean physically?"

"Yes. I know you're upset—"

"I'm not being a little sissy, Nate." Kenny screamed the words, and they echoed through the video feed. The whole school was hearing their conversation.

Duncan looked at Moreau and gave a tiny shake of his head. She tapped Benji's shoulder and drew her finger across her neck. He shut off the live feed and replaced it with a still image of Nate's face, turned back to Moreau and looked at her as though he was asking if she approved.

She shrugged. What else could they display? Maybe the kids in the school would think the feed was frozen. The only ones who'd know different were Kenny Jensen and his hostage.

"Kenny, who's with you?"

"That's what you're worried about? Be a blow to town pride if I mess up the golden boy's hand, won't it?" This was followed by the sound of a thud and another scream, like someone crying out in pain, but from a short distance.

"Can you tell me why you have Randy there?"

"Sure. When you give me the goddamn video camera so I can tell the whole school what he did."

"Why don't you start by telling me?"

"No. I want everyone to know."

Duncan put the phone on mute. "What do we do, sir?"

Freeman ran his hands through his hair. "You shouldn't give a terrorist a platform." He dropped his hands to his hips. "But we need to keep him talking until ERT gets here."

"Giving him the video camera would do that," Moreau said.

"Your gut?" Freeman asked her.

"Maybe he knows something we haven't pieced together yet."

249

THE SPYING MOON

Freeman looked at Duncan and nodded.

"Benji, can we reach the school?"

"It has a wireless transmitter and a fully charged battery. You can pick it up like it is and take the stand with it."

Duncan put the phone back on speaker. "Okay, Kenny. How would you like me to do this?"

"You can bring the video camera to the front door."

"Okay. Moreau and I will carry the equipment."

"Just you. Unarmed."

"I'm not sure my sergeant's going to agree to that, Kenny. But you're family. I'm not going to shoot you."

"Fine. Just bring it to the door."

"I'm going to need something from you, then."

There was a short silence before Kenny said, "What?"

"Let me talk to Randy."

Kenny laughed. "You won't need to worry about that. He's gonna have the starring role in my broadcast."

He cut the call and Duncan stood up.

Freeman passed him a Kevlar vest. "You should wear a helmet, too."

"No. He needs to recognize me and know we kept our word."

Moreau stepped back as Duncan exited the vehicle and Benji slid the tripod with the camera on it out and down to the door. Freeman helped them lift it down and once it was on the ground Benji did a quick check to make sure it was still transmitting.

When he gave Duncan the thumbs up, Duncan nodded at Moreau. She exited as the bright morning sun streamed down straight into her eyes.

The night of Sammy Petersen's death, Moreau had felt like the darkness of night was a physical force that closed in on her and made it hard to breathe. Today, the brightness of the light closed in on her and it felt just as oppressive.

"Be safe," she said to Duncan.

He nodded and McIver and Savage moved to either side of

her as they watched Duncan slowly took the video camera along the sidewalks in the garden area, around the benches, and to the front door of the school.

The coyote mosaic stared out at Moreau and she felt a shiver run down her spine.

Once Duncan reached the door he held his hands out as he backed away, and Moreau felt her lungs fill.

Then Duncan stopped. "I'm reaching into my pocket for my phone," he called out. His left hand remained raised high as he fished out his phone, tapped it with his thumb and held it to his ear.

Someone inside eased the door open. Duncan picked up the video camera and tripod, lifted them over the threshold and then stepped back. He was still holding the door open and paused. It appeared Kenny was exchanging some words with him, but what Duncan was saying was not within earshot.

"What's taking that damn feed so long?" Freeman asked nobody in particular as they watched the entrance of the school.

Duncan stepped back and let go of the door. Then he raised both hands in the air, turned around and walked back behind the armed officers who formed the perimeter.

"What could you see?" Freeman asked him.

"Blood coming from Randy's hand."

"Nobody else was in the hallway?"

"Not that I saw."

Duncan and Moreau followed Freeman back into the large van where Benji worked.

"You all want to pretend you care?" Kenny said as part of his face and the upper part of Randy's head filled the screen. "I'm going to show you why Sammy died."

He stepped back and pulled Randy with him, revealing the fact that he still had a gun pointed at his brother's head and his other arm was wrapped tightly around Randy's neck.

The older Jensen boy's face was red and he pulled on Kenny's arm. Kenny let go and shoved him down, below the area the

THE SPYING MOON

camera was focused on. They could see just enough to tell that Kenny was swinging his leg back and then forward and they heard a cry.

Presumably from Randy, after being kicked.

Kenny kept the gun pointed at the ground as he pulled up his phone. "Let me show you what the golden boy did."

He held his cell phone up to the screen as a video started.

"Oh no," Benji said.

"What?" Freeman asked.

Moreau groaned. "This is the video Phil Willmott found. It could be the motive for Sammy's murder. We believe the girl is Ellie Everett, and Benji was working on trying to identify the males in the video."

"How does Ellie connect to Sammy?" Freeman asked.

"They were involved. In a still from the video you can see the tattoo she has on her wrist. It matches the tattoo Sammy had." She pulled up the image on her phone and showed him.

"It's the same symbol from that piece of paper we found in his backpack," Duncan added.

"And he videoed this?"

As though he could hear them, Kenny pulled his phone away from the video camera. "He raped her. My brother. The golden boy. He raped Ellie Everett. Sammy knew about it and he was going to tell. George didn't know Sammy found the video. He started telling people it was Sammy that raped her."

Kenny's leg swung back and forward again, although to them only his hip and the top part of his thigh were visible on the screen. A yelp from Randy confirmed impact. "You useless sack of shit. You're a rapist and you killed my best friend. You made me leave early, and I saw Uncle Abe talking to Ellie's sister, telling her what George had said. That it was Sammy who hurt her. You're all a bunch of lying assholes."

Moreau and Duncan exchanged a glance as another voice came into focus in the background of the school's video feed.

"No no no no no. Don't, Kenny, please."

252

A girl's voice.

"Stop, Ellie. They have to know. They all have to know why Sammy died."

This was followed by noises and a blur of color as someone jumped up and pushed Kenny back and another figure tackled both of the Jensen boys. What sounded like a thud was followed by a grunt and a girl screamed as the camera was knocked to the ground and a gunshot exploded from outside the mobile command center.

Within seconds smoke filled the lobby. Moreau, Duncan, Freeman and Benji watched the live feed as a blur of black legs ran by and people started to clear the building.

When the smoke dissipated all that the video feed showed was a slow trickle of blood spreading out across the beige floor.

Chapter 32

By the time Moreau and Duncan got out of the vehicle the front of the school was a sea of emergency response personnel, armed officers and streams of students pouring from each exit in the building. Behind them other officers fought to hold parents back, who hugged each other or their children and cried, while reporters set up as close to the scene as they could get.

Moreau noticed Seth Gorden behind the police tape. He offered her an apologetic smile before she turned her back to him.

It was four hours later when Kenny's body was finally removed from the lobby. Creaser walked behind the gurney silently. Moreau held back as Duncan approached him and got permission to see his cousin.

He unzipped the body bag and looked at Kenny's face. Even from where she stood, Moreau could see how similar it was to Sammy's. In the struggle for the gun, Kenny had been shot through the head from right to left.

Moreau turned around as McIver and Savage walked over. "Freeman's ordered us to file our reports about what happened and then go home."

"To hell with that," Moreau said. "We still have work to do."

McIver glanced over her shoulder and she turned to see Duncan approaching.

"Alyssa did a runner," McIver said. "She's gone."

"How can we close this, then?" Moreau asked. "We have no guaranteed proof that she's the one who injected Sammy, and we still don't know where she got the drugs."

"Yes we do," Duncan said as he marched to his vehicle.

Moreau ran after him and got into the passenger seat before he could leave.

"Get out, Kendall."

"Not a chance, Nate. I'm not letting you go there alone."

He turned the key in the ignition and backed away from the school wordlessly.

Chapter 33

Moreau checked her messages as they drove over and confirmed she had what she needed for what Duncan was going to do, with or without permission.

Duncan didn't wait at the gate or call his uncle when they reached Abe Holt's property. He rammed his Rodeo straight through and tore up the hill.

"We had a search warrant, you know," Moreau said as she held up her phone.

"Forward that to me," Duncan said as he stopped his vehicle and got out. "Open up," Duncan shouted as he banged his fist into the front door. Moreau heard heavy footsteps rushing toward them from inside and then the door flung open.

"What the hell do you want? I told you to stay away. I've got every right—"

Duncan pushed past Abe. "I want to know what the hell you had to do with Sammy Petersen's death."

"Not a goddamn thing," Abe snarled. "Now get out before I call your buddies and have them arrest—"

"Nate?"

He turned.

"Kelly." All the anger seeped out of Duncan's voice.

"What the hell is...?" The voice approached from down the hall and stopped short. Moreau looked past Duncan to see a woman who looked familiar.

The middle-aged hooker from Mary Jensen's neighbor's

256

house.

"What the hell is he doing here?"

"Mom, please." Kelly moved beside her brother and grasped his hand.

He squeezed her arm. "It's okay." He took one of his cards from his pocket. "Call me."

"Go to your room, Kelly," Monica Duncan snapped. The girl didn't move as Monica walked toward the entrance and smacked Duncan across the face.

She lifted her hand to strike again but he was too quick and grabbed her wrist. "Don't think I won't arrest you."

Monica laughed. "Fucking no good for nothing ungrateful sack of shit that you are, you would."

Duncan dropped her arm and turned back to look at Abe.

"Phone records put a call coming in here Friday night and I know Alyssa Everett was here. I know you lied to her and told her that Sammy assaulted her sister."

Abe's steely-eyed stare didn't alter as he smirked. "You think you know so much, why aren't you taking me in?"

"We are," Moreau said. "And we have a search warrant." She held up her phone before she turned Abe Holt around, patted him down and cuffed him.

Once she was done she took her partner's cuffs and did the same thing with Monica so that Duncan wouldn't have to arrest his mother in front of his sister.

Ten hours later Moreau and Duncan dragged themselves into the conference room and sank into their chairs silently. McIver and Savage arrived a few minutes later.

"Freeman asked me to give you this," McIver said as he passed Moreau an envelope.

She opened it and read the single sheet inside. The room and everyone in it faded away as her mother's face flashed through her mind and then dissolved into a blackness that she felt de-

THE SPYING MOON

scend into her stomach and she reminded herself to breathe.

Duncan hadn't said a word since they'd searched his uncle's property and as the room came back into focus Moreau noticed McIver turn his gaze away from her to her partner.

"Nothing?" McIver asked.

"We found a syringe in a vent," Moreau said.

"Prints?"

"Wiped clean."

"That woman on the hill. You think it's Alyssa, right?" Savage asked.

Moreau thought about the bruising on Sammy's wrist and shoulder. Alyssa couldn't have done it alone. Someone had to have helped...She straightened up in her chair. "Maybe."

"My sergeant's happy," Savage said. "The gun we found yesterday and the one recovered at the school today both had serial numbers that could be restored. They were stolen in the robbery I've been following up on."

"Which means that there's a gun-running network spreading throughout Western Canada, probably into the United States," McIver said.

"Did you find anything at the mines?" Moreau asked. Duncan sat and stared at the table wordlessly. He hadn't spoken in hours.

"It looks like that's where Chuck and Rich were staying, along with some others."

"What were they doing out there?"

A booming voice from behind Moreau answered. "Storing drug shipments and transporting them by foot through the wilderness to various points along the highways."

She didn't need to turn around to know who it was. The Aboriginal man she'd failed to detain twice walked around her chair and rested his hands on the empty one beside her.

"The second scent trail, that led to the old mines. That's where Rich had come from," McIver said.

Moreau and McIver exchanged a glance before she looked

back at the new arrival.

"Detective Hosteen," he said as he sat down.

"Of course you are," Moreau said.

Freeman walked into the room and made his way to the end of the table. "I know it's late and it's been a long day, but I want to say that you've all done exceptional work. And I want to remind you that I tried to send you all home earlier."

"We weren't finished," McIver said. "We aren't finished."

"No, we aren't. In fact, that's what I want to talk to you about. With the gun-smuggling connection to our murders and drug investigation, Raina Savage has been offered a transfer.

"We're going to be a cross-designated team with authority to pursue investigations on both sides of the border because of the gun-smuggling connection. Detective Tal Hosteen is our main contact from Similkameen, and he operates on Canadian soil with full authority of the law."

Moreau looked at Freeman. "You knew who he was and didn't tell me?"

"Hopefully that ends now," Freeman said. "And that's why you're here. I wanted a Native officer who could have access to Tribal lands on both sides of the border." He glanced at Savage. "I guess we've got that covered."

Moreau wondered if she'd be welcomed as readily as Freeman thought. Since her mother's disappearance any time she'd tried to learn about her Native heritage she'd been reminded that she was half white.

Half a missing woman nobody else cared about and half a man who'd raped her mother. A man she didn't know and didn't want to know.

"What about the leak?" Savage asked.

"Alyssa's missing and Alec Chmar's gone too."

Moreau slumped down in her chair even further. "He was alone with Chuck after Levi questioned him."

"Did he say anything?" McIver asked.

"He leaned in close and spoke so low I couldn't hear."

THE SPYING MOON

"Is it possible he wasn't a willing participant? That Alyssa was involved with the drugs and Chmar didn't know?"

"He did impersonate you," Moreau said.

"He what?"

"Alec went to at least one of the witnesses near Holt Hill to ask them about what they saw the night Sammy Petersen died and he identified himself as you."

"And you're sharing this now?"

"We only found out yesterday," Savage said.

McIver looked at Duncan, who held up his hands. "When she said McIdiot has been there I thought it was you. If I'd known you were being impersonated I would have put money on Saunders."

"He still isn't talking." Freeman cleared his throat. "I know we haven't wrapped everything up with a nice, neat bow. The Petersens did call to thank us for finding out the truth about Sammy's death. Duncan and Moreau's hard work on that investigation has brought a family a sense of peace, even if we haven't made an arrest yet."

Moreau thought about that. They didn't have to feel a sense of guilt if it wasn't suicide. They hadn't missed the signs. They hadn't failed their son.

Freeman continued. "George Jacobs confessed to the murder of Rich Robeson. He confessed to anyone who'd listen and then, when McIver and Savage started to question him, he lawyered up."

"But you like him for it?" Moreau asked McIver.

"He knows more about Rich than the papers reported."

"Both Hosteen and Willmott connected George's crew to Rich and Chuck," Freeman said.

"Rich had come forward as a witness," Hosteen said. "He started giving me names, but when he went missing I didn't have enough to make any arrests on the drug trafficking. If George Jacobs, Doug Terry and Arnold Hardee found out they had a motive for his murder, though. Rich said they were the ones who were bringing supplies out to the old mines and re-cruiting street kids to take bogus possession charges."

"But Doug and Arnold don't drive," Moreau said.

"George drove, but Doug and Arnold were right there with him every step of the way."

Freeman looked at Moreau. "I let Tal have a look at the phone records we got on the Petersen case. There was enough there to support George's confession. He was in the area where Rich's body was found during the window for the estimated time of death."

"And the break-ins? We know Chuck was responsible, but why?" McIver asked.

Moreau thought about that. "George's truck was in the shop. He was probably just hungry."

"George's confession technically solves Rich's murder, but I believe Doug and Arnold were with him," Hosteen said, "and I believe they're the ones who were responsible for Sammy's overdose."

"Why?" Duncan asked.

"Why did they kill him or why do I believe they're guilty?"

"Yes."

"I think you'd have a better chance of determining a motive than I would. The thing that connects Sammy and Rich is the gun, and we know George wasn't on the hill the night Sammy died."

"You've been following everything." Moreau knew it was a good sign for the team; they could use someone who had the investigative skills Tal Hosteen had demonstrated, but his interest in her wasn't something she understood. Why had seeing her in the woods that day prompted him to go to her home, especially since he could have gotten Freeman to give him her file?

"There are still questions we want to answer and I expect that as we dig into the lives of Alyssa and Alec we're going to learn a lot of unpleasant things," Freeman said.

"I don't think they were working alone," Moreau said.

THE SPYING MOON

Everyone looked at her. She thought about Zadecki's story about him and Michaels giving George a walk after an alleged assault that was never reported, that from how Zadecki told it they could have charged George.

Should have charged George.

Michaels. The first to respond to the scene of Sammy's death.

What had Kenny said? They thought it was Sammy who raped her.

"With the thick trees and no campfire, there was one thing that never made sense. Friday night there was a report of a gunshot. Michaels was first on the scene. He stated he thought it was a hunter, nothing serious, and left the station to do a drive by, but the alcove where they had the party is well off the road and tucked away. If you don't know where the path is you'd never find it."

"So how did Michaels know to walk down that path?" McIver asked.

"That's the sixty-four thousand dollar question. Add in the fact that Mrs. Griffin saw a police car go up the hill before the gunshot," Moreau said.

Freeman crossed his arms. "We've lost this round with Abe Holt. He's been released on bail with only minor charges. Claims he knew nothing about the syringe and that Alyssa was upset about Holt letting boys party on his property, which was the only reason she was there the night Sammy died. We don't have Alyssa so we can't refute that. The cooler and everything you found at the dump can't be traced to Holt or anyone conclusively. Half the town gets their trash picked up on the same day and there was no physical evidence to prove that cooler was ever on the Holt property. The prosecutor says when our evidence surpasses Holt's reasonable doubt they'll move, but until then they won't touch him on the drugs or Sammy's death.

"But we aren't going to give up. We're going to do what we can to put a stop to the illegal smuggling and make our streets safe."

262

"And Phil?" McIver asked. "What about him?"

"His memory is intact. He'll report to work next Monday. Savage and Moreau will move into a house in town, and Willmott will get his old place back."

Freeman started to walk out of the room. "Go home. Get some sleep. We're through the first leg of the race, but we still have a long way to go," he said.

As soon as Freeman was out of sight, Hosteen spun back and forth in his chair. "Guess this means we'll be spending a lot more time together," he said to Moreau.

"Maybe this time I won't have to hold you at gunpoint."

He stood up. "I'll have to find a way to get a look at your new bedroom somehow." Hosteen walked past her and left the room without giving her a chance to respond.

"Someone's a fan," McIver said. To Moreau he looked like he was holding back his grin, although his eyes betrayed his amusement.

"I'll meet you at the jeep." Savage said to Moreau as she stood up and tugged on McIver's arm.

"Wait," Moreau said as she shut her eyes. "I was supposed to go to Burns Lake."

"Kendall, we all saw the story. You don't have to explain," Duncan told her.

She held up her hand to him. "Yes, I do. I had a contact who'd remained anonymous. We were going to meet when I arrived." She swallowed and took out the piece of paper from the envelope Freeman had asked McIver to give her. "I-I guess she had my name and some information in her wallet."

Savage picked up the paper. "She's dead?"

Moreau's mouth felt pasty, like she was sick with the flu. "She told me she had a lead and I couldn't get away."

Savage put a hand on Moreau's shoulder and gave her a light squeeze.

"I know this isn't your first choice, Kendall," McIver said. "But I can make some calls. I have a friend stationed in that

THE SPYING MOON

area."

Moreau nodded and after a few seconds of silence she said, "You have a friend?"

Savage squeezed her shoulder again and McIver smiled as he followed Savage out of the room.

It was quiet for a moment before Moreau asked Duncan, "Are you okay?"

He lifted his head and looked her straight in the eye.

"Me? What about you?"

"Nate, he was your cousin. I could tell you cared about him."

Duncan nodded. "And I didn't know about your mother. What I said, about you not understanding what it's like to have your family torn away—"

"It's not your fault."

"It was a shitty thing to say. Everything I'd been feeling for years came out in—"

"You couldn't have known. I never—" she considered her words, "—opened up to you. After my mother...I was a foster kid, you know? Another Indian raised by the government. Chuck, Rich. I could have been just like them."

"But you aren't. You were strong. You worked hard to get here, in spite of what you'd been through."

"So did you."

Duncan stood up. "But unlike my family, something tells me your mother would be proud."

Chapter 34

Moreau and Savage drove to the cabin in silence. When they got inside Savage tried to console Moreau.

"I'm not thinking about my contact," Moreau said. Why had Michaels been heading up the hill before the shot was fired? Why had Alyssa really been arguing with Abe?

Why kill Sammy Petersen? He knew about Ellie's rape, but that didn't give Alyssa a motive for his murder. And using drugs that hadn't been cut? That would only attract attention to the local drug trade. Would a crew that had worked so hard to misdirect the police at every turn make that kind of mistake?

Kenny's death had ensured the town knew that Sammy hadn't taken his own life and now Mary Jensen had one son in a jail cell and the other in the morgue. Kenny's death had left a gaping hole in the investigation into Sammy's murder, and neither one of the remaining suspects made sense.

Alyssa was Ellie's sister. Wouldn't she know the truth about the rape? They had reason to believe she had access to the drugs, but she lacked motive.

The only other people she knew had been on the hill that night were Arnold and Doug. Hosteen liked them for Rich's murder, but she was still having a hard time seeing it.

Michaels may have staged the crime scene but he lacked a clear motive for risking his career to steer an investigation away from the drug trade unless he was involved, and they had no evidence to suggest that.

THE SPYING MOON

Savage boiled a kettle of water and made a pot of tea. She let it steep, poured two mugs and passed one to Moreau.

"You know the funny thing about that photo of the coyote? They're pack animals, but there you have one coyote all on his own.

"When you work narcotics in the city you get the wholesalers who distribute product. You get the corner boys who take the money. You get the alley boys who hand out the product. You get runners and lookouts who make sure nobody's doing business when police are around.

"This case...you're looking for one person who fits in the frame when it could be that there are a lot of people who share the blame."

Moreau wondered about that, and she was still thinking about Savage's words the next morning when she returned to the station.

It had been a week since she'd arrived in Maple River, and what had transpired since hadn't been what she'd expected.

She imagined that the crime scene techs and Brian Bradrick and Constable Zadecki had felt similarly when she'd placed calls to them that morning. No warrant was necessary for what she needed. Moreau and Savage arrived at the station and Moreau went back to page one of the first report about Sammy's death. She was only vaguely aware of McIver, Hosteen and Duncan arriving and keeping their distance while she took over the conference room table with a sea of papers.

Zadecki arrived first and handed her a statement without a word.

He left and Moreau kept placing papers until Brian Bradrick arrived. He nodded as he passed her more papers, and went to the far end of the conference room to watch.

When she set the last paper down she exhaled. There was only one thing missing.

A knock on the open door remedied that as Benji handed her a file with nothing but a nod. She flipped it open.

266

Corporal Phil Willmott entered the conference room.

"Phil. We haven't moved out yet," Moreau said as she looked up.

He nodded at the table. "Tell me you have something on this and I'll forgive you."

She glanced at McIver, Duncan, Hosteen, Bradrick and Savage, who were at the far end of the room, as she placed the new report on the table. They moved closer and she started to walk them through it.

Arnold and Doug may or may not have been involved with Rich's murder, but cell phone records put them and George Jacobs in the area where Willmott had been attacked, and later, they'd made calls from that same area just before the fire.

"Somehow, Sammy found out about the video. He knew who had raped Ellie, and he was going to tell."

She tapped another paper. "There was enough on Sammy's video recorder that could be recovered to show that after Kenny left that night, Randy argued with Sammy. He tried to get him to keep quiet, but Sammy wouldn't listen. Randy leaves, but the argument continues with Doug and Terry.

"The video ends with them grabbing Sammy and him trying to break free as he dropped his camera. It was just after eight o'clock."

"Doug and Arnold killed him to keep Randy's secret," Duncan said. "And it had nothing to do with the drugs?"

"Probably because they were the ones who held Ellie down in the video." Moreau pointed at another piece of paper. "Ellie made a statement this morning, and Constable Zadecki brought Doug and Arnold in.

"When they killed Sammy the presence of drugs in his system was a new problem. George had a confrontation with Ellie. She says he was trying to get her to keep her mouth shut about what happened. Michaels and Zadecki come along, grab George and while Michaels and Zadecki were leaving him outside of town, Doug and Arnold started to panic. That's when we have these

THE SPYING MOON

calls between them and George, and then from George to Abe Holt.

"Kenny saw Alyssa at Abe's when he left, and that was hours before Mrs. Griffin saw her on the road. She wasn't there to argue about boys partying on the property.

"I think she was there doing business. When she found out about Sammy she realized they had to try to steer the investigation away from drugs." Moreau tapped another paper. "That's when we have her calling Michaels, who Mrs. Griffin confirmed was on the hill before the gunshot."

"And the DNA from the back of his cruiser matched DNA recovered from chewing gum that had prints connected to beer cans at the scene. Beer that was consumed well after the actual time of death."

"That's what we couldn't figure out," Duncan said. "How did the person who pulled the trigger get off the hill? The only vehicles going up or down after the nine-one-one call were—"

"Cop cars," McIver said.

"If Zadecki hadn't come clean with me I wouldn't have had a reason to have Michaels' car checked."

"This seems sloppy, though," Savage said. "Nobody knew Sammy was dead. Why desecrate his body and do it in a way that ensured someone would call the police? Why not dispose of him the way they did Rich?"

"Sammy was a good kid from a good home and if he went missing there would be search parties combing the woods for miles. You hadn't found Rich's body yet, and Chuck was still out at the mines," Duncan said. "A manhunt could have spoiled everything."

"I hate to rain on your parade, but can you put the needle in someone's hand?" Bradrick asked.

Moreau nodded. "Benji's second report." She pointed to it. "They'd wiped it clean of fingerprints, but there was DNA on it that matched the other samples. Sammy must have put up a hell of a fight. One of them got stuck before he did."

"This should be enough to compel their DNA," Duncan said. "Nicely done."

"Actually, we already have the DNA, thanks to you, Nate. That chewing gum you recovered that day we talked to George, Doug and Arnold? Benji connected that to Doug Terry. We can prove he was there and that he got off that hill in the back of Michaels' squad car."

Moreau looked at the people standing across the table from her. A week ago she hadn't been able to stand McIver. She hadn't even known Savage, but in the past two days everything had changed.

"Savage reminded me that I needed to look for more than one suspect, that it was possible these crimes didn't connect the way we thought they did. McIver, we wouldn't have found Rich's body if it wasn't for you pushing for tracking and recruiting Bradrick and Tony." She looked at Duncan. "You've been with me every step of the way and sometimes ten steps ahead of me."

"You put this all together."

"Not without a lot of help." She looked at Hosteen. "And I'm sure you did something useful at some point."

"I'd like to be useful now and question Arnold and Doug."

"That will have to wait," Freeman said as he entered the room. He scanned the sea of paperwork set out on the table and handed Moreau a new folder. "George Jacobs was found dead in his cell this morning. He hung himself."

"You've got to stop leaving Saunders in a cell next to our suspects."

Freeman's eyes narrowed as he passed her a second folder.

And a hundred kilometers away a patrol had found a car with an APB out on it. A Taurus with a deceased male and female inside.

The pictures confirmed Alec and Alyssa had both been shot in the head.

She passed the folders to Duncan silently. His face paled a touch as he closed the file, handed it to McIver and reached for

THE SPYING MOON

his coat.

Freeman shook his head.

"You can't be on this, Nate."

"You brought me here because you thought my past was an asset."

"And it is. But this time…" Freeman shook his head.

Moreau studied the paperwork spread out over the table. The evidence connected enough dots to close both murder cases and they'd gotten closer to the drug trade in the process. They may not have all the answers Freeman wanted, but the task force he'd fought for was finally ready.

"This is just the first leg of the race," she said. "We've made a lot of progress and we still have a long way to go. The drugs have been flowing through here for a while. We aren't going to close the file on the trafficking today and what's out there, in that car, that could help us get closer to the source of the local drug trade." She looked at Duncan. "But that isn't how you want to remember her. No matter what happened in the past."

"She's right. Moreau will go with Detective Hosteen. You can question Doug and Arnold."

"Respectfully, I'm not happy about this, sir."

"Don't worry, Nate. Nobody's happy about this," Moreau said, "and if I have to bring Hosteen back at gunpoint, Freeman won't be either."

Freeman's face paled as Hosteen grinned and headed for the door. Moreau thought Freeman was about to rescind his order as she started to follow Hosteen.

"I thought I wanted Moreau on this team," she heard Freeman say as she reached the door.

The last thing she heard as she stepped into the hall was McIver's voice.

"Trust me. You do."

One of Sandra Ruttan's most painful childhood memories is of her mom driving to the town dump, prying her stuffed lamb from her arms and tossing it in the garbage. She was a walking disaster in her formative years. At age eight she was hit by a car while riding her bike home and her head was cut open. Just before her ninth birthday she was running along the beach and landed on broken glass. Her foot was partially severed. The muscle had to be stitched back together, leaving some uncertainty about whether she'd walk again, and the doctor was so fed up with her screaming he told her if she didn't shut up he'd cut her foot off.

After her tenth birthday she fell down a waterfall and almost drowned. Her later adventures have included being in Seville when they found several tons of explosives set to blow up the Semana Santa parade and being in a car crash in the Sahara Desert. There is absolutely no explanation for how she's managed to stay alive as long as she has. Check to see if she still has a pulse at her website, http://sruttan.wordpress.com/.

On the following pages are a few
more great titles from the
Down & Out Books publishing family.

For a complete list of books and to
sign up for our newsletter,
go to DownAndOutBooks.com.

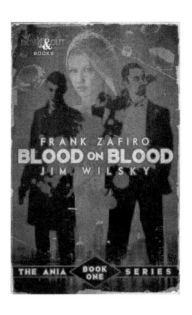

Blood on Blood
The Ania Trilogy Book One
Frank Zafiro and Jim Wilsky

Down & Out Books
978-1-946502-71-1

Estranged half-brothers Mick and Jerzy Sawyer are summoned to their father's prison deathbed. The spiteful old man tells them about missing diamonds, setting them on a path of cooperation and competition to recover them.

Along the way, Jerzy, the quintessential career criminal and Mick, the failed cop and tainted hero, encounter the mysterious, blonde Ania, resulting in a hardboiled Hardy Boys meets Cain and Abel.

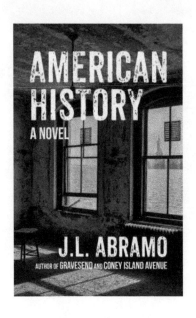

American History
J.L. Abramo

Down & Out Books
September 2018
978-1-946502-70-4

A panoramic tale, as uniquely American as Franklin Roosevelt and Al Capone…

Crossing the Atlantic Ocean and the American continent, from Sicily to New York City and San Francisco, the fierce hostility and mistrust between the Agnello and Leone families parallel the turbulent events of the twentieth century in a nation struggling to find its identity in the wake of two world wars.

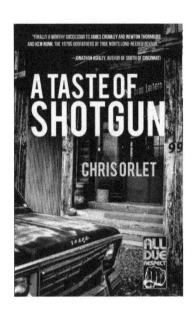

A Taste of Shotgun
Chris Orlet

All Due Respect, an imprint of
Down & Out Books
July 2018
978-1-946502-92-6

A local drug dealer has the goods on Denis Carroll. That shooting at his tavern five years ago? Turns out the cops got it all wrong. Now, after five years of blackmail, the Carrolls have had enough. When the drug dealer turns up dead, Denis is the prime suspect. As more bodies pile up, they too appear to have Denis' name all over them. Is Denis really a cold-blooded killer or could this be the work of someone with a grudge of her own?

In this darkly humorous small-town noir everyone has something to hide and nothing is at seems.

Texas, Hold Your Queens
A Mason Page & Farrah Tyler Novella
Marie S. Crosswell

Shotgun Honey, an imprint of
Down & Out Books
978-1-943402-74-8

When the body of an undocumented Mexican immigrant is found abandoned on a roadside, Detectives Mason Page and Farrah Tyler have no clue how a throwaway case that neither wants to let go will affect their lives.

On the job, Page and Tyler are the only two female detectives in El Paso CID's Crimes Against Persons unit. Off the clock, the two have developed an intimate friendship, one that will be jeopardized when the murder case puts them on the suspect's trail.